The Steps of the Sun

The Steps of the Sun

Joanna Trollope

St. Martin's Press
New York

THE STEPS OF THE SUN. Copyright © 1983 by Joanna Trollope. All rights reserved. Printed in the United States of America. No part of this book may be used or reproduced in any manner whatsoever without written permission except in the case of brief quotations embodied in critical articles or reviews. For information, address St. Martin's Press, 175 Fifth Avenue, New York, N.Y. 10010.

Library of Congress Cataloging in Publication Data

Trollope, Joanna.
   The steps of the sun.

   1. South African War, 1899-1902—Fiction.   I. Title.
PR6070.R57S8   1984   823'.914   84-2079
ISBN 0-312-76165-1

First published in Great Britain in 1983 by Hutchinson & Co. (Publishers) Ltd.

First U.S. Edition

10 9 8 7 6 5 4 3 2 1

For my father
South Africa – November 1981

Acknowledgements

Research for this book took me to South Africa in the autumn of 1981 and I am most grateful for all the help so freely given by the City Library in Johannesburg. I should also like to thank Pitch Christopher for generously allowing me the run of his library in Ladysmith, George Tatham for a memorable afternoon spent on the battlefield of Spion Kop, and Dr Kenneth Biss for great help on contemporary medical matters. And to my mother, grateful thanks for the title of this book.

J.T.

Who countest the steps of the sun,
Seeking after that sweet golden clime
Where the traveller's journey is done . . .

William Blake

Part One

1

On the eve of Queen Victoria's eightieth birthday, Matthew Paget got drunk with a handful of friends from his college and unharnessed all the horses from the two last horse trams plodding east down Oxford's High Street. The protesting tram drivers were bundled up into a loose human parcel and left on the pavement for the police and the horses were turned free to clatter stablewards over Magdalen Bridge.

Wearied by the humour of this episode, Matthew and his friends made unsteadily for their college, only to find it already locked against them. They were forced therefore to jostle each other round into Merton Street and make use of an illicit and perilous route over steeply pitched roofs and a spiked wall to gain entry. The climb ended in a leap of fifteen feet onto cobbles. No bones were broken, but outlined against the light May evening sky, fluttering on the spikes of the wall, were black shreds and rags ripped from gowns and trousers. Five minutes later, having been assisted up his staircase by a man even drunker than he was, Matthew passed out in his sitting room with his boots still on and his head pillowed on a battered copy of Lecky's *History of Rationalization*.

His scout woke him at six.

'No call to celebrate Her Majesty's birthday with your boots on, sir, if I may say so.'

He had risen at five in order to dress and breakfast and achieve the bicycle ride from Botley by six. Duck was not a fastidious man – to which the dust-furred wainscotting and panelling and the thick clots of fluff under sofa and chairs bore witness – but he drew the line at finding his young gentlemen sprawled on the dirty carpet when a bed, made by his own hands, awaited them not ten feet away.

'Had to climb in,' Matthew said, sitting up by inches.

Duck twitched the gown that Matthew had cast on the sofa. It fluttered like witches' rags.

'So I see, sir.'

'Could you mend it, Duck?'

'Mrs Duck, maybe, sir – '

Matthew hauled a few shillings from his pocket.

'Thank you, sir. I'll see what can be done.'

Matthew said, on a faint note of inquiry, 'Coffee . . . ?'

'All in good time, sir. It quite puts me out, sir, if you aren't in your bed when I come in.'

Matthew stood up, sordid to himself in every fibre.

'I'll go then. Wake me at nine.'

His room was just as he had left it. Duck operated on the same principle when it came to tidying up as when washing up, that there was no point in dealing with either until the situation was desperate. The books that were Matthew's lifelines – Darwin's *The Origin of Species*, Buckle's *History of Civilization*, George Eliot's novels, Matthew Arnold's poems and tracts, every word of John Stuart Mill – lay in a disordered heap by his narrow bed. A print of Holman Hunt's *The Light of the World* (given to him by his mother) and one of Botticelli's *Primavera* (given to him by his sister Frances) stood on the floor, leaning against the wall, and across Christ's robe someone had written with a thick fingertip, 'Dust me'. Besides the bed there was a washstand, two bentwood chairs ('Maid's furniture,' his mother had said, 'Can the college find you nothing better?'), a cricket bat and riding boots, tumbling piles of clothes, and a birdcage that had once held a canary, now deceased, which Matthew had won at the St Giles' Fair.

On his bed was a crumple of paper, thrown there by himself the previous evening. He picked it up and smoothed out the creases.

If you won't see me for dinner, I shall catch you for breakfast. I will be with you at nine, bringing champagne.

Hendon Bashford

Matthew swore, pulled off his clothes and boots, and slumped into bed.

*

'When I breakfasted at Christ Church on Tuesday,' Hendon Bashford said with his colonial twang, 'Lord Ripon was there. And his younger brother. We drank six bottles of champagne between five of us in an hour.'

'Pretty slow going.'

'Oh, well, there was ale as well, you know. Lord Ripon has his bread sent in from Marston. It was the lightest you ever tasted. I said to them, "You ought to try bread made from mealie meal, like our Kaffirs eat." They laughed like anything.'

'Did they.'

Duck put tea and coffee pots down on the table. 'Haddock's ready, sir.'

'Hendon?'

'I'd prefer chicken.'

'There isn't any. I didn't order chicken.'

'Fish, then. Roll on the salmon season.'

'Have you ever caught one?'

'No. First time lucky this summer – at your cousin's invitation naturally.' He broke a roll in pieces and began to float them in his coffee.

'Must you do that?'

'Lord Ripon never objected. Do you suppose I can ask for an invitation from him for the summer? Ask him out to dinner and everything first, of course.'

'No.'

'Might try it all the same.' He peered at his fish fork, then blew on it and polished it with a yellow silk handkerchief. He wore a high-buttoned suit of chalk-striped worsted, a black moiré tie with a huge gold pin thrust vertically through the knot, and two signet rings.

'Why did Will send you to me?'

Hendon struggled briefly with fishbones.

'Your cousin? Well, he didn't precisely send me, but as I said I was coming to Oxford to look up a few introductions my father's company gave me, he mentioned you. And your father is an archdeacon of course.'

'I imagine you would prefer him to be an archbishop.'

Hendon nodded.

'Of course.'

13

'I can't do anything for you, you know. I don't really know the men at the House you seem to want to know. I hunt a bit, but I'm not a member of the Bullingdon.'

'Lord Ripon is.'

'Where did you meet Will?'

'At the Reform Club. It was my grandfather's club and they let me have a room. I just talked to anyone I thought looked likely.'

'Likely for what?'

'What I want.' Hendon pushed his coffee cup towards Matthew and began to pile marmalade on toast. 'Introductions, that sort of thing. A chance to have a good summer here, Scotland and Lords and Henley and so forth.'

Matthew pushed the full cup back again. 'Is that what you've come to England for?'

'Of course,' Hendon said calmly.

'Isn't there any – social life in Johannesburg?'

'Not like this. There's nothing to talk about but gold. I intend to have a wonderful summer and maybe find myself a wife. It would be a great thing to take a blue-blooded girl back to South Africa. Is your sister good-looking?'

'Much too good-looking for you,' Matthew said rudely.

Hendon regarded him. 'Odd, that. I wouldn't have said you were good-looking. Tall, I grant you – and I envy you that – but a bit raw-boned. I always feel red hair looks odd on a man. Come to Ascot with me? I'm making up a party.'

'No thanks.'

'Not a racing man?'

'Not a betting one.'

'You're in the wrong set here, you know,' Hendon said, 'I wonder you have any fun. Women?'

Matthew stood up. 'Never without one.'

'Funny. You don't look the sort. I've had a wonderful time since I came. English girls have much better skins than South Africans. I suppose it's the sun. I haven't been to bed sober in two months and I haven't missed one chance of a good bet. I'm thinking of staying on for the steeplechase season. Cigar?'

'No thanks.'

Matthew folded up his long limbs on the window seat and gazed morosely down into the High Street.

14

'Don't smoke?'

'Not often.'

'But you drink. I heard about last night. You missed the proctors by seconds, you know. Why don't you buy some shares? Will has.'

Matthew turned. 'What shares?'

Hendon blew a thick plume of blue cigar smoke and leaned back in the chair. 'Eckstein's of course.'

'What are you talking about?'

'My father was a director of Eckstein's. They own Rand Mines, subsidiary of Wernher–Beit. Going in for deep mining. Can't fail.'

'And Will bought some shares?'

'Certainly. You should too. That's partly why I'm here, to drum up some support for the gold kings.'

'You're certainly going about it the right way.'

'I know,' Hendon said. 'I know what I'm doing. England couldn't fight a war in South Africa without money from people like Rhodes and Alfred Beit.'

'There isn't going to be a war.'

'Of course there is. You can't let the Boers have it their own way. Why should they?'

Matthew swung himself upright. 'And why should we? We've already redrawn the border of Cape Colony to include Kimberley now that we know there are diamonds there. We can't go on helping ourselves to bits of the world we fancy just because they happen to have gold underneath and other people on top.'

' 'Course we can. You don't know the Boers. They're a bunch of Dutch peasants. This champagne is pretty rough. It was all the hotel had. I say, are you a republican? Will didn't warn me.'

There was a knock on the door and Duck came in with a kettle in one hand and a white envelope in the other. 'You're to have this at once, sir.'

Hendon watched him rip the envelope open. 'Anything interesting?'

'Oh, yes,' Matthew said with some savagery, 'you will find it most interesting. I'm summoned to see the Master.'

*

15

In the autumn of 1897, when Matthew went up to Oxford, Archdeacon Paget had congratulated himself on having won a significant victory. Matthew's schooldays had been a turbulent and distressing affair, crisscrossed with rebelliousness, flirtations with agnosticism and liberalism, and an ability to lead others astray in his wake. At whatever cost to his own feelings, the Archdeacon had made the supreme – and eloquently publicized – gesture of offering Matthew the alternative career of the army. It was likely his cousin Will would join the army and the boys had been brought up together. The Archdeacon did not add that he felt the Church might not be able to accommodate itself to Matthew's uncomfortable opinions but preferred to project the new scheme as a personal sacrifice. Matthew heard him out in silence and then announced he was going to his father's old college at Oxford to read theology. Late that night, in the shelter of their four-poster bed, the Archdeacon had confided to his wife that he had always had a way with the recalcitrant young.

'You most certainly have,' Mrs Paget said warmly and turned to say softly into her pillow, 'even if you have no conception of what it is.'

Matthew arrived in Oxford in early October with an allowance of £450 per annum from his father and a box of books of which none bore any relation to theology. He bought his gown and cap, went to Ryman's in the High Street for engravings for his sitting room and Grimbley Hughes in the Cornmarket for fig-flavoured Viennese coffee and a whole Stilton cheese (which the mice in Duck's pantry made short work of), and was admitted ceremoniously into the university. Once admitted, he made his announcement. He did not wish to read theology, he said, but modern history.

Shock prevailed, both in his college and in the Close at Salisbury, though in the case of his sister Frances it was a shock of delight. Modern history was a raw and new school, a mere forty-seven years old, and in any case the university was not accustomed nor prepared to countenance such arbitrary changes of mind.

Dr Bright, Master of Matthew's college, was of the

opinion that he should be sent down at once. The Doctor was convinced that the business of the university lay in the teaching of the humanities and mathematics and he believed the agnosticism, currently so rife in Oxford, was a direct result of the new schools of physical science and medieval and modern history. Besides, if he were to keep Paget, he might infect the whole college with unorthodox ways of behaving, in the manner of a rotten apple in a barrel of whole ones. It was best he should be returned to Salisbury and subsequently put into some solid regiment, one maybe that would exhaust his energies by sending him to India.

The Dean of the college, a timorous man, attempted to reason with Matthew, to treat him as a straying lamb. He had, he said, a certain sympathy with a man whose beliefs were a little shaken. He did not expound upon his personal reason for this sympathy which was that he felt the Church of England was, if anything, too vulnerable, too tolerant: indeed, if the Church of Rome had not seemed to him to have an unhealthy edge of passion to her dictates, he would gladly have fled to the safety of her well-defined embrace. As it was, the only embrace the Dean knew was that of his wearisome sister, who lived alone in a damp cottage on Boars Hill and existed solely for his ritual weekly visit. Because of all these influences churning in his brain, the Dean's method of reasoning with Matthew made his purpose entirely unclear to both of them. The Dean was left feeling that he had attempted to grasp some huge and prickly thing that had not so much eluded him as seemed not to have noticed him at all, and Matthew banged down the staircase thinking, 'Poor little feeble fellow.'

Matthew then set about a personal lobby of the historical faculty of the university, even going so far as to beard the Chichele Professor, Frederick Powell, in his rooms at Oriel. Powell was taken aback, but patient, and explained that Matthew's case was a matter for his college, not the university, and that the Master's word must be taken as final. On Matthew's return to his room after this interview, he found a letter from his father waiting in his rooms.

'Am I to assume,' Archdeacon Paget wrote, 'that your apparent docility in conforming to my wishes – and naturally those also of your mother – in reality masked a scheme which you hoped would secure you three years' study at my expense in a subject which you know I abhor and consider dangerous to a degree?'

Matthew wrote 'Yes' on a postcard, signed it, and dropped it in at the porter's lodge to be posted. He then returned to his rooms where a farewell party had established itself, bent upon drinking a term's allowance of wine in one evening.

In the morning, an unexpected summons came. It was from old Prideaux, regarded as the college joke and an undoubted inhabitant of its walls since its foundation in the eleventh century. He saw only dimly – and therefore was never entirely sure if he had the proper complement of pupils at a tutorial – but his brain was as sharp as his eyes were clouded. His father had been an archbishop, he had one brother who was a bishop and another who was a judge, and he himself was internationally acknowledged as an authority on Euripides. The Master stood in awe of him.

'What can he want with me?' Matthew said.

'He's probably made a mistake. It isn't you at all. But you had better go.'

'Had I?'

'At the double.'

Old Prideaux knew exactly who Matthew was and lost no time in explaining why he had sent for him. 'It seems to me, Mr Paget, that there is nothing whatever the matter with your mind, merely with your manners. I dislike your method of attempting to achieve your academic ends, though doubtless you had your reasons, but I am in sympathy with your desires. Unlike your father – whom I knew as a boy – I am wholly in favour of the windows opening upon the academic life of this university. This will surprise you to hear since I am generally regarded as being too old to have any opinions other than retrospective ones. I share your enthusiasm for the study of modern history though no doubt my reasons differ. Your father read theology and his father before him. What did you expect?'

'Exactly this,' Matthew said, 'which was why I had to resort to subterfuge.'

Old Prideaux gave a wintry smile. 'I see your difficulty. And I see his disappointment. In your token acquiescence you were already, in his mind's eye, the curate of Flamstead in Hertfordshire, which living this college has in its gift. The present curate is moving on in a year or so. I have spoken to the Master, Mr Paget.'

'To any good effect, sir?'

'Certainly. You are permitted to change schools. I allow myself the pleasure of telling you this, since it is by my good offices that it has come about. I only hope it will not precipitate a flood of young men who do not know their own minds.'

'I know mine. And I am truly grateful, sir.'

'You will of course apply to be made exhibitioner of this college. And you will enter for both the Stanhope and the Marquis of Lothian's Historical Essay Prizes. You will repay this college for its understanding by adding a little lustre to its reputation, Mr Paget.'

By the end of his second term, Matthew had secured a Linton Exhibition in Modern History with a value of £40. In the summer of 1898 he was runner-up to the Honourable Richard Denman of Balliol in the Stanhope Historical Essay Prize, but lost his manuscript for the Marquis of Lothian's Prize so thoroughly and inexplicably that he could only suppose the winner had stolen it. He played rugger for his college's second team, hunted when funds allowed him to hire a horse, was a vociferous heckler at the Union, and drank more than was good for him. His essays were energetic and unconventional, which was, after all, only a reflection of his way of life and the frequent extravagance of his behaviour. He was lucky to belong to a college with a tradition of tolerance, even among those in authority, for in many another college his escapades would have had him sent down several times over.

In his fourth term, two sobering events took place. He almost failed his Moderations – to be plucked, as a college exhibitioner, would have meant sure dismissal – and he fell in love. The two events were not connected except that the girl he fell in love with was his tutor's daughter, and the near failure could be put down, almost entirely, to several months' voracious reading on any subject but his own and to a spell of excessively wild carousing.

The Master gave him a stern warning and his tutor summoned him to his house in North Oxford to review, as he put it, 'the shortcomings of your way of life'. Adolphus Munro lived in Norham Gardens, in a red and blue brick gothic house which had caused a sensation when it was built twenty years before. All the windows were mullioned, and filled with small, almost opaque glass panes set in lead. It had in consequence virtually no natural light, and the conservatory was so shrouded in ferns as to be sunk in green gloom even at midday. The Munros were very proud of the house and Mrs Munro told every newcomer that it had been much admired by Butterfield, the architect of Keble.

Adelaide Munro, the daughter of the house, found it claustrophobic. But then she found Oxford claustrophobic too. When her father said, as he invariably did, to new pupils, 'Oxford is less a home of learning, it is more a microcosm of English intellectual life,' she was violently tempted to shout, 'And that is all!' Nobody in Oxford lived, to Adelaide's mind, a really useful life. Useful lives, in her book, were those led by doctors and nurses, missionaries and liberal reformers. Teaching, if taken beyond school level, she saw as an end in itself to the teacher, a chance to bang the door on the world and retreat into the unassailable intricacies of the mind. To Adelaide, that was, to put it mildly, unethical. She had attempted, several times, to get away from home and go to London to be trained as a nurse, but a mother with a weak heart and three younger brothers, not to mention the difficulty of persuading any maid to stay for long in the damp basement and icy attics of Norham Gardens, kept her at home.

When Matthew arrived for his interview with her father, Adelaide showed him into the study. He thought her at once very beautiful which, in a rather stern and uncompromising way, she was. She was of medium height with a good and graceful figure, brown hair drawn severely back, and long grey eyes under heavy brows. When the interview was over – Adolphus Munro said exactly what Matthew had known he would say – Adelaide was waiting in the dark hall, her dress blobbed with blue and red reflections from the glass in the front door, and drew him into the drawing room for tea. Her mother was not there, being too weak that day to leave her bed, and the boys were not yet back from school. Adolphus Munro came in to retrieve a cup of tea and a slice of ginger-bread and retired to his study to mark the essay Matthew had brought with him as a sort of peace offering and symbol of future good intent.

Adelaide and Matthew sat either side of the fire on chairs upholstered in plum-red cut velvet and talked. She was, he discovered, almost three years older than he, and the discovery filled him with awe. She had been a member of the Peace Society since her eighteenth birthday and enjoyed the distinction of having had several letters on the desirability of continuing peace published in the *Daily Chronicle*.

'Of course, the editor Mr Massingham is very sympathetic to the views I express. I always write under a masculine *nom de plume* because I don't suppose my letters would be considered otherwise.'

'You should meet my sister Frances,' Matthew said. 'She is a tremendous believer in women's rights.'

Adelaide blushed very slightly and said she would love to. She then revealed that she was an occasional correspondent of Miss Florence Nightingale, who had promised to recommend her particularly to St Thomas's Hospital when she was able to leave home and seek her own career. By five o'clock Matthew was full of ginger cake and excited admiration. Two weeks later, after several such interviews, he was in love.

Adelaide Munro proved a steadying influence. Matthew admired her practical view of things and thought he detected an unspoken contempt for his past self-indulgences that made him very sorry indeed. He attended at least a third of the lectures he was required to attend, managed to be late for chapel only twice in a month, and bewildered his friends by turning them, still half-sober, out of his rooms at night so that he could work. He went home for the Christmas vacation of 1898 full of exalted feelings and steady resolve.

His sister Frances was not taken in for a moment. 'Who is she?'

A pause, then, 'Who?'

'Matthew, you can't hide anything from me. You have "Love" writ large all over you. Come clean.'

'I don't feel like being teased about it.'

'I will only tease if you won't tell.'

Matthew showed her a photograph. 'Of course, she is much more handsome than that.'

'Of course.'

'You promised not to tease.'

'I wasn't. I was agreeing. She's certainly had a wonderful effect on you. I never saw you so tamed.'

Frances told her mother on condition that she would not, in turn, tell the Archdeacon.

'Let Matthew get all the credit, Mamma, for being so industrious and soberly behaved. Time enough to tell Father if Matthew's enthusiasm for Miss Munro continues.'

It did not. He returned to Oxford to find Adelaide, so remote and decided and admirable the term before, quite ready this term to return his affection a hundredfold. She had lowered herself very cautiously into being in love, spending many nights sitting by her mother's bedside telling herself that he was only a boy and therefore must be put out of her mind. She found, however, that the more she tried to push him out, the more he persisted in remaining, and so in the end she surrendered herself to the luxury of her feelings and allowed herself to think of him every waking moment.

Her enthusiasm disconcerted him and he took to waylaying Adolphus Munro in college when he needed to see him rather than seizing any and every pretext to go striding up to Norham Gardens. It was a bitter blow to Adelaide and it was followed by another, the death of her mother on a dark grey day in February when it seemed impossible that anything should ever come to life again. Matthew called to express his condolences and Adelaide was never quite sure whether it was the death of her mother or her hopes that he had come to say he was so sorry about. He stood in the hall with the harsh light from the gas mantle falling on his rough red head and said, 'You must start a new life now. Now is your chance.'

'But the boys – '

'Can't they go away to school? Isn't there an aunt, some sister of your father's, a cousin maybe, who could come?'

22

'I – I'll see. It seems rather wicked to even begin to plan a new life with Mother only three days gone – '

'Not at all. She was the reason you stayed at home. I expect she would want you to have a new life. Adelaide – ' He stopped and held out his hands. She put hers into them. 'Adelaide. I am so very sorry.'

'Yes,' she said and took her hands away, 'and so am I,' and then she turned and went swiftly up the stairs.

Three weeks later, Adolphus Munro, having said quite candidly to Matthew that his defence of Oliver Cromwell showed a tendency to his old and undesirable ways of thinking, added almost casually, 'You may be interested to know that Adelaide is going to London to nurse. I have decided that it is time the boys tasted a little independence and my wife's first cousin has agreed to manage household affairs for me. Miss Nightingale has found her a place at the best of the nursing colleges. I wonder if you would read your final paragraph to me once more? I want to be entirely sure that I have been fair in my criticism of your thesis.'

Matthew wrote briefly to Adelaide.

Dear Miss Munro,
    Bravo! It's wonderful news that you are to go to London to do what you have so long wanted to do. I wish you every success and happiness.
                              Yours ever,
                              Matthew Paget

Her reply was as sensible and cheerful as she had been when he had first known her. She gave him her address in London and begged that he would write every so often and let her know how Oxford did. When she had gone – hoping until the train actually pulled out of the station that he would appear to say goodbye – he reverted to all he had been before her influence. Through the remainder of the Lent term, through the vacation, and continuing into the new Trinity term, Matthew did not trouble to curb his impulses. Patiently, the college authorities watched his work slacken and his wildness grow wilder. Adolphus Munro was instructed to hint that, being an influence for disruption in

23

the college, he must restrain himself if he wished to remain a member of the university. He paid little heed. And then, on 24 May 1899, two proctors and an officer of the Oxford police force requested an interview with the Master and said that one of a pair of tram drivers who had been found bound together on the pavement outside Queen's College the previous night had recognized Matthew by the colour of his hair and his participation in similar incidents previously.

'This is the final warning,' the Master said. 'You have tried our patience sorely, Mr Paget, and disappointed us very bitterly. To show you that I do not threaten idly, I am relieving you of your exhibition to this college as of the end of this term, and I shall award it next term to a member of the college who has studied to deserve it. Any more folly like yesterday evening and I must send you down altogether. It is my frank opinion that I should have disregarded Mr Prideaux and never permitted you to change schools during your first term. What is it, Mr Paget, that makes you squander your talents in this way?'

Matthew said, 'I hardly know myself, sir.'

'You must be as bitter a disappointment to your father as you are to us. The third generation of Paget to be a member of this college, and a disgrace to your name. My own inclination is to send you down at once because I feel that our generosity is wasted upon you, but I am prevailed upon by your tutor who has faith in your abilities. But I shall not be so influenced again. At the first instance of behaviour that is indecorous or of inattention to your studies, you will be dismissed this college and this university.'

Hendon Bashford was sitting in Matthew's rooms, comfortably smoking a cigar. He had his feet on the fender and a litter of newspapers round him indicated that he had been there some time. He looked up when Matthew came scowling in and brandished his cigar.

'Been plucked?'

'No.'

Hendon's face fell a little. 'I thought I'd stay. See what happened to you – '

'Would you go?'

'Had quite an amusing time,' Hendon said. 'I got on very well with your fellow, you know. I've a way with people of that sort. I say, won't you ask me to meet your people?'

'No,' Matthew said.

Hendon got up slowly and stood with calm deliberateness on the crumpled sheets of Matthew's newspaper.

'I'll get to meet your sister if I want to. I'll get to be a friend of your cousin Will's if I want to.'

'Just go,' Matthew said, 'will you? Go. You are not wanted here, you don't belong. Go!'

Hendon lunged at him. 'I'm not a bloody Boer, damn you! I'm an Englishman, just as you are!'

From the doorway, Duck said disapprovingly, 'Another scrap, Mr Paget?'

'Duck, would you show Mr Bashford out? He's just going.'

Hendon straightened his jacket. 'Wait until the war comes,' he said to Matthew, 'then see if you aren't begging for our help and money. See how you feel about belonging together then.'

Three days later, Matthew was crossing Tom Quad in Christ Church as a short cut from St Aldgate's to Merton Street. Dusk was falling and by the round pond in the centre of the quadrangle with a statue of Mercury in the middle there was a shouting group of young men and a good deal of splashing. Matthew approached them and discovered seven or eight members of the Bullingdon Club – he recognized several, including Lord Ripon, from the hunting field – ducking another who was easily identifiable by his voice as Hendon Bashford. When he was thoroughly soaked, he was hauled out of Mercury and rolled about on the grass.

'Why don't you peg him out to dry?' Matthew suggested.

'Good idea. What with?'

Half an hour and a good deal of hoarse shouting later, Hendon Bashford was found by the college porters crucified on the grass of the quadrangle, his arms and legs neatly pinioned down with croquet hoops. When unpinned and dried out, he was asked if he knew any of his assailants. He seemed very confused about most of them and quite

25

uncertain which college they came from, but of one man he was absolutely sure. Matthew Paget had been in the forefront of the attack and the croquet hoops had been entirely his idea. He said in an injured manner that he had had no idea that a visitor from abroad might be maltreated in this way at Oxford.

The next morning, accompanied by two trunks and a box of books, Matthew Paget left Oxford for Salisbury in disgrace.

2

When Jim Bashford built the Valley House for his bride in Parktown in 1869, it was, if only briefly, the talk of Johannesburg. It was generally agreed that if one had to work in Johannesburg, Parktown was the only place to live and Jim Bashford made the Valley Road intensely fashionable by erecting his Scottish baronial pile there, a fantasy of leaded windows and turrets and great studded doors. His bride, fresh from her father's farm, wept like anything when she saw it, and said, between sobs, how could she live in a house where there was no stoep to sit on and shell peas? Jim Bashford said firmly that the word was verandah, not stoep, and that the pea-shelling would be done by the servants.

The marriage itself was discussed almost as much as the house. It was Jim Bashford's proud boast that his father had been one of the first 1820 English settlers in the Eastern Cape. Therefore, it was an enormous surprise to all those who fully expected him to go home to England when it came to choosing a wife to discover that he had only ridden as far as a farm to the southeast of Pretoria and come back, not with the flower of some lesser aristocratic family, but with old Jan Dreyer's younger daughter. Johanna was very pretty, to be sure, with none of the heaviness that marked so many of the faces of Boer women, but her English was atrocious and her manners and habits uncouth to a degree. She sat miserably in her mahogany-panelled drawing room in a jungle of potted palms, her feet resting on a zebra skin, and waited for callers in terror. When they came she offered them the strong bitter coffee her mother had taught her to make, which they refused, going away to the next drawing room in glee to recount every detail of her awkwardness. She suffered acutely and in silence, living for the early evening when Jim Bashford would come home from the Rand to cross-examine her about her day, entirely unaware how profoundly her subservience excited him.

Once a month at first, she went home to Dreyersdal. She used to cry every time the farmhouse came in view, a low simple whitewashed building, with wooden shutters and a flat roof, the doorways adorned with pairs of springbok horns. Her city clothes were never much admired, except by her sister Bettie, who was three years older than Johanna, and unmarried and very perturbed about it. She was supposed to go into the kitchen and join in as if she had never been away, taking down her apron from where it had always hung and settling to the tasks that had been hers since she was a child. Her mother spoke of love only in her prayers, never to her children, and old Jan Dreyer had accepted too splendid a bride price for Johanna to regard her any more as anything other than Jim Bashford's property. She cried even harder when leaving the farm than when arriving, but hardly knew why.

When she had been married four years, she stopped going to Dreyersdal. Her three brothers had all brought home wives and the farm was alive with babies. In addition, Bettie had married Christiaan van Heerden, whose land marched with Dreyersdal, and also she herself was pregnant. In February of 1874, she gave birth to a son in the huge gloomy bedroom of the Valley House where Jim had made love to her with brisk efficiency every Tuesday, Thursday and Saturday of their married life. She wanted to call the baby Jan but Jim said he was to be Hendon, after the celebrated settler from the Eastern Cape.

Babies made her life much more bearable. Hendon was followed three years later by Daisy and after that the lovemaking nights were reduced to Tuesday and Saturday and then only to Saturday, and Johanna sank with relief into the world of the nursery. Gossips told her that Jim had a mistress set up in the neighbouring suburb of Yeoville, but Johanna hardly cared. She sang Afrikaaner lullabies to her children and fed them mealie porridge and took them to play hide-and-seek in the Glen, a nearby grove of eucalyptus trees. She bowled hoops with them along the soft dirt roads of Parktown and took them down the southwards-leading footpaths through the red fields, so that they could all gaze at the prospect of Johannesburg and the mine dumps that were the refuse of its wealth.

When Hendon was twelve his father woke up to the fact that his English was almost as heavily accented as his mother's. The tutor and governess who had been hired from Cape Town for the children were banished and Hendon went to school in Johannesburg with the sons of other English settlers. There he learned to despise his mother's background and passed his contempt on to his sister Daisy. Johanna bought a rocking chair and put it on the verandah and sat there, day after day in the winter months, knitting and stitching, just as her grandmother and mother did on the stoep at Dreyersdal. She wrote to her sister Bettie and begged to be allowed to visit her and, when the invitation came, she behaved with uncharacteristic authority and compelled Hendon and Daisy to accompany her.

The Van Heerden farm was altogether a less homely affair than Dreyersdal. It was built of stone and, although it had the usual tin roof, it was gabled and had a porch trimmed with wooden fretwork. It was filled with heavy red mahogany furniture and every table was shrouded in bobble-edged plush. There was a harmonium in the sitting room, European china in the dining room, and a crucifix above every bed. For Bettie, the house was a dream come true.

Like her sister, she had two children. The boy was a year younger than Hendon, the girl was two years younger than Daisy. Daisy wore plaid silk with plaid silk bows in her hair, and her skirts were held out by flounced petticoats trimmed with hand-worked crochet. Her cousin Alecia wore a dark stuff dress and an apron. Her hair was knotted in a tight bun and she stared at Daisy horribly. None of the children would speak to each other. Johanna burst into tears on her sister's comfortable bosom and Bettie patted her and said next time, maybe next time . . .

The monthly family visits were resumed, only to the Van Heerden farm, not Dreyersdal. The children had to accompany their mother every time – it was the only thing upon which she ever insisted, for otherwise they were allowed to do as they wished. Hendon and his cousin Gaspar settled for an uneasy truce but Daisy and Alecia made no such effort. Their mutual contempt was impressive in children so young. Daisy imagined that Alecia craved her clothes and envied her accent, her piano playing, and her city polish. It was true that Alecia envied her, but not for any of those things, for what Alecia would have sold her soul for were Daisy's books, Daisy's chances to learn music and languages, in short the chance of education that Daisy regarded merely as a tiresome chore. Alecia could read, but there was no reading matter at the Van Heerden farm that was not religious or related to the breeding of the wide-horned Afrikander cattle for which her father was so renowned. She longed to beg Daisy for the loan of books but could not bring herself to do it. Instead she continued to stare.

At meals on the farm, the children were not permitted to speak. Oom Christiaan said grace with his hands folded and his eyes closed, and the whole table said Amen. Then the eating began, several courses of heavy Afrikaaner food all put on the table at once and fallen upon, and Oom Christiaan would talk to his brother, and sometimes Tant Bettie would whisper to her sister, and the children would remain quite silent, Gaspar shovelling in food, Hendon attempting to imitate him, Alecia staring between mouthfuls, and Daisy disgustedly pushing round her plate shreds of tough beef and mounds of butter beans cooked to a pudding with vinegar. After every meal, Tant Bettie would give each child a spice biscuit shortened with mutton fat. Daisy always gave hers to a dog.

Christiaan van Heerden's black labourers lived in a collection of rondavels some hundreds of yards from the farmhouse. A rich strong smell hung over the place and the children playing in the dust and rubbish between the huts mostly had umbilical hernias. Tant Bettie distributed home-brewed medicines to the sick and blankets in summer – which the women wore proudly as garments – but Christiaan seldom paid his labourers. If you did, he said, they only drank. When Daisy was fourteen, six of the labourers ran away to work in the mines in Johannesburg, and when she told her father he laughed.

'What else did Van Heerden expect? Boers! Worst nigger drivers in the world.'

The servants at the Valley House were paid regularly. Daisy watched her father do it as a Friday morning ritual. Some of them did drink, it was true, because there was always a lot of wailing and banging about on Friday nights and Saturday mornings in the servants' compound. Daisy never went there; her father forbade it.

When Hendon was eighteen, his father took him into Eckstein's, the gold-mining company of which he was a director. From then on, Hendon became his father's constant companion. He went to Kimberley with him to meet the great Alfred Beit, co-founder of Wernher–Beit which owned Eckstein's, and Hendon found a little man like a stout monkey dealing in diamonds in a small wooden office, just, he said, to keep his hand in. He put an uncut diamond like a lump of rough and clouded glass into Hendon's hand.

'What do you think that's worth?'

Hendon shook his head.

'That's fifty carats. Medium quality, say twenty-five shillings a carat. Not more than sixty pounds. Disappointed, eh?'

Beit took Hendon and his father springbok shooting in a buckboard. It was a memorable outing for Hendon. He was a good shot – his father had seen to that – and he so excelled himself that morning that the older men began to cheer at every success and laugh and beat him on the back. His father was in high delight. At lunchtime they stopped under a group of thorn trees, the branches dangling with the round grass nests of weaver birds, where laden tables awaited them in the shade. Also waiting was a big expensively dressed man with an expression of arrogant petulance and a curiously high voice. Jim Bashford put a hand on Hendon's excited arm.

'Steady,' he said. 'Go easy. That's Cecil Rhodes.'

Rhodes was a legend to Hendon, as he was to every English-speaking South African settler Hendon had ever met. Founder, with Alfred Beit, of the new British colony, Rhodesia, to the north of the Transvaal, creator of the de Beers monopoly of the Kimberley diamond fields, sometime

Prime Minister at the Cape, Rhodes represented everything Hendon had been taught to admire since he had been wrested from his mother's influence. His story was of the romantic stuff of schoolboy dreams – the penniless son of a Hertfordshire curate coming out to South Africa with nothing but poor lungs and a volume of Greek poetry as possessions and ending up veritable lord of all he surveyed. The glory of the morning's slaughter died out of Hendon as if icy water had been poured over his triumphant head. He got out of the buckboard and stood with uncharacteristic uncertainty in the dust beside it. When it came to his turn to be presented, he stammered. If it had not been for his youth and looks and that stammer, Cecil Rhodes might have taken no further notice of him.

'No need to be afraid,' Rhodes said. 'If you are your father's son, you're as good an Englishman as I am.'

Hendon blushed in fierce gratitude. When they sat down to luncheon, Rhodes called for Hendon to sit by him. Hendon could eat nothing. Rhodes tore ravenously at scraps and pieces, pushing food about his plate, talking all the time, but never to Hendon. Then, sated, he leaned back in his chair and opened his high-buttoned coat and the diamonds on the watch chain across his bulky body shot out rapiers of white light.

'Well!' he said suddenly to Hendon. 'And what does Majuba mean to you, boy?'

Hendon looked anxiously at his father. Jim mouthed back at him covertly. The table waited in silence.

Hendon said, stammering again, 'Shame, sir.'

'Hah! Shame! For whom?'

'For – for us, sir. For the British.'

It had been the most violently insisted upon history lesson of Hendon's school career. When he was only a small boy, a sailor-suited four-year-old with a thick accent and a taste for Kaffir corn, the British had annexed the Transvaal, his state, in the first stage of an effort to federate South Africa. This had led to what Hendon's history master, a clergyman for whom godliness came a very poor second to imperialism, called the first Boer Rebellion. Paul Kruger, President of the Transvaal, gathered his Boers together from their farms and unleashed their shooting skills upon the British, defeating them in a bloody slaughter on Majuba Hill and losing not one man themselves in the process. Hendon saw this as treason, his uncle Christiaan van Heerden as the rightful defence of a Boer republic whose independence Britain had recognized almost thirty years before. To Oom Christiaan, Paul Kruger was as much a hero as Cecil Rhodes appeared to Hendon.

'I tell you, nephew,' he would say, thrusting his great spade-shaped beard at Hendon, 'I tell you this, boy. We owe all we have to that man. He is a man of God. I tell you that. All his life he has struggled to give us this land, our land, the land God ordained for us, we Boers. The British drove him out when he was a boy himself, drove him beyond the Orange river, beyond the Vaal river, where our people could live as God ordained that they should. Paul Kruger is our father in God. I tell you that.'

The history master in Johannesburg had prepared Hendon to retaliate at least a little.

'The Great Trek only happened because the Boers would not give up their slaves!'

'And you, I suppose, have none? Your mother, she scrubs your floors and makes your porridge, heh?'

'At least my father pays ours!'

Oom Christiaan would come closer then, exuding the rank smell of stale tobacco and sweat.

'And what happens, boy? They spend it on drink and loose women. They beat their wives. They are like animals. I tell you that. They must work like animals and I will look after them like animals. In the Bible, boy, in the Bible, is there one black man mentioned who is required to do more than hew wood and draw water? One? I ask you that, boy, I ask you that.'

Hendon, who privately agreed with at least this aspect of his uncle's view of life in the Transvaal, would let the argument slide away at that point. Oom Christiaan would grunt, jab Hendon in the chest as a signal of victory, and tramp out to his cattle. Only over Majuba, when Hendon was eight, did his uncle actually exult in being right.

'There!' Oom Christiaan had shouted. 'There, nephew!

There, boy! God is with us! He gave us this land and He will help us keep it!' He turned to his sister-in-law. 'And you, Johanna, you should be ashamed. Ashamed! To let this boy of yours be pumped full of English foolishness. I tell you this. If the Englishman and the Kaffir want to stay here, they must do so on our terms, God's terms. We will give the vote to the Uitlanders when we please, when God pleases. You married in folly, Johanna, now you reap the fruit of that folly. But this boy, to let this boy believe such foolishness, that is a wickedness, a sin against Holy Writ. You should leave the boy here on the farm and I will show him the path of righteousness, I will make a godly man of him!'

For ever after, Majuba and its bloody defeat and shame had been inextricably tangled in Hendon's mind with the nightmare possibility that his mother, weak-willed in her fear and awe of any strong-minded man, might indeed leave him at the Van Heerden farm. Even ten years on, actually sitting so close to Cecil Rhodes that he could have touched the stuff of his sleeve, a chill gripped Hendon's heart at the mention of Majuba.

'And what,' Rhodes said, enjoying himself, playing with his watch chain, 'and what shall we do about that shame?'

Alfred Beit leaned forward to hear Hendon's reply and he had a feeling his father was holding his breath. He licked dry lips.

'Avenge – avenge ourselves, sir?'

It was the high moment of Hendon's life. Rhodes, Hendon's hero and the most powerful man in Africa, broke into a high whinny of laughter and put his arm about the young man's shoulders. And then the whole table burst into tumultuous applause.

If he had been his father's companion before, Hendon now became his confidant. His feelings for his mother, at the most those of affectionate tolerance, dwindled to embarrassment and contempt. He was made a member of his father's club in Johannesburg, given two polo ponies with a promise of more if he distinguished himself, and taken to meet his father's mistress who fascinated him physically and repelled him in every other way. She was as much his father's property as his

34

mother was and, as such, no more significant except for sexual purposes than any other woman Hendon had ever met. His father talked about her – which he seldom did – as if she were one of his English horses or gun dogs. But chiefly Jim talked to Hendon about South Africa and England and Cecil Rhodes. He reminded Hendon ceaselessly of what Rhodes had said during that unforgettable luncheon on the springbok shoot.

'Don't you forget it, my boy. Not ever. England, he said, stands in the vanguard of human progress. There is no civilization like it and no place on earth that wouldn't benefit from it!'

Hendon did not forget it, but not for the high-minded reasons that his father supposed. The attention of Rhodes that great day had most certainly been the most bragged-about incident in his life and it had given him a standing among the young bucks of Johannesburg that no one else could touch. But he also liked to be, hands in pockets, in his office in Eckstein's, looking at the map of the world pinned to the wall and seeing just how much of it was coloured pink. The only thing that marred his satisfaction was that he knew himself to be only half English. But he could do something about that. His father was right behind him, his sister Daisy was more anti-Boer than he was, and his mother, rocking tiresomely on the stoep with her damned knitting, well, she could just be ignored. She looked all right, for heaven's sake, indeed there was still strong evidence of the voluptuous prettiness that had seduced Jim Bashford, and as long as she kept her mouth shut – which anyhow she mostly did, except to the servants – all was fine and good. To be English, accepted English, even admired and adulated English like Rhodes, became the aim of Hendon's life.

In the spring of 1895, just after his twenty-second birthday, Hendon asked his father for leave to go to England. He had wits enough to know he was not indispensable to Eckstein's for six months and that his post as a fairly minor executive was thanks to his father's standing in the company rather than to his own talents. The request led first to some prevarication from his father and then to a second and extraordinary interview with Cecil Rhodes which was

35

disconcertingly quite unlike the first. The upshot of it was that Hendon was not permitted to leave South Africa. He knew too much and yet too little to be a safe ambassador for Rhodes' plans in London and Rhodes ordered him, quite bluntly, to remain in Johannesburg until the next stage in Rhodes' plan of campaign for annexing the whole of South Africa for the Empire had been achieved.

Hendon sulked a little but had no choice but to agree. A year before he had met briefly in his father's office a small frail man with a nervous manner and a powerful allure who was introduced to him as Dr Jameson, Administrator of the Chartered Company by which Rhodes ran Rhodesia for the Crown. Dr Jameson was, it transpired, in Johannesburg for a particular reason, and that reason, gathered in the Eckstein boardroom and fortifying itself with champagne (the best, Hendon noted, at nearly 80s. a dozen quart bottles), proved to be a mustering of the most distinguished Uitlanders in the city, the British and foreign businessmen to whom Kruger and the Volksraad were denying the franchise. Their anger at being treated thus was dramatic. Dr Jameson's suggestion for dealing with the problem was equally so. Hendon, adding Cape brandy to his champagne to give it a kick, thought the solution admirable.

Dr Jameson, backed by Rhodes and by Alfred Beit, proposed that he should raise sufficient troops from Rhodesia to raid Johannesburg and wrest it, literally, from Kruger. He thought he could find five or six hundred men and the Uitlanders – with one or two exceptions, Hendon noted, men who were making quite enough money out of Johannesburg to render them indifferent to having a vote or not – promised to raise an equal number at least to support the raiders when they came sweeping into the city. It seemed to Hendon an idea gallant and spectacular enough to be worthy of the Empire and said so to his father that night over cigars in the smoking room at the Valley House.

'To be kept tight under your hat, my boy.'

'Of course. I know that.'

'Like to ride with them? Won't attempt it for a year or more. He'll need the time to get arms and men.'

Hendon looked down at the suit his tailor in Commissioner Street had sworn to be impeccably English in cut. 'Not much.'

His father said, 'We won't deal with these Boers by sitting back and watching. Power politics aren't a spectator sport.'

'I don't want to fight,' Hendon said.

'You're a good marksman.'

'That's different. Soldiering has never appealed to me.'

His father poured port and sighed. 'Hendon, I'd like to feel – you were prepared to pull your weight. Do your bit.'

'Not that way.'

'How then?'

Hendon shrugged. Englishness to him was the cut of his clothes, his ability to carry his drink, a swaggering proficiency on a horse and with a gun and a cricket bat, a bloody-minded disregard for any obstacles to the pursuit of what he saw as these gentlemanly pleasures. Englishness was certainly not stampeding into Johannesburg with a bunch of toughs from the wastes of Rhodesia after months of training in some obscure and dusty outpost.

'Maybe I'll help them when they get here.'

'*Maybe?*'

'I don't know. I haven't made up my mind. And you?'

'Money raiser,' Jim Bashford said shortly, 'and I wish I could think you'd be a help to me there at least.'

After that, his father made no more stirring speeches to him about South Africa and the Empire. They talked of business and the price of gold and horseflesh and property. Dr Jameson, Hendon heard, had set up a secret camp in Bechuanaland, at a place called Pitsani, and Rhodes and Beit had established a committee in Johannesburg to round up Uitlander support. Hendon kept well out of it all, listening hard but contributing nothing, paying daily visits to the Stock Exchange in Commissioner Street, buying riding boots from Strachan's and English pipe racks and tobacco jars from Belcher Brothers, the importers in Saver Street, and slumming it with his friends by getting drunk in the Fountain Bar. It seemed to him, after a year had passed and life in Johannesburg, still in the grip of the Volksraad, had not altered at all, whatever Dr Jameson was plotting at Pitsani, that a change would be desirable. And where more desirable than England? He was surprised that his father did not immediately acquiesce and even more surprised to find himself confronting Cecil Rhodes. What Jim Bashford in his disappointment in Hendon had found it difficult to say, Cecil Rhodes had no trouble in making very plain.

'If you were a vigorous ally of our cause, young man, I should let you go. But you're not. I don't say you're pro-Boer, but you don't want to lift a finger to achieve what you would like to enjoy when achieved by others. Your idleness makes you a security risk. There is plenty of pro-Boer support in London and you would be so seduced by England that you wouldn't smell danger. You'd tell all to any flatterer, and you know enough to be useful to an enemy. You don't, however, know enough to be useful to us. If I'd thought you could raise one penny piece more for us, you would be on the next ship. But you couldn't. No one would believe you. And don't take revenge on me by blabbing in Johannesburg. Any leaks of the scheme and I shall know it is you.'

Frightened and humiliated, Hendon went back to his cronies. Out of defiance he actually made an effort at Eckstein's and achieved results good enough for Alfred Beit to say to his father, 'That boy of yours responds better to the stick than the carrot, eh?'

There was little news from Pitsani and Hendon supposed that the whole plan was about to die a natural death, particularly as the Uitlanders in Johannesburg appeared to be going about their very profitable lives largely unconcerned with the grievances that had seemed unbearable less than a year before. On New Year's Day 1896, Hendon played cricket and took four wickets. In the evening he took his sister Daisy to a party, drank far too much of his favourite mixture of champagne and brandy, and punched a man who was trying to kiss Daisy. Instead of being grateful, Daisy was in tears of indignation because she had very much wanted to be kissed and the screams that Hendon had misinterpreted were all part of the excitement of the tussle in a dark corner of the verandah. They went home together, Daisy sobbing and Hendon swearing, and were put to bed by Johanna who crooned in Afrikaans to them as she had done when they were small and tumbled over. At dawn Jim woke Hendon and told him that the Jameson Raid had failed. Rhodes had given no final word that Johannesburg was ready so Jameson had taken matters into his own hands and ridden nearly two hundred miles with his men without rest. They had reached the city of gold and found that the Uitlanders, far from racing to meet them with the enthusiasm they had counted on, were tucked up safely in bed and had made peace with Volksraad.

'They've taken him to gaol in Pretoria,' Jim said. 'He was weeping like a girl. He lost most of his best men.' He looked down at Hendon, sour-mouthed and dull-eyed from the excesses of the previous evening. 'It's all over. You can go to England when you want to.'

It was, however, two years before Hendon booked his passage to Southampton. He had meant to. Indeed, once his hangover had cleared sufficiently for him to bear to lift his head from the pillow, he had sent one of the clerks from the office off for that very purpose. But, as luck would have it, his hand was stayed, first by a bout of influenza that kept him tied to the house for weeks and then by the sudden death of his father, knocked down by runaway oxen as he was entering the Bank of Africa one morning and dying within hours of massive haemorrhaging. The scenes that followed disgusted Hendon. His mother abandoned herself to absolute grief, even to the extent of being found weeping on the opulent bosom of her husband's mistress in the drawing room of the Valley House. The Van Heerdens came in from the farm, outspanning their oxen in the road outside the house like any peasants, and standing about the house in granite attitudes while Oom Christiaan read from the Scriptures. Even the old people came from Dreyersdal, with Johanna's brothers and their wives and hordes of blunt-featured children in stout garments and stouter boots. Daisy sat in the drawing room under protest and sighed audibly and fanned herself with copies of *Johannesburg Mademoiselle*.

When eventually they had all gone and Jim had been buried with as much splendour as his children could dream up, Johanna went back to her chair on the stoep to rock and knit and cry every so often and talk to herself in Afrikaans. Daisy shed her mourning at once and spent her days with girlfriends, trying on hats and opera cloaks at Pearse Brothers, the dress shop in Von Brandis Square, or having photographs taken in languishing girlish groups, and gossiping. Hendon inherited his father's shares in Eckstein's but not, for obvious reasons, his position. He and Daisy entertained a good deal and he kept his eyes and ears open and waited for his chance to get away.

It could not be long, he felt. The failed raid had united the Boers dramatically, not only bringing about a military pact between the Transvaal and the Orange Free State but causing President Kruger to spend more than a million pounds in equipping his burghers for their next brush with the British. Hendon had little intention of being around when that happened, and when he looked at the muddle and corruption of Kruger's administration – even with the new white hope of a young lawyer called Jan Smuts to sort it out – he couldn't see that the uneasy peace could go on for long.

'I'll come to England with you,' Daisy said.

'No, you won't.'

'Hendon!' She pouted at him, swishing rose-pink moiré skirts and forgetting that he was as impervious as a stone to what she imagined were her pretty little ways.

'I shall go to England alone. When I've seen the lie of the land, I'll send for you.'

'How do you know there'll be a war?'

Hendon sighed. 'I've told you before. A dozen times. The Uitlanders still haven't the vote. And anyway, there's the gold. Do you suppose we shall let the Boers hold on to that?'

'But what will happen to me?'

'You'll go to Cape Town.'

'But I don't want to!'

Hendon picked up the paper. From behind it he said, 'Of course you do. Everyone will be going. It's much more English than here.'

Daisy was silent for a minute. 'What about the company then?'

'Eckstein's? Oh, nothing will harm that. That's one reason why we must have the British in. Kruger lets anybody

40

have monopolies right, left and centre; we've got to lower the cost of working the mines. Take off all Kruger's customs duties and so on.'

'Father would say you were running away. And you are so!'

'Father isn't here to say anything.'

Daisy glanced towards the stoep. 'And Mother?'

Hendon crumpled the paper down and looked at his sister over the top. 'Mother? Back where she belongs. On the farm.'

In March 1899, Hendon Bashford boarded the SS *Caernarvon Castle* at Cape Town for Southampton. Behind him in Johannesburg he left the rumblings of imminent war and his mother twenty miles outside the city sobbing in her sister's overfurnished and grudgingly provided spare bedroom. The only person on the Van Heerden farm who did not make her feel entirely unwanted was her niece Alecia who brought her wild flowers from the veld and handfuls of coral-red wild plums from the garden hedge and sat by her chair listening to her nostalgic babble.

Daisy travelled to Cape Town with her brother and was happily lodged with a school friend whose family had moved from Johannesburg a year before. Cape Town was preparing itself for war too, but in the lighter-hearted manner of a city making ready to house, feed and amuse an army. The Mount Nelson Hotel, where Hendon spent three most enjoyable nights, anticipated brisk trade in the shape of a steady stream of British officers and their wives.

Hendon put a substantial sum into an account in Daisy's name at the British Bank of South Africa and gave her and her school friend a farewell luncheon at the Mount Nelson. Daisy cried a good deal but then champagne always made her laugh or cry and even though she was his sister Hendon had to admit she looked less awful than most when crying. The two girls stood on the quayside and waved handkerchiefs and shrieked inaudibly at him and then the great steamship swung out of the harbour and away from South Africa. There was, Hendon reflected with satisfaction, nothing after all to keep him there any longer.

3

'Dear God,' Will Marriott said, 'what can have possessed him?'

'Whom?' his mother said absently, engrossed in her own letters. 'God?'

'Matthew. He has been sent down. Sent down! For tying up a couple of cabbies and pinning some South African to Tom Quad with croquet hoops.'

'Will,' his mother said, 'don't be silly.'

Will brandished a letter.

'It's all here. A letter from Matthew. He is at home and in disgrace.'

'My poor sister.'

'My poor mad cousin. What was he thinking of?'

'He should have gone into the army. With you.'

'He would have destroyed the regiment. The Archdeacon sounds in a rage beside which Hell's furies pale. Matthew says nobody will speak to him.'

'Not even Frances?'

Will coloured a little. 'He doesn't mention Frances.'

'May I see the letter?'

Will rose and moved round the breakfast table towards his mother. She said, 'Oh, do be careful!' the moment he stirred, so unused was she, in her sheltered widowed way, to having a man move, however gingerly, among the possessions she now treasured more than people. Will felt like some Gulliver at home these days, floundering along an obstacle course of porcelain and lace and blown glass that echoed with little female cries of panic. It seemed that his robust father might never have lived there, so utterly was his vigorous, athletic and leathery presence banished in all its manifestations.

'Don't, mother. It makes me gun shy.'

'I can't bear it when you tramp about.'

'But I *tiptoed*.' He lifted one foot. 'Look. Slippers.'

'You make them sound like boots.'

'I'll stand to attention while you read Matthew's letter. I can do it for hours.'

'Do lieutenants have to?'

'Not for as long as second lieutenants. Do read it.'

'I wish you wouldn't blaspheme.'

'I didn't – '

'I distinctly heard you say "Dear God".'

'Ten minutes ago. I won't again. I won't even breathe.'

Beatrice Marriott read for a few moments and then said, 'How distracting you are.'

He said patiently, 'How shall I not be distracting?'

'In another room. Or the garden.'

He looked with relief out of the window.

'The garden then. Ten minutes.'

There was early-morning summer glory outside, a kind of damp golden excitement. The grass glittered with dew and the sky was as delicate and clear as an eggshell. It was going to be a wonderful summer, everyone said so and *The Times* had that morning confirmed it with news that old Kruger had climbed down over the matter of foreign settlers' rights to vote in the Transvaal. He had offered the Uitlanders a retrospective seven-year franchise and Chamberlain had reported the news to *The Times* lobby correspondent at once. Will was glad in one way but sorry in another. He had been looking forward to some action, to something other than Aldershot rule books and classroom campaigning. And there was something more to his urge for action than the impatience of peacetime soldiering, a something rooted in his belief in England and the English, in English greatness. It dazzled Will to think of the greatness of England, the splendour of this tiny nation, not particularly militaristic and with only a smallish army, which had built a huge empire in which it had been an influence for peace and honour and admirable administration. Will believed utterly in the duty of the strong to help the weak, the superior the inferior, the rich the poor, and he saw the English as evangelizers and guardians, protectors and enlighteners. The chance to protect British subjects in South Africa, black and white, and to

43

enlighten those who were as reactionary and blinkered as old Kruger, Will saw as duty and he could not but be disappointed when the opportunity to shoulder that duty so eagerly looked as if it had been erased by diplomacy.

The books that lay beside Will's bed would not have had a moment's tolerance from his cousin Matthew. Will had, at Matthew's instigation, read Mill and Darwin and Buckle and had come away from them dissatisfied. His own bibles were Kipling, anything and everything that poured from Kipling's pen, but particularly 'The Light that Failed', and a book by Alfred Milner, now High Commissioner for South Africa, called *England in Egypt*. Will loved that book. Nothing else he had read described in such splendid and moving and morally sound terms the excellence of the English as colonizers. When, the year before, all Milner had described had come to pass with Kitchener's victories at Fashoda and Omdurman, Will had begun to regard Milner as something of a visionary. He believed passionately in what Sir Alfred was doing in South Africa and longed to be there, soldiering and spreading the British influence for good.

Out of the open window Beatrice Marriott said, 'It's a very incoherent letter, Will.'

'He's pretty angry, you know. With himself, I shouldn't wonder.'

'Shall you go to him?'

'At once, if you don't object. What is this rose called?'

'Chateau something. I never can remember. Don't go for a moment, I must put up something for you to take to Harriet. My poor sister. What a trial those children are to her. Not to mention the Archdeacon.'

Will came up to the window. 'I think she likes it, you know. Aunt Harriet loves a good row.'

'Nonsense.'

'Anyway, Frances isn't a trial to anyone.'

Beatrice waved the letter. 'Oh, my dear boy, Heaven forbid I should have had such a daughter. All those terrible unfeminine notions of emancipation and other foolishness. Even the Queen says such thinking is unwomanly, not that I suppose Frances cares a jot. When you come in, perhaps you would stay in your bedroom or the smoking room? It's the

44

maids' day for washing the glass. No wonder my nerves are all to pieces. Matthew is the last straw.'

'I'll telegraph Salisbury to say I am coming. What luck I've some leave – '

'Your slippers are wet through.'

'I stood on the grass. I was thinking.'

'You need a wife,' Beatrice said, withdrawing into the room. She reappeared briefly and added, 'Or a nursemaid.'

Sighing, Will reached the doorway and kicked off his slippers. Then, stooping to retrieve them, he made his way up the staircase in stockinged feet to the bedroom that had been his since boyhood.

On Salisbury station Matthew was waiting, huddled in clothes more appropriate to January than July. He ran forward to greet the train, pounding beside Will's carriage and shouting senselessly into the hiss of brakes and steam.

'Thank you,' Matthew said. 'Thank God you've come. It's a frightful business. Heaven knows what happens next. I'll have to go to Australia and build railways.'

'You are a perfect idiot. What did you think you were doing?'

'I didn't think. I just did. Perhaps I shouldn't have gone to Oxford at all. But I liked the work. And the fooling around. I hope you are prepared for absolutely silent meals.'

'Won't they talk to me either? As your ally I suppose not – '

'We can but see.'

'Matthew – '

'Yes?'

'I wish you didn't squander yourself so.'

'I call it living,' Matthew said, and shouldered Will's bag.

'There's a porter.'

'I like carrying it. It's slightly too heavy for comfort and that suits me excellently. Do you know what doesn't suit me?'

'Salisbury,' Will suggested.

'You have it. Salisbury. Designed for old ladies and older clergymen. But I've no money, not a penny. Father has seen to that.'

'Are we walking to the Close? You can't carry that thing.'

'Of course I can. Strong as an ox. Ask my scout. He said he had never seen anyone break so much furniture. Will?'

Will hurried to catch up with his cousin. 'Yes?'

'Who is this scoundrel called Hendon Bashford?'

'He's not a scoundrel. At worst he is a rather charmless colonial and he is going to make my fortune. I met him in London. Did he come to find you at Oxford?'

'And witnessed my downfall. I thought he was a blackguard. He has no social principles. He's almost as appallingly imperialistic as you are.'

'Am I in for a Little Englander tirade?'

'Certainly not. A republican one, perhaps, before the day is out. Do you know what that weasel wanted? Introductions to what he sees as the right people, and one to Frances on the off chance he might consider her handsome and blue-blooded enough to take home to Johannesburg.'

Will said angrily, 'Even her little finger is too good for a man like Bashford.'

Matthew smiled tolerantly and swung Will's bag from one shoulder to the other, narrowly missing his cousin's eye with the corner. 'He's got what he wanted so far, you know. He's going to Yorkshire with the Ripons and someone else is taking him to fish the Dee. For sheer effrontery he has no equal. How is he going to make your fortune?'

'I've bought shares in Eckstein's. It's a subsidiary of Alfred Beit's company, Cecil Rhodes' crony. Sounds quite copper-bottomed. Do we have to go this fast?'

'I thought soldiers were fit.'

'They are. I am,' Will said in some desperation, dodging and weaving between the pedestrians surging up the slope to the station, 'but not for crowded streets, not carrying things – '

'Oh, of course not. You have horses for that.'

'I don't, blockhead. I'm an infantryman. Do you know, Matthew, that a cavalryman fully dressed and kitted up can weigh three times as much as when he is naked?'

Matthew stopped abruptly and a small boy cannoned into his knees. 'Poor bloody horses.'

'Matthew – '

'Yes?'

'What did – Aunt Harriet say about my coming?'

'Nothing to me. I told you. But I heard her ordering your bed to be made up.'

'And – Frances?'

'She said she knew you would come, that you wouldn't fail me.'

'I wish you wouldn't put me to the test.'

'I won't much longer. It's by cattle boat to Sydney for me.'

'Stop,' Will said.

They were at the great gateway to the Close. Even though the gates were open, it was as if a shutter had fallen behind them, blocking out the rumble of wheels and clatter in the narrow streets. In front lay the Close, its turf as smooth and neat as green velvet and at its heart the Cathedral, the owner of the tallest spire in England.

'I love it,' Will said. 'It amazes me every time I come. It's so fragile and so dramatic.'

'You're a romantic, Will.'

'Probably.'

'What would any other nation do with you, I wonder? Only England produces men like you.'

'Don't you feel English?'

'At this moment,' Matthew said, setting off purposefully again, 'I feel of no fixed abode in either body or mind. Australian railmen would suit me excellently.'

'Stop talking about Australia.'

'Where else do you suggest?'

'South Africa.'

'Aha. Hungry for a little war mongering? Well, you'll have to swallow your disappointment. There isn't going to be one. Will –' He paused and looked down at his cousin. 'Australia may be a red herring. But I have to do something. And I think it should be far away where the breakages can't be heard in Salisbury. And I might need your help.'

'Anything. You know that. I wish I didn't want to add "within reason" but I do. I wish you could think of something constructive. I wish you weren't so damned perverse.'

Matthew gazed skywards. 'In current Oxford parlance, Will, I am a pretty average rotter.'

'And, from your tone, pleased to be.'

Matthew looked at him again, intently. 'Oh, no. Not pleased at all. Do you imagine I would have lounged about here since the end of May unless I was in such a state of confusion that I couldn't stir myself to do otherwise? Quite apart from the fact that I am penniless. And why the hell do you suppose I asked for *you* if the inner man in me wasn't screaming for help?'

Harriet Paget was fidgeting about in the hall, blowing dust off the ledges in the panelling, adjusting the Chinese vases on the oak press, fiddling with her hair. It wasn't that she didn't like having visitors – on the contrary, visitors were a vital ingredient of the isolated and highly political life of the Close – but their arrival always unnerved her. Once they were settled in and had eaten their first meal and had grown bold enough to leave books and pipes and pieces of embroidery about, she wanted them to stay for ever, to become part of the family. But she couldn't bear the welcome, the initial awkwardness, the explanations about bathrooms and mealtimes, and the ritual inquiries about journeys. It always seemed to take her several hours to remember what people were like, even Will, whom she had known since his cradle and sheltered as much if not more than his own mother.

He had grown quite handsome, she thought, peering through one of the sash windows that flanked the front door. Henry hated her to do that, he would have liked her to sit in state in the drawing room while the household ran smoothly round her. But she had a habit of making friends with the servants and that of course was death to stateliness. Henry wanted her to emulate the Bishop's wife, a huge upholstered woman so devoted to status and hierarchy and precedence that ordinary conversation was quite impossible with her. Dear Will! Not of course as striking as Matthew, but so pleasant looking with his open friendly face, and his clothes certainly made Matthew look, well, a little disorganized. She was going to have to speak to Matthew soon, seven weeks of silence and Henry still carrying about with him a perfect overcoat of injury. She knew he was upset, she was herself, but she couldn't see how sanctimonious self-pity could help. If only Henry were a little lighter of heart . . .

'Aunt Harriet,' Will said, and opened his arms.

'I've put three pillows on your bed. Very bad for your spine but I know how you like them. And I've put my copy of *Soldiers Three* up there because I know how you love Kipling and mine is a first edition and I thought you should have it. How is your mother?'

'Washing ornaments. Thanks most awfully. For the book I mean . . .'

'Would you like a drink? It's so hot – or perhaps your room first? You must go for a bicycle ride, we all have bicycles now. Your uncle is so cross with Frances and me, he thinks bicycles wildly unsuitable for women. Really, if you come to think of it, what *is* suitable for women? Think how hard Elizabethan women worked, even the grand ones, they simply never stopped. Apparently an Elizabethan woman could never get her hands into our gloves or her shoulders into our dresses. We have dwindled through idleness. I shall order tea on the lawn. In half an hour? Rather than find Beach I wonder if Matthew would take your bags up?'

'Try asking him,' Matthew suggested.

Harriet hesitated. 'Oh, my dear. Divided loyalties are the most exhausting affair in the world. It is so difficult to abide by one's principles *and* to be scrupulously fair. Just not in front of your father, Matthew.'

He stooped and kissed her. 'When has anything ever been possible in front of my father?'

A shock went through Will. The lack of reverence and the acute perceptiveness which the Archdeacon's children had always allowed free rein in their dealings with him never failed to startle him. He started up the stairs behind Matthew. From below his aunt said, 'Bless you, my dear. Two minutes in the house and you've made me speak to Matthew.'

'But, Aunt, I didn't – '

'Just by being there. Being sane and calm and ordinary. Why does your mother have this obsession with washing china? She never did as a child, though she was always extremely fastidious. I wish Matthew was a little more. Will – '

'Yes?'

'Look under your pillow.'

Under his pillow, as they had been since his first conscious visit alone as a child of six, lay a flat tin of Terry's chocolate and an orange. He took them to the window and looked at them fondly, then he raised his eyes and saw at the end of the walled garden a tall red-headed girl riding a bicycle carefully in and out of a row of bean sticks planted in the lawn. It was his cousin Frances and she was wearing bloomers.

For tea, laid on a dangerously angled table under the tulip tree, she had changed. She wore a tall-collared white blouse, a dark skirt, a tight hard belt of patent leather, and her red curls were piled on her head. She gave Will a sisterly hug.

'Oh, the relief! I hear you have brought Mamma to her senses. Poor her, always running with the hare and hunting with the hounds. Will, you look tremendously spruce.'

'And you very different to half an hour ago.'

She laughed. 'Aren't they wonderful? So comfortable you can't imagine. They give the Close apoplexy. Now, before we plunge to the depths and talk about renegade Matthew, shall I tell you what very exciting thing is happening to me?'

'More exciting than bicycling in bloomers?'

'Not such an immediate thrill but of more lasting worth.'

Matthew put an arm about his sister. 'One out, one in. Frances is going to Oxford.'

Will's eyes widened. 'Frances!'

'To St Hilda's College. My old headmistress started it six years ago. Teacher training. A whole year of working upon Father, Will, and you know what he was like about my going to school so you may imagine what a Herculean labour it's been. Of course,' she made a face, 'I won't be a member of the university, being a mere woman, but I can attend lectures and I can take a degree examination.'

She sat down in a wicker chair and motioned to Will to do the same.

He said, 'It doesn't seem very consistent – '

'With what?'

'With what I gather you feel about Matthew's – little escapade. I thought you didn't approve of Oxford for him.'

'I don't. Matthew knows that. Not now, for him. Perhaps when he's forty, but not now.' She poured out a cup of tea and passed it to Will. 'They are wasted on each other now.'

'So you are in favour of the Australian theme?'

'No,' she said, 'I'm not.'

'Then what – '

'Australia would simply be carte blanche to run absolutely amok. What Matthew needs is a war.'

Matthew was laughing, rubbing his hands over his rough head.

Will said, 'How could any army deal with Matthew?'

'Oh, come on, Will,' Frances said, 'like it deals with all rogue elephants. Matthew, what about offering the cinnamon toast around instead of gorging?'

'I'll tell you something,' Matthew said, 'Frances may well say that what I need is a war but she joined the Peace Society a month ago. So don't go to her for consistency.'

'I may not seem consistent to you,' Frances said blithely, 'but if you look at the practicality of my views you will see that I am entirely so. I disapprove of unnecessary waste of life and cause of suffering. But I know my own brother well enough to believe that in his present state of mind a war would be ideal – exhaust his body and preoccupy his mind. I don't *like* the solution, I just see it as the best one for Matthew. That's being practical. It doesn't get in the way of my belief in peace at all and, if there *is* a war, of course I don't want it to be us bullying those wretched farmers in South Africa.'

'How can you be pro-Boer? Do you know what they are doing to British subjects?'

Frances leaned back and regarded Will over the rim of her teacup. 'And vice versa? Would any settler be there if it wasn't for rich pickings? The Boers may not be very appetizing people as such but they have worked and worked to build themselves a country.'

'It isn't theirs. It doesn't belong to them.'

Matthew said, 'It doesn't belong to either of the great white thieves. It doesn't belong to anyone but a few Hottentots. But the Boer case is ethically stronger than the British. We want the gold. They want a way of life.'

'And the gold.'

'Probably. Who wouldn't? But their greatest ambition is independence.'

'They are ignorant and unprogressive,' Will said. 'They need us, it's our duty – '

'Here's Mamma,' Frances said. 'Talk to her about it. She is wholly on the side of the black men and says whoever wins, they will lose.' She stretched out and put a hand on Will's sleeve. 'Don't look so perturbed. I want England to be great too. But I think she will show much more greatness by restraint and entering into arbitration than by tramping all over other people's land and gobbling it up into the Empire.'

Harriet sank into a chair and fanned herself with a newspaper. 'Oh, my dears! Everywhere is like an oven with the door left open. Now, Will, tell us what you have been doing.'

'The usual thing. Marching about and shouting at the men, you know.'

Frances said, smiling, 'It sounds as if you could do with a war too.'

'You know I could. But not for the same reasons.'

'Father,' Matthew said levelly.

Archdeacon Paget, sepulchral in black, his fine legs buttoned into gleaming gaiters, waited on the edge of the terrace until observed by each one of the group on the lawn below him. Satisfied at last, he grasped the lapels of his coat in large well-cared-for white hands and descended the stone steps with majestic tread. He was renowned for his physical presence and his ability to fill any church or cathedral where he preached with a devoted and rustling horde of single women.

He kissed his wife and daughter on the forehead and held two fingers out to his nephew. 'William. Welcome.'

'Thank you, sir.'

'Ah! Tea. Might one inquire why the lawn bristles with poles?'

'I was bicycling, Father. It's to practise balance and is immensely difficult.'

'I hope you were suitably clad.'

'Certainly I was. For bicycling.'

The Archdeacon lowered himself into a chair, accepting

tea and toast, ignoring his son. 'Now, William. And how did you leave your mother?'

'Very well, thank you, sir.'

'And your soldiering?'

'It could do with a little variety, sir. But I wouldn't change all the same.'

The Archdeacon swallowed his tea and sighed and held out his cup for more. 'It was the meeting of the Deanery Synod today, most ineffectually chaired. William – ' he paused, took back his cup, drank again, slowly, and put the cup on the grass beside his chair. 'William, I shall not beat about the bush. You would not be here if you did not wish to assist us in the trouble and grievous disappointment that has fallen upon us. My anger has burned itself out but it has left me bowed, broken. You will know the hopes I placed in your cousin, the breadth of mind he was shown to accommodate his arbitrary changes of mind and unprincipled behaviour. And you see how I am repaid? I cannot exaggerate the blow it has been to me. My old college, my father's college – '

Matthew stood up. His father paused but did not look at him.

'If you want me,' Matthew said to Will, 'I shall be in my room.'

Harriet said, 'Please, my dears – ' and stopped, half choking.

Will watched Matthew walk away and then found his uncle's eyes fixed upon him.

'When I have your attention, William – '

'Of course, sir.'

'It is not that I seek your advice. You are yourself too inexperienced in the ways of the world to comprehend fully the magnitude of the problem, the depth of the disgrace. But I should like your help in the short term. I trust you are not at the end of your leave?'

'No, sir – '

'In that case I feel a bicycling tour would be a constructive exercise for your cousin. And you are the only companion of any common sense he would acquiesce to. It would be your task to bring some order to the confusion of his mind before he embarks on the course I have chosen for him, the only course open to a renegade who brings nothing but shame and wretchedness upon those around him.'

Harriet and Frances were leaning forward. The Archdeacon gave them both a significant look and then rose from his chair. 'As soon as it can be arranged, Matthew will sail for Canada. An ex-parishioner of mine from long ago has begun a timber enterprise on the west coast and is prepared to take Matthew on for three years. At the end of that time, he may come to see what he has squandered and what pain he has caused.'

There were tears standing in Harriet's eyes. Frances's face wore a hard and shuttered look.

The Archdeacon put a hand beneath his wife's elbow. 'Come, my dear. The details are for your ear alone. You will remember that we dine at seven, William?'

They moved away towards the house together, Harriet fumbling in her pocket for a handkerchief. 'Canada,' she was heard to say faintly, 'oh, oh, Canada – '

Will stood where he was, as he had risen when his aunt was drawn away, looking down at Frances. He observed, through all the tumult of his feelings and in a helpless, melting way, how badly she had put her hair up and how, every time she moved, great prongs of ineptly placed hairpins caught the sunlight harshly.

'Frances.'

She looked up at him. Her eyes were angry and dry. 'Canada is just another name for Australia.'

'Yes,' he said, 'I'm afraid it is.'

'He will go to pieces there. You know he will. Matthew needs a *cause*.' She stood up and grasped Will's lapels, taller than he by an inch or two. 'You know about causes, Will. You have one. Matthew needs one, craves one, would burn himself out in the service of the right one. It's so awful to see him at the moment, so languid and indifferent and aimless. Don't you see?'

'Yes,' Will said unsteadily, 'I do see. May I tell you what else I see?'

She took her hands away. 'Not that, Will. We agreed.'

'I can't stop,' he said.

'Will. We have been through it all. I would drive you mad,

54

in the long run. You know I would. You aren't even comfortable with the idea of bicycling in bloomers, are you, let alone flirtations with liberalism? Don't you meet other girls?'

'Yes.'

'Well then?'

'That's just the point. Not one is remotely like you.'

She grinned. 'But I'll bet you have fun. Aren't they all in love with you, Lieutenant Marriott?'

'There's no point in every woman in the world being in love with me if the right one is not.'

She put her arm through his. 'The atmosphere in this house is catching. It's making you melodramatic. Now what can we think of to cheer you up?'

'Leave me uncheered. Can I ask you something?'

'Anything except one thing.'

'I mustn't propose again?'

She nodded.

He drew away and put his hands in his pockets, jabbing at a daisy root with the toe of his boot. 'Do you love me at all?'

'Yes,' she said.

He sighed. 'I know what that means. As a brother. You don't even see me as a grown man, do you? I might be three, not twenty-three.'

'You were a duck at three.'

'It's a rotten thing to say, but I wish I had the power to break your heart.'

She watched him kicking the daisy. 'Will, I don't want to be in love with anyone. I've so much to do. To be perfectly honest, love would simply be in the way at the moment.'

'No pallid curates hanging about?'

She smiled, showing perfect teeth. 'We feed them to Matthew.'

'I will take him bicycling, you know. I've got nearly two weeks. I'll keep him with me as long as I can, perhaps I'll find him rooms near the regiment. Until his ship sails, that is.'

'Matthew is not going to Canada,' Frances said.

'Is he *your* cause?'

She looked at him. 'Yes,' she said. 'Yes, he is. For the moment.'

55

4

In the first week of October that year, only a few days before Frances Paget was due to arrive in Oxford, the Peace Society held a meeting in dingy public rooms off the Marylebone Road. For all that, the hall was full since the main attraction, the speaker, was H. W. Massingham of the *Daily Chronicle*, founder of the South African Conciliation Committee and a powerful voice for peace.

It was not, viewed objectively, a very prepossessing gathering, Frances thought. She had come up from Salisbury by train, ostensibly on a mission entrusted to her by her father but in reality on her own version of that mission coupled with a chance to attend the meeting. Archdeacon Paget had said that of course he did not mind if Frances read about peace, but he did not want her mixing with its promulgators, people, in his view, of half-formed notions and doubtful loyalty to the Crown. Whether that was true or not she was not yet experienced enough to know, but the sea of sombre serge and pale earnest faces about her was not particularly encouraging.

Perhaps she had read too much and let her imagination make for her a delightful world of enlightenment that did not exist. Perhaps it was not proper to believe deeply in sober and noble things and look animated and charming while you were about it. No, that was nonsense. Look at Belloc, look at Wilfrid Scawen Blunt who was wonderfully attractive, look at that young man, Ernest Temple Hargrove – a name the Archdeacon would fling at Matthew in derision – who had rebelled against his parents and flung himself with great gusto and dash into the international arbitration movement! And then look at the three women over there, earnestly talking, dismal in their charmlessness. It wasn't clothes so much – heavens above, Frances thought, looking down at her own rather clumsy assemblage of garments, who am I to criticize anyone for that? – as an absence of spirit, of lightness. Energy pervaded the meeting, to be sure, but it was the energy of sober dedication not the spontaneous outcome of lively belief. Perhaps Father was right, perhaps reading is better . . . But then, what use to anyone is solitary reading?

Someone said, 'Forgive my impertinence, but is there any chance at all that you are Miss Paget?'

Frances drew her eyes from the crowd. There was a young woman before her, shorter than she and regarding her with a lively interest.

'But – yes – '

'You must forgive me. After seeing your name here on the list of new members I have often hoped to see you here. You are so like your brother. The hair is unmistakable. I am Adelaide Munro. My father was your brother's tutor.'

'Miss Munro!'

Adelaide trusted she was not colouring in the least. 'I joined the Society seven years ago. I come to almost every meeting. I am training in London, you see.'

'Yes! Yes, of course. To nurse, was it not?'

On the platform the chairman of the meeting was clapping his hands and clearing his throat for silence.

Adelaide looked round. 'Discouraging-looking crowd, isn't it? But they mean what they say. I must introduce you to Emily Hobhouse, she is a tower of strength and so wonderfully well intentioned. Come and sit here at the side with me, for some reason one can hear much better.'

Frances followed Miss Munro through the crowd and lines of wooden chairs to a secluded corner by a pillar. It was odd to think of Matthew in connection with her, she seemed so well ordered, so decided, her brown hair quite smooth beneath a neat hat, but then, of course, under her brief influence he had gone to lectures, remembered to change his shirt, stayed sober and law-abiding.

'Do sit, Miss Paget. There is no need to hurry. I've heard Massingham several times and he is always late. I used to write letters to the *Daily Chronicle* when I was living in Oxford, and he published several. I pretended I was a man.'

She looked at Frances, bit her lip, and said more quickly than she had intended, 'I – I was so sorry to hear of your brother's troubles.'

Frances clutched her handbag to her. She looked quite wild for a moment and Adelaide began to repent that she had spoken of Matthew at all. Then Frances said, in a perfectly ordinary voice, 'It's been a long summer. It was all very unfortunate.'

'I'm so sorry. I should not have mentioned it.'

A large woman brushed heavily past them, momentarily obscuring them from each other in a swirl of mothball-scented skirts.

Frances said eagerly, 'Oh, no! Indeed you should! I'm – I'm so glad you made yourself known. I wanted to know you – then, when you were friends. Everything Matthew does concerns me so nearly, you see, we are only a year apart in age and in many ways he seems to me the younger, though he isn't.'

'And what will happen to him now?'

Frances swallowed. 'That's – that's one reason why I could come to today's meeting. My father has a bad attack of gout and is confined to an armchair, so I was deputed to come to London and buy Matthew's ticket for Canada. It was all arranged. I only had to collect the papers.' She clutched her handbag again.

'Canada!'

'A timber-felling company – '

'Ladies and gentlemen! Silence, if you would be so good – '

'But the war!' Adelaide whispered.

'I know, I know – '

'It makes me so angry! We've worked in this Society for years and this summer I really thought we were winning. But of course the country *wants* war, can you believe it?' Adelaide snorted.

On the platform, H. W. Massingham shuffled his papers and cleared his throat. 'Ladies and gentlemen – '

'Will you have a cup of tea with me?' Adelaide said.

'I should be thankful to. I feel uplifted and cast down all at once. He spoke with such beautiful sense and all for nothing.

58

There are troops on the high seas from all over the Empire heading for South Africa and we sit in a dreadful hall in London and talk about stopping them.'

'One can't give up trying,' Adelaide said. 'Come in here. It's where I usually go.'

The Peace Society had surged, it seemed in a body, into the teashop and an atmosphere charged with high argument and toasted buns. Adelaide led Frances among crowded tables, stopping here and there to shake a hand, to a squashed corner by the hat stand.

'Not comfortable, I'm afraid, but private.'

Frances sat down and rubbed her hands over her face. 'Days like this, living history – '

'I know,' Adelaide said, 'and so incongruous that the English take refuge from them in cups of tea. Shall I order? Are you hungry?'

'No, no thank you – '

'Tea for two, then. Just tea. May I call you Frances?'

'I wish you would.'

'Will you tell me more about Matthew?'

Frances looked at her. Her long grey eyes – very fine eyes – were quite steady. 'He ran wild. He didn't seem able to stop.'

'My father had such hopes for him, he admired his brain so much.'

'That's the trouble. Most people admire Matthew's brain and I sometimes feel he doesn't give two straws for it himself.'

'I hated to see the waste.'

Frances smiled at her. 'I could see you did.'

Adelaide blushed fiercely. 'It's an awful fault of mine. I can't bear to see waste. It's the same at the hospital, though obviously in terms of human endeavour it's much worse. That's really why I joined the Peace Society, I think. A feeble gesture to stop any more waste. And look what's happening.'

Tea arrived on a metal tray, banged down on the table. Adelaide began to pour out. 'It's so stupid. Of course I'm glad Matthew isn't going to be involved in the war. You could tell that by just looking at me so it's no use pretending otherwise. But I don't like the Canada scheme. More waste. What will he do out there? What sort of people will he mix with? Milk?'

'Please. Adelaide – ' Frances picked up a teaspoon and began to score quick lines in the tablecloth with it. 'Adelaide. Matthew *is* going to South Africa.'

Adelaide stopped pouring.

'That is what I have been doing today. It's all part of a scheme we laid in the summer, Matthew and I and our cousin Will Marriott, who's in the army. They went bicycling – they were *sent* bicycling – together in July and came back with the plan and we completed it today. If there was a war, and we all felt in the summer, whatever anyone said, that there would be war, Will would obviously be sent, as a regular soldier, and Matthew would volunteer. Not here of course, where he could be stopped, but in Cape Town. He thinks like me about war, this war, but he says he would rather *be* there, see the situation properly, and of course he wants to disobey our father. Father says go west, so Matthew goes in the opposite direction. Will sails tomorrow for the Cape so we had to put the plan into action today. I collected Matthew's passage and sold the tickets to Will, who says he has a friend who will dispose of them. Then with the money I booked him on the *Orient* to Cape Town. It sails on 14 October, the same day as General Buller leaves for South Africa. His ticket is in my handbag.'

She put her hand to her face for a moment. It shook a good deal. Then she said with false brightness, 'So now you know it all.'

'Oh, my dear – '

'It would be easier if it wasn't so confused, if *I* wasn't so confused. I hate the idea of war, I hate it. I don't want Matthew to go, I don't want Will to go, I don't want any wretched soldier to go. But Will believes in what he is doing, believes England can only do good, great good, wherever she goes, however she does what she does. And Matthew is looking for the Holy Grail. Do you suppose it is any more likely to be found in South Africa than in a logging camp in Canada?'

Adelaide poured more tea. 'And your parents?'

'They will know nothing until a letter arrives postmarked Cape Town not Vancouver. My poor mother. I suppose,' she smiled wanly, 'my father might even miss the point and

60

see it as Matthew's capitulation. A soldier of the Queen after all.'

There was a pause and then Adelaide said, 'There is very little you can do about someone like Matthew. I agree with you. I abhor the idea of war and yet there's something in the whole horrible business that would suit him. He needs to exhaust himself. I think you are very brave, I do indeed. You have to stay and bear the brunt of things at home. Your parents won't like the secrecy. How could they?'

Frances began to gather up her possessions. 'I must go. I mustn't miss the train. Matthew will meet me at Salisbury.'

Adelaide rose. 'And I must be back on duty. Will you keep in touch?'

'Of course – '

'And wish Matthew godspeed. From me.'

Although her father had given her money for a second-class railway ticket, Frances travelled third class and would return the extra money to the Archdeacon. It was a tiny, and she knew useless, sop to her conscience. She sat in the corner with her eyes closed and felt, in an impersonal way, the odd tear slide from under her shut lids and slip down her face. There was so much in life, it seemed, that one's head could manage and one's feelings could not. Everything had been so clear in the summer, her own opinions so lucid, her courage so high, even her conviction that Matthew's disgrace was only his own disrupting way of making a new beginning, so firm. And now here she was, eager party to a scheme which involved sending the two young men closest to her in life off to a war which she abhorred in every way, both particular and general, and also included the deception of her parents which, even in her most buoyant moments, filled her with bitter distaste. And going off to Oxford, which had seemed such a modern and free-spirited thing to be doing, now appeared to her just rather a silly and selfish enterprise in the context of war.

'Life must go on,' the Archdeacon had said and Frances had known that what he meant was that his must, the same in every detail of regular comfort. But, for those who could

61

not obscure their fears with the mechanics of pleasant living, life going on would need a superhuman effort.

She had needed one today, saying goodbye to Will. He had been magnificent himself, enabling them both to behave beautifully. They had lunched together in the little house his mother kept but seldom used behind Pont Street and Will had eaten normally and talked normally and said comforting easy things like 'When I'm back after Christmas' and 'I want regular letters – there's a splendid service to Cape Town, you know. No excuses' and Frances, who had always been in charge of their conversations before, was quite helpless and pushed her goujons of sole round and round her plate until they fell to pieces and she was embarrassed at the childish mess she had made. Will made her drink a glass of Madeira after lunch and then he walked her into Hyde Park and very briskly across it and put her into a cab at Marble Arch for her meeting. She let down the window.

'No going native, Will. It happens to Englishmen who go to outlandish places. They preach imperialism and become seduced by the conquered.'

'No little Hottentot lady, then?'

Francis grinned. 'I wasn't thinking of her. I was thinking of a Boer farmer's daughter.'

A small spasm passed over Will's face and then he laughed and said, 'Think of me the next three weeks. Parlour games and amateur dramatics all the way to the Cape, they say,' and then he kissed his hand to her and turned and went quickly back into the park.

She knew why he had briefly looked so pained. He didn't like her sounding so carefree over the possibility of his flirting with somebody else. He had liked it at lunch when she couldn't manage herself and he had steered the way for both of them. When he was there, believing so entirely in what he was about to do and excited at the adventure, it was quite easy to be carried along with him, not to think too hard herself. But now, alone in the railway carriage with an old man snoring in his sleep and two raw boys eating chestnuts, it wasn't easy in the very least. She didn't share Will's belief, she was frightened by the ill-defined force of whatever was driving Matthew, she was sorry for her mother, exasperated by her father, and scornful of the prospect of going to learn how to teach in a college at Oxford. It didn't seem to her, at this very moment, grinding out of Basingstoke, that she had a mind at all, let alone the one she was so proud of, which had given her, in the past, such confident pleasure.

Adelaide Munro came into her thoughts, trim and decided, her beliefs unshaken by the seeming ineffectiveness of the cause to which she was pledged. Frances pictured her on the ward, starched and capable and busy, and was comforted at the image. She sat up straight, blew her nose with finality and glared at one of the boys who had dropped his chestnut peels all over the carriage floor.

On the morning of Saturday, 14 October, a vast and cheering crowd gathered at the dockside at Southampton. There was a good deal of flag-waving and shouting and two men had climbed a crane with a clumsy home-made banner which read, 'Pull old Kroojer's whiskers'. None of this patriotic fervour, Matthew knew, pushing his way through the packed bodies, was for him, nor indeed for the SS *Orient* and the troops it would carry to Cape Town. That afternoon, the *Dunottar Castle*, berthed at some distance from the *Orient*, would bear away General Sir Redvers Buller whose Army Corps, at a cost of £10 million, was intending to send the Boers back at the double to their Bibles and ploughshares.

Indeed, there was no one at all to see Matthew off. He had asked that there shouldn't be. Quite apart from the fact that his destination would be discovered, he did not want to be wept over. His mother had almost managed not to, at Salisbury station, and he was grateful for that. He went up the gangplank of the *Orient* in great strides and turned at the top to look down at the quayside and the crowd. The sight filled him with a queer exhilaration, there was a sniff of freedom in the air, a taste of danger and adventure. He raised both arms in the air and began to flap them vigorously at the upturned faces below.

Part Two

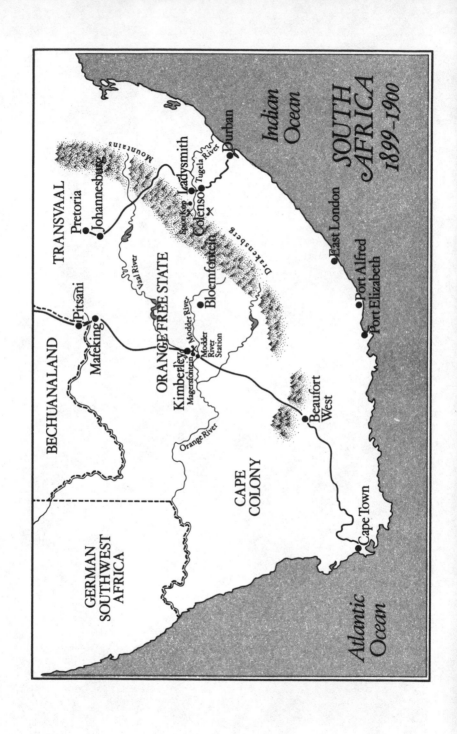

5

Daisy always wrote to her mother in English. Johanna could read it, but she didn't like to in her brother-in-law's house where life almost obliterated any memory she had of the Valley House with its English books and newspapers. When the letters came, she would wave them feebly and say, 'Aie, aie, what use are these to me?'

And Oom Christiaan would say, 'Put them on the fire. She only sends tales of foolishness from the Cape. She is as silly a girl as you deserve to have in all your weakness over her.'

Johanna knew Alecia would help her. She would hand the letter to Alecia and some neat sleight of hand would take place over the fire and later Alecia would bring the letter to her bedroom and she would read it to her in a whisper. Tant Bettie thought they were praying together.

If it were not for Alecia, life would have been intolerable. Even before they were all sure there would be fighting and the men were still at home, the house and the yard busy, Johanna had not been happy. True, she could hardly remember when she had ever been happy and was inclined to think that it was only for the split second before Jim Bashford proposed to her and she had realized, gloriously, that he was going to. Now, of course, happiness was out of the question. Her children were gone – Daisy wrote irregularly, Hendon, up to heaven knew what in England, never – her husband dead, leaving behind such a wealth of infidelity as quite ruined his memory for her, and her sister and brother-in-law had taken her in because the Boer tradition of family loyalty demanded it and it seemed more natural she should go to her sister than to the brothers and their wives at Dreyersdal. The Valley House had become lonely and alien towards the end but she had grown used to servants trained to English ways and to being able to please herself. On the farm she had to please Christiaan in the name of pleasing God. It was back to the harsh domestic burden of her childhood, the allotted tasks, the shouting at the black servants, the words of the Scriptures being the hour-by-hour, minute-by-minute stuff of daily talk, the coarse heavy food, the stiff dark clothing and stout boots, the smell of unwashed humanity, and the proximity of animals. By her bed she had a photograph in a claret plush frame of the drawing room at the Valley House, but after a month Bettie took it away. She said it displeased Christiaan as the farm was now Johanna's home. It was horribly true. On Hendon's instructions the Valley House had been let to a director of Cecil Rhodes' company, Consolidated Goldfields.

A week after the photograph had been taken away, Alecia brought it back, removed from its frame and folded in a piece of paper. Alecia had not spoken much to her aunt since she had come to live on the farm, except for the merest formalities, only stared as she had stared at Daisy as a child. Now she knelt by her aunt's chair and said in an English so thickly accented it was hardly intelligible. 'Hide it. Hide. Under your bed.'

Together they slipped the photograph under Johanna's mattress.

'You teach good English,' Alecia said as they knelt together by the bed. 'I learn you. I learn *from* you.'

'Your father – '

'Not know.'

'But why? Why do you want to learn English?'

Alecia pulled a book from the pocket of her apron. She held it out to her aunt.

'*Rob Roy*,' Johanna read, 'Sir Walter Scott – '

Alecia said rapidly in Afrikaans, 'I must read. I must. I cannot go through life reading only the Bible. I want to read English. Daisy gave me this. She hated it. She gave me a book every time she came, she didn't want them. I've taught myself but it's so slow, it's terrible it's so slow, and I have to hide to read. All the books are hidden. Will you help me?'

'My dear, my dear, my English is so bad, your uncle always said it was only fit for the kitchen – '

'Teach me that, teach me! I only need the beginning.

68

Daisy gave me a dictionary. She hated that book worst of all.'

'That is why you brought me back my photograph?'

'Not only why.' Alecia stood up, folding her rough hands on her apron. 'You always look as if you want to cry.' She looked round the room, at the heavy solid furniture of which her mother was so proud, scattered with her aunt's silly pretty possessions, legacy of her light contact with more sophisticated tastes. 'I will bring you flowers. For this room.'

She brought a sheaf of canna lilies and stood them in an earthenware milk pitcher on the floor. She began to bring things most days, a handful of tiny peaches, a frond of frothy yellow wattle blossom, blown birds' eggs. Johanna did not really care for these offerings, she would have preferred manufactured things, but she took them in the spirit in which they were given. The English lessons took place intermittently throughout the day, at the sink, kneading dough, feeding the poultry, stripping the mealie cobs for porridge, boiling the great cauldrons of laundry. It was easy to do in low voices under the cover of activity and the black women singing. Alecia began to read *Vanity Fair*. She understood the language and nothing of the story.

When Johanna had been at the farm almost a year, everything changed. It changed, it seemed to Johanna, overnight. One late September evening she had been sitting by the light of the foul-smelling tallow candles hooking rags into sacking for kitchen rugs; the next morning only, the yard was full and men and boys were away to the war. President Kruger, Oom Paul as they all thought of him, had called up his burghers in the Transvaal to defend their republic as the British were sending ten thousand soldiers to South Africa, and the Van Heerdens were responding to his call. Each man was to take his own horse, his own gun, his own billy can, his own coffee and mealie meal and biltong, the sun-dried leathery strips of game and spiced meats, and, provided only with ammunition from the republic, he was to go off to join the commando of his choice. Gaspar was very excited. He wanted to kill an Englishman.

'I'll bring you back their heads! The heads of the rooineks!'

69

They were taking two black farm labourers mounted on tough little Basuto ponies. They did not know where they were going beyond assembling in Pretoria, a twenty-mile ride. Christiaan van Heerden's usual method of communication was by shouting and this day was no exception. He shouted at his wife and daughter and sister-in-law, he shouted at the black labourers gathered in the rubbish-strewn dust outside their rondavels, he shouted at his son, his horse, at other members of the Middelburg Commando who had come to collect him. Then he kissed Alecia and Johanna on the forehead, his wife savagely on the mouth, leaving her with her hand pressed to her bruised lips, swung himself into his saddle, and thudded from the yard. In the confusion and excitement, Gaspar forgot to say goodbye at all.

Tant Bettie went back to the kitchen and wept into her hands. 'My man, my boy, my man – '

Alecia left Johanna to comfort her, clucking and soothing in the Afrikaans of their shared childhood, and went out to the great barn behind the house. The threshing floor was thick with aloe and prickly pear leaves which Christiaan had ordered beaten to a mash which could be fed to the cattle if the rains did not come. There was no one there. Until her mother had finished her weeping and assumed the authority she had been left with, no one would do anything. The morning was still and clear and fresh, damp with spring. Alecia climbed up onto the huge wagon in which her mother had come as a bride with the vast mahogany and velvet wealth of her dowry, and reached up to loosen a stone of the wall. In the space behind were two books wrapped in torn scraps of cheesecloth, *Rob Roy* and her dictionary. The dictionary was not proving much help with Scottish dialect. In the gloom of the barn, her lips moving soundlessly, Alecia settled down to read. She promised herself ten minutes, every day, no matter what happened. Today her father and her brother had gone off to save their land from being conquered by the English, to defend the Van Heerden farm, her home, but still she must read.

Hooves sounded in the yard. Someone shouted, a man. Unhurriedly, Alecia wrapped up her books, put them back

70

in their hiding place, replaced the stone, and climbed down from the wagon. There were half a dozen men in the yard, all mounted but one, and he was standing by his horse's head and shouting, just like her father.

'Can I help you?'

The dismounted man whipped off his slouch hat revealing a head of brilliant red hair. He was enormously tall and had a rhinohide whip coiled round his waist.

'Your father. We are looking for your father. All the burghers are called up.'

'We know,' Alecia said, standing before him and shading her eyes from the sun. 'Father has gone twenty minutes since. To Pretoria.'

The red-haired man smiled. 'You must be Alecia. I dandled you when you were a little bit of a thing. I'm your father's cousin, Daniel Opperman. Red Daniel.'

She nodded, smiling back.

'I wanted your father in my commando. With the men from Carolina. And your brother.'

'They've gone with the Middelburg Commando.'

'I'll find them. I'll catch them up.' He paused. 'Your mother?'

'In the kitchen. She is upset.'

He shook his head sympathetically. 'It was very sudden. But we must be ready. The British will declare war any day and we want to be ready for them, lined up on the Natal border. Your brother, is he a good shot? Like your father?'

'Yes,' Alecia said, 'almost better.'

Red Daniel looked around the yard. 'And you will help your mother here. Till we come back.'

'And my aunt.'

Red Daniel spat. 'The aunt who married an Englishman?'

'Yes.'

'Just as well he is dead, heh?'

'Do you hate the English?'

Red Daniel looked round at his companions. They were all laughing.

'Hate them? No, indeed. Who gave you such an idea? I want them to come in here and take our land and our farms and our gold and our women and all the things that God in

71

His wisdom has given to us by His word in Holy Writ. I want to give all that to the rooineks. I am just going to the Natal border to give them a welcome. A big welcome.' He pulled a rifle from its sheath beside his saddle. 'See that? That's a Mauser rifle. The Germans make them. So light we can fire with one hand. Much more accurate than anything the British have. That is what we will welcome them with.'

He bent and kissed her, smelling strong and animal like her father. Then he turned and mounted his pony, sitting easily in the saddle.

'You women,' he said, 'you women will keep our farms for us. We will bring our freedom back for you.'

'You want a British soldier's head?' one of the others shouted.

'No thank you,' Alecia said. 'My brother says he will bring one and I don't want that one either. If I wanted one I would shoot him for myself.'

Bettie came running from the house, her face blotched from crying, carrying calico bags of bread baked slowly dry to rusks. She went from man to man, handing up a bag, calling blessings up to them, godspeed.

Red Daniel said, 'Christiaan will be back. You sow the seed, he will be back for the harvest.'

'It's the calving – '

'She will help you,' Red Daniel said, patting Bettie's hand, looking at Alecia. 'She knows what to do. Keep her busy, keep her busy. When it's all over it will be time to find her a husband. Come, we must be going, I've a commando to get in shape.' He looked round, grinning at his men. 'The Carolina Commando are going to send the British flying.'

The next day, there was a letter from England. Bettie said nothing but her disapproval needed no words. She had been up since dawn, Christiaan's small revolver strapped to her waist, turning the labourers out of their rondavels, making lists, delegating. The back of the envelope was embossed with a name of a London club and both it and the letter were of thick stiff paper. Freed from Christiaan's presence, Johanna read it in the kitchen, spreading it out on the table among the butter beans she was shelling for drying.

'It's Hendon,' she said to Alecia. 'It is as well your father is not here. He is on the side of the English. He is coming to Cape Town with the English general and he will stay there.'

'What will he do? Will he fight?'

Johanna looked down at her letter. 'I do not think so. I think he will try to run his business interests. That is what he says. He asks do I need money – but he does not ask do I need him.' She spread her hands. 'I cannot go to the Cape. Not alone.'

'Ask him to come here.'

'He is with the English!'

'I forgot,' Alecia said. 'In spite of everything, I cannot forget he is my cousin. What I forget is the sort of cousin he is.' She held out her hand, 'I think we should burn this letter. Don't you?'

Hendon Bashford arrived in Cape Town on the last day of October. It was a pity to have missed some excellent sport in Scotland by being on the high seas, but as his hosts had been on the same troop ship there really had been no alternative. And in fact the ship had been pretty jolly, all things considered, each day starting with a gymnastic class on the starboard side of the upper deck – dress: pyjamas – and ending with a pretty reasonable dinner of a dozen or so courses. The last night on board had been quite like some of the best evenings he'd had in London. Dinner had begun with lobster mayonnaise, meandered through chaudfroid of pheasant and several joints to a dressed ham and then all sorts of nonsense to please the ladies, like *gêlée aux liqueurs* and *crême à l'ananas*, and then cheese and salads and dessert and some reasonably handsome port. He'd been as sick as a dog but not before a much-applauded rendition of a song he'd composed about the Bay of Biscay, all about seasickness, with every verse ending in the refrain,

> Steward! Stand by with the old pail
> As you'll frequently have to do!

He had then drunk a bottle of Pol Roger and half a bottle of brandy and two majors had held him over the rail while he threw it all up into the ocean. He had a dim recollection of

73

hearing one of them say that if that was the alternative to Johnny Boer, he wasn't sure he was fighting on the right side, but he wasn't at all clear about the accuracy or the sense of that. To be sure, the colonel of the regiment had been somewhat frosty the next morning but then English officers could be on the stiff side and one shouldn't take any notice.

After all, there were plenty of people who had taken a great deal of notice of him. Hendon had had a wonderful summer. He had been to Henley in white flannels and a high-lapelled striped blazer and consumed lobster and champagne without ever going near the river except to push somebody in. He had been to three army balls where the supper rooms glittered with regimental plate, eaten oysters galore, and danced with a great many pretty girls with beautiful skins, dressed in silver gauze and pink crepe de Chine and osprey feathers, only a few of whom refused to dance with him again. He had fished in Scotland and on the very first day the ghillie had caught two salmon he had passed off as his own. He had shot grouse in Yorkshire, played cricket and croquet (the sight of the hoops gave him a slight qualm still), acted in drawing-room comedies, and in every house taken maximum advantage of his host's cellar and daughters. He had played cards three or four nights a week and had cheated, if he possibly could, on every one of them.

It was only at the last house before his departure – or before, as he had hoped, he went north to Perthshire for what promised to be a distinguished and wealthy party – that any kind of rebuff came. He was met in the hall by his host, the father of the young man whom he had relieved of £200 at bridge the week before. His host was as straightforward as any man Hendon had ever met.

'I fear, Mr Bashford, that your reputation has preceded you. I have no wish at all to entertain under my roof or in the company of my wife and daughters a man as deficient in honour and scruple as your behaviour recently has shown you to be. I shall not order your luggage brought in. On the contrary, I shall request that you rejoin it in the carriage and are taken forthwith to the railway station.'

Hendon shrugged and went back to London. It was August and London was empty. He telegraphed to all the

74

houses he had visited during the summer and they politely regretted that their houseparties were full and there was not a bed to spare. For almost four weeks Hendon rioted in London with whatever company he could find and then discovered that he preferred drinking other people's champagne to his own. He wrote to Perthshire asking if he might come earlier than planned and was called upon at his club in London by the son of the house.

'Awfully sorry, old boy, but the whole thing's off. For us young ones anyway. We're all off to the Cape, it looks like. Just as you said.'

'I don't mind,' Hendon said. 'I don't mind none of you being around. Won't bother me.'

'Thing is, old boy, you can't go north. The pater's got wind of something, some lark or other, and, not to put too fine a point upon it, he won't have you. Between you and me, I think you ought to go back to South Africa. It's where you belong after all. And I should think the Cape will be fairly jolly with the army pouring in. Why don't you think about it?'

It seemed, in the circumstances, a fine idea. Five weeks later, being hugged by Daisy, dressed to kill in pale yellow with a hat smothered in primroses, it still did. Swaggering through the crowd in the sunshine, ordering his splendid new English luggage into the carriage, being greeted by officers here and there, it still seemed an excellent plan. The Taggarts, Daisy's schoolfriend's family, had booked him a suite at the Mount Nelson, already full of officers and their wives and accompanying intrigue.

'It's all parties!' Daisy was saying, squeezing his arm. 'I never get any sleep, I'm turning into an old hag. Look at me! Isn't it shocking? And I need heaps more money. Are you going back to Johannesburg to get some?'

'No.'

'But will we have enough? I keep meaning not to spend it, but I still do. It just melts away, however hard I try. Have you brought some from England?'

'Yes,' Hendon said, 'yes, I have. Lots of people wanted to invest in Eckstein's but I can't do anything about that till the war's over. So we'll use that for the time being.'

Daisy fanned herself vigorously. 'Thank goodness for that. I've ordered so many things, you can't imagine. There's a ball at the hotel tonight, to welcome the general, it's so lucky you're here. Hendon?'

'Yes.'

'Did you write to Mother?'

'Yes.'

'Do you know, she writes to me in Afrikaans! I can't understand a word. Is she coming down to the Cape?'

'I didn't ask her to.'

'She'd be miserable. What would she do? She's much better off where she is.'

Will was not in a dancing mood. His regiment was off in two days, by train up the western railway to the Orange river, which gave him the fidgets, and in any case the news from Natal was not of the sort to celebrate. He had arrived in Cape Town ten days before and for over a week they had all fiddled about unloading stores and putting guns together and having endless kit inspections while gloomy news rolled in from the north, starting with the dismal and shaming information that, on the western front, both Mafeking and Kimberley were now under siege. Things looked a little brighter just after their arrival, with General Penn Symons taking some hill called Talana from the Boers, but then it seemed that Penn Symons had been mortally wounded and that, worse still, Colonel Möller and his small company of cavalry and mounted infantry had surrendered, and so whatever splendour there had been in Talana had ebbed away. Then came reports, a day or so later, of a battle at a place called Elandslaagte, near Ladysmith, where Möller's shameful white flag had been avenged, and the cavalry, with howls of 'Majuba! Majuba!', had ridden three times back and forth across the defeated Boers, hacking at them with sabres and lances.

'Excellent pig-sticking,' someone said heartily to Will.

Will felt something close to envy. Not for the slaughter but for the involvement. Down here in the Cape, in this lush green place with its pretty Dutch houses and vineyards, it was like being confined to a drawing room when you longed with all your heart to be on the football field. They said it was much uglier up there in Natal and even more so in the Transvaal, where the action was, miles and miles of wild red nothing with thorn trees and rocky outcrops and distances beyond imagining. Someone said that Ladysmith, where Sir George White, in command of all the British troops in Natal, had set up his base, was absolutely the back of beyond, a sort of South African Aldershot, a place that had grown up as a crossroads for the great cattle drives across the northern republics. Most people, especially those given to armchair strategy, said he should never have gone that far north, should never have crossed the Tugela river. It did seem odd, Will thought, that the great British army should end up having such battles as Talana and Elandslaagte all for the defence of an insignificant and dusty hole such as Ladysmith sounded. Of course, it had the railway, and it was on the way to Pretoria – and that was everything.

And then worse things had begun to happen. White sent out regiments from Ladysmith to try to secure surrounding vantage points and disaster struck. Names began to shower down on Cape Town – Rietfontein, Pepworth Hill, Nicholson's Nek – all of them causing fury and despair. The British had been defeated, soundly and repeatedly, and tired troops were stumbling back into Ladysmith with nothing gained and a great many lives pointlessly lost. People were calling yesterday 'Mournful Monday' – only *yesterday*, Will thought, and here am I, hanging about some damned ballroom when all I want in the world is to be up and at them.

The room had been hung with green garlands, and behind the stage where the band was playing a huge Union Jack had been suspended, as well as several regimental colours, including Will's own. Every corner was crowded, there was hardly any room to dance, even if he had been inclined to. He'd spent most of the evening lounging about with fellow officers, all of them binding on about the incompetence of everyone in the army, particularly those in Natal, except themselves.

'The thing is,' Dick Rawlings said to him, 'that the Boers have absolutely no military discipline at all. It amazes me that they can fight at all. They choose their own commando, they push off home when they want to – '

77

'They ride and shoot like the very devil,' someone else said.

'But we know what we're doing! I simply don't see that they stand a chance. I can't imagine what's going on in Ladysmith. Even the 92nd with its tail between its legs – '

'No uniform either,' Will said, 'and if they all look like old Kruger heaven help them – '

'Ponies and muskets! Coffee pots hanging from their saddles. Bloody coffee pots!'

'What we have to do,' Dick Rawlings said, 'is relieve Mafeking and Kimberley.'

Will said, 'That's what we are going to do. Or are you going somewhere else on Thursday?'

'Don't be a fool. I mean we must relieve them quickly. It's a matter of prestige as well as strategy. If we don't we shall have awful trouble with some of the Dutch colonists down here who are just waiting to see what happens before they show their true colours.'

'I don't think they do matter,' Will said. 'Not as much as Natal. That's where we should be going. To Ladysmith. Not to the Western Front at all.'

'But there's the railway – '

'Oh, the railway – '

'And in any case the Western Front via Bloemfontein is the best way to get at Pretoria. And the ports can supply it.'

'Then why relieve Kimberley at all?'

'Kimberley first, fathead, then take those troops with us to Bloemfontein and on to Pretoria.'

'No. *No.* Concerted push northwest from Ladysmith to Pretoria. We are deployed over far too wide an area as it is – '

A commanding woman in violet satin loomed over their table. 'Are you gentlemen not dancing?'

They leaped guiltily to their feet.

'I am Mrs Taggart of Cape Town. I thought that British officers could be relied upon for their gallantry. I have two charming young ladies here and they are in need of partners.' She seized Will and Dick by the arm in huge capable hands and spun them onto the dance floor.

'My daughter Grace. And Miss Daisy Bashford.'

78

In front of Will was a girl as pretty and luscious as a Persian kitten. He held out his arm. 'Miss Bashford?'

She took it giggling. 'Oh, this is too embarrassing! I'd been forbidden to dance with the man I was dancing with. Can you imagine? Mrs Taggart actually pulled me away from him! In front of everyone! I could have died. She said I had to dance with someone else from a good regiment and never ever with Major Simpson again – '

'I'm Will Marriott. My regiment is honoured – '

'Do you know Johnnie Simpson?'

'No.'

'He's the wickedest thing – '

'Would you care to dance, Miss Bashford?'

She swung into his arms, exuding little puffs of rose-geranium from ruffles of white gauze.

'Do you by any chance, Miss Bashford, have a brother by the name of Hendon?'

She nodded. 'Nobody's speaking to Hendon. He got off the boat from England only today and he got drunk at supper and insulted Mr Taggart. I expect that's why old mother Taggart is in such an awful mood.'

'I met Hendon in England.'

She pouted. 'He wouldn't take me.'

'And now he's back?'

'Yes. I can't think why. He seemed to meet just heaps of people in England.'

'He was certainly seen about.'

Daisy looked at him with her wide open gaze. 'Marriott, you said?' She eyed his shoulders disparagingly. 'Lieutenant Marriott?'

'Captain actually. As of 1 November.'

She rolled her eyes at him. 'Big boy.'

'I think you must be the prettiest girl in Cape Town.'

'Oh, you soldiers! All this naughty talk and then off you go and leave us broken hearted! Look – look over there. There's Major Simpson and he's not dancing at all!'

Will slipped his arm more firmly round her waist. 'All I can say, Miss Daisy Bashford, is that Major Simpson's loss is definitely my gain.'

79

6

The western railway ran northeast out of Cape Town, over the Groot river, and into the Witteberg hills. Five hundred miles later its rusty single track brought trains into Kimberley, having run through Beaufort West and De Aar and over, interminably, the Great Karroo.

'Look at that, sir,' Will's sergeant said. 'I saw it when I was up 'ere in '86, fightin' in Bechuanaland.' He turned slightly aside and remarked to the soldier behind him, 'Four 'undred miles of bugger all.'

Someone had told Will that spring brought the only greenness the veld knew. If that was so, it had forgotten the Great Karroo. Orange-red earth strewn with boulders rolled away and away beside the train, beyond the train, behind it. A few thorn trees cowered among the stones and every so often a curious cairn-shaped cluster of rocks rose out of the earth, a flat-topped hummock of stones balanced together in the manner of dry-stone walling in the West Country.

'Kopjes,' Will said to himself, 'kopjes – '

There was nothing else. The train, an incredibly long snake of trucks, stretched away to the far horizon; eight thousand men, forty to a truck, open cattle trucks at that; flat wagons with swivelling turrets on which the guns were carried, the field guns and naval guns, the great fifteen-pounders and the field artillery's howitzers. Besides them were the cattle trucks of horses, wagons of mule carts, boxes of ammunition, crates and bales of medical supplies, food stores – and somewhere, no doubt in the general's own baggage, a small and secret wireless set made by Marconi that no one quite knew how to work.

Will had only met General Methuen as the merest formality. That summer, bicycling along the lanes of Wiltshire with Matthew, they had stopped at Corsham Court,

80

Methuen's birthplace, and been given mugs of cider in the kitchen courtyard. It had not been significant to Will then; he had only thought of his slaked thirst and with mild envy of a man who owned as much land as Lord Methuen being the unconscious provider of the cider. Now he was GOC of the British Forces on the Western Front, his brief was to relieve Kimberley, and Will was one of half a dozen captains in a mere one of the regiments in all the brigades under his command. When they got to the Modder river camp, there would be twelve thousand fighting troops and an additional three thousand service units of ammunition columns, field hospitals and engineers. Before that, they would camp on the Orange river and de-train to begin the march to Kimberley, seventy-five miles of foot-slogging across that endless red veld.

And beyond the Orange river lay, of course, the Free State. That was the river the Boers had crossed to independence, over sixty years ago, some pushing even farther north, over the Vaal river, putting as many miles between themselves and domination as they could. Will expected something of the Orange river. He visualized it broad and shining, a sort of symbolic pathway to a new life. It proved to be a muddy stream flowing reluctantly down a wide and sticky river bed, but its banks were fringed with willows dipping soft green fronds towards the water. The railway crossed the river some miles east of Hopetown over a bridge that astonished Will by its ramshackle appearance. It was constructed of planks, strongly reminiscent of a tree house he had had as a child, and along its length railway workers were suspended in rope slings, painting the metal lattices that held it together in scarlet paint. In the angles formed by the railway line and the river lay the camp, line upon line of regimental bell tents, a mile and a half of orderly military occupation, and, beyond that, the huts of the Africans and the railway workers, and beyond them the vast russet distances of the veld. The only other thing that awaited them besides the camp was a dismal piece of news. Sir George White's field force was now besieged at Ladysmith.

It was the dust, Will discovered, that featured most in camp life. It lay on his tongue and crept inside his ears and the rims of his eyelids, it coated his hands and his clothes and his papers and his fork and spoon and mug, it obscured features and landscapes, it made every surface powdery, every distance veiled. They all spent the first days polishing, fighting a battle against the dust on buckles and buttons and stars. Then the order came that this was to stop. The officers were to be as inconspicuous as the men. Will's colonel looked down the glittering line of his junior officers.

'We have a new problem here. The enemy is invisible. Quite where they are we don't know, but they seem to know more about us than vice versa. The Mauser, well aimed, can pick a man off at a mile, and in this sunlight every button that's polished makes us shine like Christmas trees. That's what went wrong with Colonel Gough's reconnaissance patrol – could be seen a mile off. And was.' He paused. 'All buckles and buttons to be painted out. A mixture of brown paint and dung is suggested.'

He left them staring downwards at their tunics.

'Hell,' Will said, 'we'll look like sandbags – '

'That's the aim.'

'Why so much fuss? The Mauser magazine is only five shot. Our Lee Metfords have ten – '

'It's the accuracy. And the distance. Someone said they can shoot at grazing height. Come on, what's a few buttons?'

'It seems – a little like giving in.'

'We don't have any choice. They seem to know more than we do, damn them.'

Nobody seemed to know how many Boers there were, or where they were. It was said that there were nine thousand besieging Kimberley alone, but what about those vast spaces between the Orange river and Kimberley, the empty distances where Colonel Gough's patrol had been mown down by invisible enemy, shots from their smokeless rifles whining through the hot air? How many Boers there? How to attack an enemy when you could not find him? How to find him?

'There's the observation balloons.'

'It's too far. The heliograph to Kimberley helps.'

'Not much. Why don't we use more patrols?'

'Look what happened to the last one. In any case, we haven't enough cavalry.'

'Only the Tigers – '

'Even they get picked off.'

'I expect it will be a night march and fisticuffs when there's trouble.'

'Anything, anything. Just no more hanging around.'

Will took baths in a tin tub in front of his tent. The tub was so small he could only bathe sections of himself at a time. The cardinal rule was that one must never, ever remove one's sun helmet in the sun, even if one had removed everything else to wash. He wrote home to Frances:

> It's such a blessed relief to take one's puttees off, you cannot imagine. My sergeant is very hearty about it all and says by the time I get to Kimberley I shall have forgotten I have any feet, it will be so long since I have seen them. Our food is pretty good but that won't be the case when we leave camp. I long to leave, to be up and doing. I know you don't understand me but I want to do something chivalrous and honourable. For England, not for myself. It isn't that I am anti-Boer, you know that; in fact, when I see this country I can't but admire people who want to stick up for it so, but I want to see England governing here. She *must*. It's only that way that there will be proper justice for everyone and no oppression. It doesn't seem that there is any way you can explain that to the Boers except with bullets so that's the road we must go down. I have been promoted to captain. Unfortunately my new glory is obscured by brown paint for camouflage. Write and tell me of giddy doings in Oxford. Write soon.

Lord Methuen was in excellent spirits. He sat at a camp desk in his tent, his long heavily moustached face crowned by a slouch hat, firing off memoranda and telegraphs. Will, summoned to see him on a matter of horses for war correspondents, found himself much infected.

'A week after we leave here, Marriott, we'll be breakfasting in Kimberley!'

Kimberley was difficult to picture. Will saw it as a mixture of great wealth and great raffishness and squalor. It contained the biggest man-made hole in the world out of which the first diamond had come thirty years before. It also contained Cecil Rhodes and a great many African mineworkers kept, Will was told, in dreadful compounds roofed in wire mesh. This disquieted him a good deal. It sounded altogether like a combination of an American gold-rush town and a Southern plantation before slavery was abolished, and all the worse for both those likenesses. He wondered, if it wasn't for Cecil Rhodes, would they trouble to relieve Kimberley at all?

In the dawn of 21 November, they were at last on the move. They did not strike camp, even going so far as to pile more thorn branches onto the fires to disguise their departure, and having crossed the Orange river, began to march along the railway line to the north and Kimberley. Each man carried his own kit, a greatcoat a blanket and a groundsheet, his rifle and ammunition, water and his semicircular mess tin fitted into a leather case. Will, trotting softly beside Dick Rawlings, was humming. The huge South African sky began to fill with light stealing up from the horizons all round as if a dome were being lifted from the earth to let the daylight in. The thorn trees, he observed as he jogged past, were growing new soft red thorns and little tufts of brilliant green leaves and every so often a wheeling flock of egrets went overhead, ice blue in the new light. The smell of the earth rose up to him in the dust churned up by eight thousand pairs of tramping feet, the strong, rich, spicy smell of the earth, and the air was filled with the sounds of the army, the creak and jingle and thud as the three-mile column crept northwards to the Modder river.

'Right,' Dick said. 'Now you've had a battle. Want another?'
'We won! We won!'
'We lost nearly three hundred men.'
Will said, 'I can't sit still. I can't. I want to go up that hill again – '
'And see again what we saw at the top?'
Someone else said, 'The Boers jogging away calmly at their leisure as if we hadn't hacked our way to the top of the hill believing ourselves the victors?'
'But we got the hill!'
'They only lost a hundred and fifty. We lost twice that. What price victory?'

Someone handed Will a cigarette.

'It's always like this, the first time. You can't believe you're still alive so you tell yourself it must have been worth it. You want to do it again to prove there is no chance to it.'

'Belmont,' Will said, 'the battle of Belmont. The way the Guards went up the hillside. I'll never forget it. Straight up, crag after crag, as if they were walking upstairs – '

'The Grenadiers lost thirty-six alone.'

Will looked round at the others. Their faces were filthy, eyes and teeth white in the firelight. He stood up. 'I'm going to see the men. Couldn't sleep anyhow.'

Some others stood up.

'Come with you.'

'And me – '

Dick said, 'Try to tell them it was worth it.'

Five miles up the railway line, the Boers were waiting again, at Graspan. The men of the Free State had simply ridden away from Belmont and entrenched themselves in the ridges between Lord Methuen and the point where the railway crossed the Modder river. Precisely how many there were, no one could tell. They held on to their positions under heavy fire until the sheer weight of Methuen's troops drove them down into the veld, leaving a hundred burghers fallen on the hillsides. There was nothing, Will thought, lying exhilarated and wakeful that night, to stop them from relieving Kimberley; from Kimberley they would sweep eastwards into the Free State to Bloemfontein and onwards in an irresistible rush to Ladysmith, relieving the thirteen thousand men confined there, and then they would all turn to the northwest, this marvellous dauntless army of the British Empire, and take Johannesburg – and, once that was done, on, onwards to Pretoria itself. And then back to England, to the cheering and the exultation, leaving only the clean lines of incorruptible British administration behind, to lay this new jewel at the feet of the old Queen, Empress of India, Empress of South Africa . . . Will put his hands behind his head and smiled up at the million stars that glittered fiercely out of the huge night sky.

*

The Modder river, everyone said, was delightful. There were two resort hotels – one, the Island Hotel where the Riet river joined the Modder, was a particular favourite with Cecil Rhodes in times of peace. It would, Will was promised, remind him of England. There were willows and pleasant riverside walks and ducks and rowing boats. Of course, the Boers were there at the moment and they had, predictably, blown up the railway bridge, but that was only a temporary setback. They could be cleared away in a moment. The plan was to march down the veld to the river, breakfast on its southern banks, ford it, and send whatever Boers were waiting on the northern banks about their business. It was 28 November, three days after Graspan.

Will, with the left hand of Lord Methuen's two brigades, was tramping through the tough veld grasses, in the best of spirits. To his right the railway line ran north to Kimberley, ahead of him irregular blots of green indicated the Riet river, flowing to meet the Modder a mile to the east. Their goal was the Rosmead dam, the furthest point to the west that anyone expected any Boers to be. He peered ahead. 'Can't see anyone through the trees.'

'Never can, sir. It's fightin' in civilian clothes that does it. Can't tell a Boer from a koppie.'

Will looked down at his feet. 'Earth's changing.'

'That'll be the river, sir.'

'Sergeant. There isn't anyone there. Here, have my glasses – '

There was a pause.

'They'll be there all right, sir. Flat on their bellies the far side. In the scrub.'

'We aren't a quarter of a mile away – '

The first bullets came sizzling through the grasses at knee level. There was a frozen moment of incredulity and then they were all flat on their faces while Mauser fire spat at them from the river, hissing across the veld like hailstones. Will raised his head cautiously and his helmet was spun off his head in a second.

'Christ! Christ!'

'Don't move, sir. Stay right down.'

'Where are they?'

'Dug in the river banks. Trenches in the southern bank, sir.'

'Trenches – '

'Done it before, sir. Long ago as '81. Haven't seen 'em do it in a river before, thought they only liked hilltops – '

'There isn't a hill round here. What do we do?'

'Flat on your face, sir.'

'Tell the men not to go for water. No one is to move. What about the artillery?'

'No cover, sir. Helpless as we are.'

They lay for three hours. The smallest movement and the rain of fire, never ceasing, grew to a storm, helmets spinning over their backs, hands shot through, lifted water bottles punctured and spilling their precious contents into the earth. By turning his head sideways, as he had to do cautiously every so often to ease the blazing sun on his face, Will could see the backs of Highlanders' knees to his left, burnt red raw, blistering and angry between kilt and stocking. He wasn't sure if he fell asleep at intervals or whether he passed out, but black blots of unconsciousness dropped upon him every so often, only a relief from a savage pain in the base of his skull. Two men near him sang softly at intervals, snatches of jaunty Scottish nonsense:

> Wha sa' the forty-second?
> Wha sa' them gang a' war?
> Wha sa' the forty-second
> Marchin' doun the Broomielaw?

The fire would increase, crackling like knotty wood set alight, and the song would vanish, drowned briefly by the Mausers, and then it would drift back to him:

> Some o' them had tartan troosies
> Some o' them had nane at a'
> But wha sa' the forty-second
> Marching doun –

Men began to groan round him, some wounded, some burnt beyond bearing. He wasn't sure if the man beside him was dead or fainting.

'It's the dumdums, sir – '

'I thought they were forbidden, that no one used them – '

'Tell that to Johnny Boer, sir!'

He stole a glance at the man's hand, imagining the bullet embedded in the flesh swelling inside it unbearably. His own throat was so dry, his craving for water so strong he had to clench every muscle in an effort to lie still. It couldn't be done. He raised his head with the utmost caution.

'Look, sergeant!'

Ahead of them in the dark band of rushes that fringed the river, soldiers could be seen inching forward on their bellies towards the water.

'General Pole-Carew! They're moving!'

The fire from the river had become more sporadic all of a sudden, the steady fusillade of the past three hours broken, only spattering in bursts.

'They're tiring!'

Will pulled his shoulders from the ground. Nothing happened. Ahead of him the 9th Brigade were standing up now in the rushes and hurling themselves forward towards the river. Will leapt to his feet.

'Come on! Come on! Forward!'

The British field guns began to open up, pouring shot into the river while the soldiers thundered down under its cover. As they pushed through the rushes, stumbling over rocks and those who had fallen, the Boers, men of the Free State, could be seen scrambling up the far bank of the river, some of them firing as they went. And then it was into the river with the North Lancashires, the Highlanders, slipping and sliding through the mud, leaping the newly abandoned trenches and plunging into the brown water to capture and hold the northern bank.

When we opened fire the next morning [Will wrote to Frances], there was no one to reply. They had all gone. Three Boer generals, Prinsloo and Cronje and De La Rey (he is only armed with a Bible, I'm told), and three thousand men, absolutely cleared out. We were first in their headquarters and there was nothing there but rusk crumbs and a lot of empty gin bottles. My face is burnt like a sunset and most of the Highlanders can't bend their knees. The Boers didn't lose a hundred men. We lost 450 I'm sorry to say. But we won.

*

88

'We are to march at night,' Will said, standing in the doorway of the mess tent, 'Halfway this afternoon, bivouac, the last half tonight.'

'Who says?'

'The Brigade Commander. Wauchope. I've just seen him.'

'But why at night?'

'We've over six miles to go to where the Boers are dug in. We have to do it by night for a dawn attack. That's why.'

They bent over the map spread on the camp table. It was ringed with mug stains and speckled with cigarette burns.

'Look. That's where they are. That kopje called Magersfontein. The one you can see from here, the one that looks like a ship. They're going to do a Belmont on us, dug in on the hilltop.'

'So we'll flush them out. Just like before.'

Will straightened up and looked round. Of the six captains who had left Cape Town with him, there remained five. Dick Rawlings' body had been pulled from the Modder river a fortnight before, wedged against the boulders of the northern bank where he had fallen, almost ashore.

Will said, 'It's the order of the khaki everywhere. Aprons over kilts, no sporrans, nothing. We have to be halfway up that kopje before they even know we're awake.'

'I haven't seen them up there, digging. I've watched pretty consistently.'

'Use your head. Would they dig trenches in daylight?'

'So it's to be a short night – '

'We leave this afternoon, bivouac dusk till midnight.'

'And tomorrow? Bayonets?'

'Bayonets.'

'A pretty bloody breakfast then – '

Will went to the doorway and squinted up at the immense African sky. It was a strong clear blue, regularly dotted with small fat white clouds sailing along in steady formation.

'Last stop before Kimberley. The signals say they have food for more than another month, but we shouldn't let the Boers get their breath back.'

'Damn the Boers',' someone said, 'What about mine?'

As the day wore on, the small and comfortable clouds

began to pile up into darker and more ominous masses, and the breeze which had done no more than ruffle the veld gathered strength and veered to the northwest. By mid-afternoon the wind was chill and sharp, whirling among the kilts of the 3500 men marching northwards behind the artillery batteries. It was monotonous going. The veld was dun-coloured, flat, dotted with dark patches of scrub and the wind whipped spirals of dust and sharp twigs against faces and knees. The railway, that lifeline to which they had clung since they left the Cape, grew farther and farther away to the west; ahead there was nothing but the rising dome of Magersfontein kopje upon which nothing stirred. Then the sun went in abruptly, engulfed in clouds, and a thin rain began to fall.

About three miles from the kopje, they halted by a low eminence in the plain. Headquarters Hill it was to be. The rain grew harder and colder. Will went among his disconsolate men, sharing a blanket and groundsheet in pairs.

' 'Oo's idea was it to leave our greatcoats be'ind, sir?'

'I couldn't tell you. Not a very bright one in the circumstances.'

'Cigarette, sir?'

'No. No thank you. And not for you, either. No smoking, no camp fires. Hungry?'

'No, sir. Could do with a smoke, though – '

'And me – '

'Me too, an' all – '

'You've only got to get through till midnight. Then we'll give it to them. Clean run to Kimberley.'

'Pickin' up di'monds in the streets – '

'What I wouldn't do for a fag – '

'No coat either – '

'Bleedin' climate, 'ot as 'ell one minute, brass monkeys' business the next – '

' 'Ow the 'ell are we going to see where we're goin', sir?'

Will tensed suddenly. A crash like that of artillery had sounded ahead of them, to the north.

'Our shells, sir – '

'Our shells!'

It was hopeless. Confine these wretched men to a wet

bivouac, forbid them fags and fires so as not to alert the Boers
– and then begin this bombardment. He peered into the
dusk. The din was growing and the air was full of great
gobbets of rocks and earth.

'Lyddite – oh, great God. *And* shrapnel – '

A voice beside him said, 'Permission to smoke then, sir?'
Will wheeled round.

'No,' he said furiously. 'No. No, you bloody well may not.'

At midnight they were lined up in the customary file
formation, a huge block of over three thousand men. Down
the left-hand edge of each file ran a long rope, knotted at
intervals of ten feet. Each man on the extreme left of his
file held a knot. Almost no one had slept. The rain had
become more sporadic but the incredible fireworks of an
African thunderstorm, accompanied by crashes of thunder
that sounded as if the world were breaking apart, had made
any rest but the most fitful impossible. Huge jagged lengths
of lightning, pink and apricot and blue, danced and quivered
on the kopje ahead of them, filling the sky with sparks,
illuminating the whole plain for a second with their savage
and dangerous light. Even through closed eyelids, Will could
see them, like irregular searchlights being flashed intermittently into his face. They were still doing it as the brigade
moved forwards towards Magersfontein, and on the march
the forks of lightning seemed to dart actually among them
all, never lighting any hazard up long enough to see it, only
adding a taunting dimension to the difficulties and confusion
already there.

'We ought to broaden out a bit,' Will said. 'We're in such a
dense mass. We can't be much more than half a mile – '

'No orders, sir.'

Ahead, the outline of the kopje began to swim out of the
dimness. The sky behind it was lightening mercifully, the
blue of a good day pushing at the heels of the storm.

'Praise be for that, I'm soaked through. Oughtn't we to fix
bayonets?' Will said, peering forward into the dawning day.
'Half a mile be damned, we aren't four hundred yards!'

Out of the dimness to his left came the order, floating
across the ninety lines of packed and tramping men, 'Open
order! Open order! March!' and then, as he turned to his

own soldiers, a sheet of flame half a mile wide blazed from the foot of the kopje with a roar of rifle fire. Blinded and deafened, the huge mass of men broke into a heaving sea of frenzy. Will, plunging forward, shouting 'On! On! Advance, damn you, advance!' found himself packed tight in a company of Seaforth Highlanders, not his own men at all, but they followed him, shouldering through the mêlée, and only when on the edge of the brigade realized that they were as duped as they had been on the Modder. Flat on his face in the red mud of the veld, while the bullets sang and whined about him as they had done a fortnight before, Will could have wept. Of course the Boers had not dug trenches on top of the kopje. They had done what they had done on the Modder and the British had given them plenty of time to do it. They had dug trenches in the plain and that is where they were crouched, six thousand riflemen – four thousand more than at the Modder – firing accurately and tirelessly into the Highland Brigade.

Touching his face gingerly, Will was not sure if it were covered with sweat or tears. The sun was rising, at first welcome and wonderful on his soaked clothing, then mercilessly again, drying him out, drying him up. The man beside him, a major of the Highland Light Infantry, was dead, sprawled on his back with half his head blown redly into the red earth. On his other side, a private of the Seaforths was muttering, his cheek pillowed on a flat stone, his eyes closed.

'Why didn't they tell us about the trenches? Why didn't they? And no one said about the wire. Did they? Wha' did they march us up in column for, then? Answer me tha', will you? Why didna anyone say about the trenches – '

The British artillery began, steady and heavy from behind them. Will could hear the big naval gun, Joe Chamberlain, hurling out its great shells, reputed to kill everything within 150 yards of where each one fell.

'I can't lie here. I can't do it again. I can't be pinned down again.'

He raised his head a couple of inches. Between him and the man in front was a low thorn bush, to the right of that a boulder, beyond that, about fifty yards away and well screened by low scrub, he could make out a handful of men of his own regiment. He would make for them and once he had got to them, he would make some plan. It was perfectly possible, under cover from the artillery. He felt for his water bottle. It was gone. He put his elbows down into the earth and began to pull himself, an inch at a time, across the stony space between himself and his goal.

When the shot came, he hardly felt it. The day had been so long, the strain so intense, his thirst so crippling, the slaughter so awful, worse than any time before, worse than anything. He'd worked his way round with his little band, all round the foot of the kopje, with the Boers blazing away in front of them and their own artillery thundering behind, to its eastern face. It had taken hours, creeping onwards, cursing, cajoling, losing two men, passing body after body, blood, splintered bone, torn flesh and muscle, flies, clothing everywhere. And then finally, exhaustingly, dragging themselves twice over the white dust road to Kimberley, once eastwards to be clear of their own positions then back again westwards towards the east end of the kopje where Boers were dotted in little groups, and, oh miracle of miracles, some of the Black Watch and the Seaforths had had the same idea, and were before them. They'd struggled up the lower slopes and the Boers had come at them from all sides, flat-faced men in farming clothes, their breeches patched with blanket, and he'd seen three go down from his own revolver and his men beside him gazing at the dripping blades of their bayonets. And then from above, from the Highlanders above, came a cry, or sort of mournful howl, and they began to crash down the hillside around him, back in disorder to the British line, falling around him with bullets in their backs. He started to shout again, cursing he knew not whom, trying to drive them back at gunpoint, trying to prevent his men from joining them, more incoherent at every moment, more filled with despair of every kind, for his men, for the bloodshed, for himself, for war –

A band of some half dozen was coming leaping down towards him. He tried to move forward to prevent them, caught his foot, and was hurled down the hillside like a rag doll, his revolver flying from his hand. At the bottom, lodged against a thorn tree, he made to get up. An unbelievable pain shot like a knife through his thigh. He looked down in some surprise and there, sticky as jam, was a broad dark stain, his own flesh and blood seeping upwards through the khaki drill of his breeches.

7

'I have not heard from Matthew,' Frances wrote to Will. 'No one has. Not a word since the day he sailed. I suppose you left the Cape just as he arrived but do let me know if you hear anything.'

She put her pen down and looked around the room. It had pleased her vastly for the first month of term, but now she was not so sure that it reflected how she felt so satisfactorily. A huge violet and green banner hung above her bed with a photograph of Matthew pinned to it. The juxtaposition of the two had delighted her when she had first thought of it. Besides that, the walls were entirely covered with reproductions of the paintings of Rossetti and Burne-Jones, in addition to Botticelli's *Primavera* which she had given to Matthew for his own rooms and he had never hung up. The curtains were of heavy linen, printed with stiff yellow and green lilies in the manner of William Morris, and over the chair and bed she had tossed pieces of unhemmed brocade and imitation silk bought by the yard in Oxford market. At first this random draping had seemed to her artless and imaginative; now, she thought, gazing at it reflectively, it only looked a mess.

She got up and went to the window. Really, whatever silly thing she did to her room could hardly matter less, with a view like that over the river to the Botanical Gardens. Pale December sunshine, the last of the day, lay on the gravelled path below and there was Celia Miller and Rose Hemming-Hemming, wrapped in mufflers and mittens, leaning on their bicycles and talking. Celia had been at school with her, Rose at the Manchester High School for Girls where, she said, her father had been most progressive in sending her. Men of the North Country, she said laughing, eyeing Frances, were even more stick-in-the-mud than archdeacons in the South so her father had been daring indeed.

Frances opened the window and shouted. 'Tea?'

They looked up, Celia clasping her hat against the wind.

'Can't. My essay – '

'I can. I've bought a walnut cake. If I don't give some to you, I shall eat it all myself. I'll be five minutes.'

Frances banged the window shut. She stood and watched them as they began to wheel their bicycles away round the corner to the long sheds where they were stored in numbered racks. She went to her desk and picked up her pen.

It's all so detailed, the way women live together. Even if the army is as highly organized as a women's college, it can't be so maddeningly *neat*. We have so many little rules, tiny regulations. Everything is measured and numbered and timed. My curtains are not regulation, for instance, because they hang to the floor instead of ending at the window ledge. So when we have inspections – which we frequently do – I just pin up the bottoms with hatpins. It's terribly cold. I'm allowed a scuttle of coal a day and God bless kind Mr Jaeger for thinking of this Oxford-proof underclothing. My bicycle is not a bit shocking any more – everyone rides them – but I have learned to smoke and to swear (you could help a lot with this latter accomplishment with your military background) and I ride as much as I can. It's a little frowned upon, so that's excellent. I think the Principal fears that I may want to go hunting and then I shall meet unprincipled rakes from the Bullingdon Club – and in that she is quite right.

There was a knock at the door.

Frances said, not turning round, 'Oh, Rose, I'm so sorry, I meant to go and put the kettle on at once and I got scribbling.'

'It couldn't matter less,' Adelaide Munro said. 'I'll do it now if you will only tell me where.'

'Adelaide!'

'I hope I am not a nasty surprise. I have two nights off and of course duty calls to see how father is managing those awful boys and naturally he takes no notice of them at all and they grow more awful every moment.' She put her arms round Frances and gave her a brisk hug. 'Why is it that adolescent boys smell so dreadful? Feet?'

'I didn't think a nurse would notice – '

'I notice everything about my family. Well, how is everything? How are you doing?'

Frances pulled her down onto the multicoloured riot of her bed. 'Adelaide. I am so pleased to see you!'

From the doorway Rose Hemming-Hemming said, 'Shall I be in the way? I can easily have tea alone. I have my cake for consolation after all.'

'No!' Frances said. 'No, indeed! Come in. Introduce yourselves. I am going to brave the beetles in that horrid little hole and put the kettle on. Rose, this is Adelaide. Adelaide, this is Rose with whom I fight over the need for emancipation. She has been brought up by a miraculous father so she doesn't need to see the point.'

When she had gone, Adelaide said, nodding towards Matthew's photograph, 'My father taught her brother. That is how I met them. Matthew was up here – rather briefly. Such a pity – '

Rose, who knew all about Adelaide from late-night confidences over mugs of cocoa, nodded. 'He looks fascinating. Frances is rather worried about him. They haven't heard from him since he sailed and, of course, her parents still think he has gone in the opposite direction. The longer they don't know, the more she dreads them knowing. Well,' Rose said, spreading her hands, 'wouldn't you?'

'It was a very daring plan.'

Rose said, 'She is daring. Have you known her long?'

'Oh, no! Hardly at all. Just one rather intense meeting after a Peace Society lecture.' She looked round the room. 'Are your rooms all like this?'

'Mine very much more so. Most people's rather less. Do you like it?'

'To be candid, not very much. But I think I am too used to hospitals. I grew up in Oxford, in Norham Gardens, and I have never liked it. It does seem a waste when so many people regard it as a sort of intellectual paradise and would love to be here and can't be. I've come here for forty-eight hours and I am irritated already. My father's papers are everywhere, there are books on every chair so that one cannot sit down, and my father's cousin, who is supposed to housekeep for them all, has given up completely and made a sitting room for herself out of my old bedroom. And *that*'s not much better, all stupid little cushions and mats and a dreadful Pekinese.'

Rose said, laughing, 'How you would hate our house!'

Adelaide shook her head. 'I really dislike myself for being like this. I'm always so attracted to people who have the individuality not to care.' She looked towards Matthew's photograph. 'I suppose that was why I found Ma– the Pagets so appealing.'

Frances came in with a large brown teapot and cups and a jug upon a tray. 'You would not find my father appealing, my dear Adelaide.'

'I should probably find him very sympathetic and I should not like myself for doing so. Rose says you have heard nothing from South Africa.'

Frances began to pour out the tea. Rose put her walnut cake in its box on the floor, and cut it into huge slices, pausing between each slice to run the knife along her finger and then lick off the resultant icing.

'One letter from Will. Faithful old Will. He wrote the moment he got there. But of course he was only writing about doing not very much in Cape Town and there really wasn't anything to say except how pretty it was and how many parties there were and how much he longed to be away and fighting. Not one word from Matthew and I know he got there over a month ago. I even telegraphed the shipping line and the *Orient* docked at Cape Town at the end of October. I don't expect him to write to Salisbury, but I do expect him to write to *me*.'

Adelaide hesitated. It seemed to her the moment to speak and then she thought it was not. The other side of a piece of walnut cake would do well enough. She said, 'And what do you do with yourselves here?'

Rose sat back on her heels. 'We make our own beds, we eat three meals a day, we have to be in before dark, we may not post letters two minutes away without a hat – '

'We can go to any lecture we like, we can have a man to tea with written permission so long as he is a relation or accompanied by one – ' Frances stopped and then said, giggling, bent over the teapot, 'They *say* there's to be a new rule. That you can have any man to tea as long as you push your bed into the corridor for the duration of the visit.'

She and Rose looked at each other and exploded. Rose said, 'You must think us so silly, you being a nurse – '

'It's the coyness of it, so hole in the corner – '

'I don't think *you're* silly. I think the authorities might be. Of course,' Adelaide said, regarding them, their mouths full of cake, 'you wouldn't have seen a naked man.'

'No,' Frances said, 'we wouldn't.'

'I have, of course, but not,' she added, struggling to be truthful, 'in what you might call the best circumstances. The *right* circumstances.'

'Oh, Lord,' Rose said, and put her hands to her head, 'deep waters – '

'I think she's good for us, Rose. We are just as idiotic here as Celia and I were at school. Even when we had had the whole birth business explained to us. And I often wonder if I really understood that. I mean, suppose I were to walk in here one night and find a man in my bed, should I know what to do with him at all?'

Adelaide said, 'If that happens, you don't need to worry. He will have an excellent idea of what to do with you, I promise you. Actually – '

'Actually?'

'I didn't come to talk about – any of this. I came to tell you something. I came to tell you that I am going to South Africa too.'

Frances gaped. '*You* are!'

'I really can't sit here any longer. You know how I feel about waste, and the waste out there of all those brave young men is just too awful. Suppose I only saved *one*? I know we are supposed to be winning but for the life of me I can't think how. We have lost hundreds more than the Boers and the trainloads of wounded pouring into the Cape are coming thicker and faster every day.'

'Oh, Adelaide,' Frances said admiringly.

Adelaide put her untouched cake down on the bed beside her. She slipped to her knees on the floor and began pouring more tea. 'I never introduced you to Emily Hobhouse, did I?

99

Very remiss of me. I fully intended to. Her detractors say she simply has the typical British sentimental feeling for small peoples and that she suffers from acute Boeritis. I don't agree with them. As I said to you before, I think she is wonderfully well intentioned. She wants to launch a general charitable committee for the victims of the war, women and children, caught up in it helplessly. And because she's a practical woman, she wants more than a committee. She wants to send out a team of nurses who can nurse the wounded for the time being and, while they are doing that, can keep their eyes and ears open and send her back reports and perhaps in time develop into a team to help the innocent sufferers as well as the soldiers. There are ten of us. I was the second volunteer.'

'Do – you mean, help *Boer* women and children?'

'If they need it. Why not? There must be thousands of them keeping farms going on their own. Suppose their farms are in a battle area?' She leaned forwards towards Frances. 'That's the essence of something like the Peace Society. It's peace for everyone, just as medical care should be. We are just very lucky that the war isn't happening all over Surrey and Hampshire. Think how we should feel. I don't believe in this war, but that's no reason for opting out. You are different, you are clever. Like Matthew. I just have a good ordinary practical intelligence and that tells me that there are a great many people, British and Boer, out there who might like my help. I can't stop the war, but I can mop up a little corner of the aftermath.'

Frances said, 'You make me feel ashamed. I don't believe in the war either, I am quite adamant about that. But look at me. Will gone, Matthew gone and with my help! Before it was a reality, before they had gone, I was so full of theories, so easily able to reconcile Matthew's predicament and needs and a war. But it was just intellectual cheating on my part.' She paused, then added, looking at the small photograph of Will half submerged in the tide of papers on her work table, 'I don't blame Will in the least. He believes in it all, he really does. He has just the utter conviction of British influence for good that his father must have had. I remember him saying to me earnestly that the Empire was not expansionist, that all it wanted to do was set up a structure of administration and trade in other places which would benefit quite as much, if not more, from the arrangement than Britain. He knew, given what he believes, that he was helping Matthew. I don't really know any such thing. At this moment, Adelaide, you have made me feel nothing but a muddle-headed meddler.'

'That was the last thing I intended to do. And even if there is a grain of truth in what you say, remember that Matthew agreed with you. You hardly had to force him to go, now did you?' She looked at Rose. 'Do you have brothers?'

'Not one. Three sisters, all younger. My father has been a friend of Lloyd George's for years so you can deduce what I feel about the war. I sometimes wonder,' she said reflectively, 'who was in favour of it.'

Adelaide stood up. 'I sail next week. And I go back to London tomorrow. You can at least rely upon me to write if there is anything to write about.'

'I think I envy you,' Frances said.

'Yes,' Adelaide said calmly, 'of course you do. It is always easier to be up and doing, not sitting at home worrying and helpless, waiting for news. I feel infinitely better since I decided to leave.'

'You see, suppose something happens to Matthew, suppose I never – '

'A great deal will happen to him, you may be sure of that. Now, reluctant though I may be to return to Norham Gardens and what is bound to be a most disgusting dinner – the cook can only have worked in institutions before – I must get back. Father will read throughout dinner, the boys will argue among themselves, and Cousin Grace will complain about domestic matters without drawing breath. Can you wonder I am relieved to be going?'

Frances and Rose stood up too, and surveyed her.

'Don't think,' Adelaide said, 'that you are useless. That would be a great mistake. We shall need teachers after the war more than ever and how are you to know how if you have not learned? As a girl I used to despise teaching on account of my father, if you understand me, but I am glad to say that I know better now. I'm only a nurse because I'm not clever enough to do what you do. A great disappointment to my father, I can tell you. Frances – '

'Yes?'

'Keep going to London. Keep going to the meetings.' She opened her bag and produced a card from it. 'This is Emily Hobhouse's address. I will tell her to expect to hear from you. I don't think you should do anything, certainly not yet, but I think it would help you to meet her.'

'Keep looking for him, for Matthew,' Frances said, taking the card and nodding, 'and for Will. Let me know – '

'Of course.'

Adelaide leaned forward and kissed her on the cheek, then held out her hand to Rose. 'It's been a very happy interlude. I have enjoyed myself.'

When her step had died out along the polished corridor, Frances sat down on the edge of her bed.

'More cake?' Rose said.

'No. No, thank you. Oh, Rose, one of the most awful things about all this, about the war, is all this endless saying goodbye . . . '

The Oxford term ended two weeks before Christmas. There were no examinations at St Hilda's as such, but instead rigorous tests which caused quite as much frenzy as full-blown examinations might have done. Frances, Rose and Celia sat up half the night, wrapped in blankets, sharing the contents of their coal scuttles in a hysteria of revision. Frances had no memory for quotations, Rose's was excellent; figures made Celia want to weep but she was the only one with an appetite for constitutional history; Frances loved languages of any kind, Rose said they were as foreign to her as when she had first opened her books. Sighing and muttering and scribbling copious notes, they plodded doggedly on through the syllabus, fortified by draughts of cocoa and slices of bread and butter. It was in one sense almost a relief to Frances. The day before they embarked upon this intensive programme, *The Times* carried copious information on the battles on the Western Front, and Frances saw Will's regiment mentioned three times, in three engagements, three battles in six days. There were lists of casualties, headed by the officers. Will was not among them, but it was unnerving all the same, distracting. If she was left alone, she thought about it too much, helplessly. Revision was a drudgery, but a welcome one.

When the results came, they were respectable.

'Matthew would say it was typical,' Frances said, pushing her way back out of the anxious crowd in front of the college notice board.

'Typical of what?'

'Women. He always says we are hopelessly conscientious, that basically we don't have the verve and brilliance of a man's mind – '

'And you let him say such things?'

'Oh no. I argue like anything. But I do know what he means. He wouldn't have sat up every night for a week going over every note, every word. He would have dashed at it at the last moment and, although he would have made a lot of mistakes, he would also have been more original and exciting. Men are intellectually braver – '

'Nonsense,' Celia said. 'It's only that they have had hundreds of years of being the acknowledged thinkers. Once we are used to the idea, we will be just as brave. You have been talking to Rose too much.'

They sauntered out across Magdalen Bridge to the High Street. There was a chill wind slicing down between the buildings, unwinding their long mufflers relentlessly and blowing dust and bits of straw about in eddies. The men's colleges were going down too and there were black clusters of hansom cabs outside University and Queen's and Brasenose, piled with luggage destined for the station.

'Next term it will be next century.'

'New beginnings, perhaps?'

'It's going to be a dismal Christmas. So many men away, everyone preoccupied. And I have to screw up my courage and tell the truth about Matthew.'

'I must say, I don't envy you that.'

'I should have done it weeks ago. I kept thinking that he would write, even, miraculously, write to them.'

An undergraduate came running down the steps of University College, paused when he saw them, and took off his hat.

'There,' Frances said, 'it's boys that age that are being

shot down in South Africa. They have hardly had time to be men. And the men are being wasted. Look at your brother.'

Celia's brother, a bacteriologist, was serving with the Royal Army Medical Corps, leaving behind him a promising field of research into the typhus vaccine.

'He's still in Cape Town. He must be so frustrated, torn away from his work and still not doing anything.'

'But at least he won't be put in the front line?'

'He doesn't know. If they are short of men he will. Oh, Frances, look at that!'

There was a news-vendor's stall by the nearest entrance to Oxford market. In front of it had been propped a board onto which squares of paper could be pinned and headlines scrawled.

Defeat on the Western Front [it read]. Over 200 killed. Heavy losses in the Highland Brigade.

Frances clutched Celia. 'Buy me a paper – '

The pavement at this end of the High Street was crowded, people pushing their way in through the arches to the covered market behind and laden with packets and bundles, battling out again in search of homeward trams. Jostled and nudged, Frances and Celia stood together, each holding a side of the newspaper.

'Oh, dear God, listen, "Sound defeat", it says, "taken absolutely by surprise, the Boers had dug trenches at the foot of the hill, no one saw them . . . All the Highland Regiments severely reduced, over seven hundred killed, wounded, or taken prisoner." What place? What does it say? Magersfon— oh, Celia, Celia, look "Lieutenant Marriott, wounded." *Wounded*. Oh, thank heavens, thank heavens and heavens – can I borrow your handkerchief? Wounded! Oh, poor Will, poor Will, only five weeks out of Cape Town. Celia, take this, hold this paper, I must run. I must – I must telegraph to Aunt Beatrice – '

Beatrice said, 'This will surprise you to hear, but I am very tempted to go out to Cape Town and nurse him. I know perfectly well that both you and my sister Harriet feel that I have great shortcomings as a mother. Which I do. It's a great misfortune for Will. But this circumstance is exceptional. Do you think I should go?'

They were sitting together in the small drawing room of the house in Hans Place. Frances had last sat there with Will, over two months before, gratefully drinking Madeira. There was no Madeira now. The room was very cold and smelt of dust and, as her aunt was in London merely for the day, the shrouds of grey linen had only been removed from two of the chairs, the two in which they sat.

'No,' Frances said.

'Oh, my dear. I am disappointed and relieved all at once. Should I be of no use?'

'I think you would be so distressed that you couldn't be. If it's any consolation, a splendid friend of mine sails tomorrow, a trained nurse, wonderfully capable and resourceful. She knows about Will and I am sure will seek him out and make sure he is in good hands. She has promised to write the moment she has any news.'

'Oh, my dear, the perfect solution! The relief – I came to London today fully resolved to book my passage, but of course you know the extent of my resolve in any thing disagreeable. I am sure your uncle would be most proud of Will, the reports are very gratifying – '

'Not about his leg.'

Beatrice closed her eyes. 'I am afraid I cannot begin to think about that.'

Frances murmured, 'Broken teacups, not broken men.' They had said Will's femur was smashed, that the bone had splintered in his thigh, there was talk of amputation unless such a messy wound could be prevented from going septic.

'You say your friend is a trained nurse?'

'Yes. Adelaide Munro. She is the daughter of Matthew's tutor at Oxford.'

'Poor unfortunate man, what a task.' Beatrice rose and went to the mantelpiece, poking at objects distastefully with a gloved forefinger. 'Oh, my dear, London dirt. So very, very dirty. It clings so. I suppose there is no news of Matthew.'

'Not from him. No. But I know his ship has arrived in Cape Town.'

Beatrice turned, her hands upraised. 'Cape Town!'

'Yes, Aunt. That is where he has gone, to volunteer. We sold his ticket to Canada and bought him a passage to South Africa. It was a plan made by the three of us, Matthew and Will and me.'

'And your parents? Poor Harriet. What do they make of this?'

Frances rose too. 'They don't know as yet. I am practising on you, Aunt, to be perfectly truthful. I have been shirking telling them and now I must go home and do it.'

'But this is preposterous behaviour! How *can* you have been so irresponsible, so unthinking? What a grief you must be to your poor parents!'

Frances coloured in a rush. 'Oh, Aunt. I hope not that – '

Beatrice regarded her for a long moment. 'When Will was born I wished very much that he had been a daughter. I knew I should never have a daughter then, because nothing on earth or promised in paradise would have persuaded me to endure childbirth a second time. All his childhood was saddened for me by his being a boy and my envy of my sister was considerable when you were born. I now see, Frances, that my escape was miraculous. I might deplore Will's clumsiness and inevitable masculine insensibility, but at least he is dutiful and honourable and true to the best aspects of his gender. You, on the other hand, are a shame to womanhood. You have always been undisciplined and unfeminine. My sister has never encouraged in you the softness and sweetness that is the essence of a true woman. And now, to your hoydenish and unattractive ways you add a deceit as deep as this into which I see you have dragged your poor cousin who has suffered from a misplaced weakness for you all his life. Education has taught you nothing but a disagreeable self-importance which in its turn has made you absolutely heedless of those around you. I might suppose that you thought a little of Matthew in this scheme. But did you think of your father or your poor living mother? And did you, for one moment, think of Will?'

Frances cried on the omnibus most of the way to Marylebone. She cried for several reasons which made it

106

very difficult to stop. Anger was the chief, it seemed, for a while and then that was swept aside by shame and remorse which in turn gave way to bewilderment at the seemingly arbitrary nature of men. It was hideous to cry in public and not at all what she expected of herself and a greasy stout man opposite watched her with unnerving and steady speculation. He stared with such directness that she began to worry that he was forming some hideous purpose and became very confused and got off the omnibus before she had intended and was then lost, and terrified that he might be following her. When she risked a covert look behind her, he was of course not following her at all and for some reason that made her cry more than ever, so hard for some minutes that she had to lean against the railings of a house in Upper Montagu Street and two maids came to the kitchen window in the area below and peered up at her and made faces. When she could finally stop, she found she was so tired she could hardly move forward and had to creep northwards like an old woman and it took her an unconscionable time to reach her destination. She wanted to pause and have a cup of tea and find a looking-glass before she reached the meeting, but she could not find the teashop Adelaide had taken her to and she was not in any frame of mind to be in the least adventurous and enter a strange one. She would have given a good deal to have had Adelaide materialize out of the pavement before her at that moment like some reassuring and practical genie, but of course Adelaide was half across London, no doubt packing with tremendous efficiency and the aid of a sensible and unexcessive list.

The meeting was not as crowded as it had been on the occasion she had first met Adelaide. This was possibly because there was a rival meeting that day of the newly founded South Africa Conciliation Committee which was to be addressed by the Liberal MP for Liskeard, Leonard Courtney, a loud and well-informed champion of the Boers, and many of the loyal members of long standing of the Peace Society had been seduced by this new attraction. Instead, the Peace Society could only offer a journalist from the *Daily News* which was, being almost the Society's organ, too familiar to be a great draw. Frances threaded her way between the lines of wooden chairs to the pillar she now associated with Adelaide and sat down. She kept her head bent, hoping that her hat brim and what little dingy winter daylight there was through windows of greenish glass would obscure her red nose and eyes from view, and attempted to be very busy in finding a pencil and notebook in her handbag. After a while a man came and sat on the only chair beside her and she gave covert and unhappy glances at the pepper-and-salt tweed of his trousers from under her hat brim and wished that whoever he was he had chosen any other seat in the hall.

The journalist was very dull. He was a man of statistics and his stated endeavour to prove the Boers' entitlement to the Transvaal and the Orange Free State foundered in a welter of figures. The man beside Frances began to take notes and after five minutes he gave an impatient sigh and put his notebook in his pocket. She felt she could not keep up her own pretence of writing in case he should overlook her and see that her mind was not upon the lecture at all. Of course, without a notebook she must at last look up, and he of course must look at her as any man would who had sat beside a girl with an adamantly bent head for twenty minutes.

He said softly, 'Would you care for one of these?' and handed her a dark-blue handkerchief.

She shook her head. 'No thank you. I'm trying to stop.'

He put the handkerchief away and regarded the stage for a little while and then he said, 'Why are we listening to this dreadful man?'

She smiled slightly but did not reply.

Her neighbour leaned towards her. 'As a journalist myself I am a judge of dreadfulness.'

He laid a card on her knee. Oliver Stansgate, it said, of the *Speaker*. She turned a little to look at him. He was square and sandy with an open and humorous face and he wore a caped greatcoat of green loden cloth.

'So you know Mr Belloc?'

'Intimately.'

A thin woman in the row in front turned and hissed crossly at them. Oliver Stansgate retrieved his card, turned it over, and wrote on the back, 'Tea? I know I need it and you look as if you do.'

'Please,' Frances wrote gratefully, 'yes.'

He put his hand under her elbow and steered her behind the pillar and towards one of the pairs of double doors that led out of the hall. From the stage the journalist watched them reproachfully.

'Whenever I am in this place,' Frances said, looking around, 'I seem to be in a state. Oh dear, I am so sorry – '

'Tea for two,' Oliver said firmly across her to a waitress, 'China for one, Indian for the other. And teacakes. A great many and be generous with the butter. Perhaps, Miss Paget, it is the effect that Peace Society meetings have upon you.'

'Not so much those, I think, as human beings. Particularly myself. I seem to have behaved with an inconsistency that makes me quite miserable. I really would rather not dwell upon it. Tell me about the *Speaker*.'

'It is a weekly newspaper of liberal leanings and pro-Boer sympathies. I run it with Hilaire Belloc and several others and I am delighted to say that we are rather successful. I suppose my own view is semi-socialistic.'

'Like Mill.'

'You know Mill?'

'He was one of my brother's heroes. I first read him because he is so in favour of complete suffrage, men and women, in Parliament and in local government, and then of course I couldn't stop and read on.'

'Your brother?'

'My brother Matthew. The one I have assisted in sending to South Africa. Oh, Mr Stansgate, may I have that handkerchief?'

Tea arrived, banged down as before, a regiment of little metal pots and a steaming pile of teacakes under a domed dish.

'But your brother consented to go?'

'Yes. Yes, he did. But I think he was feeling so very violent and so very confused that his decision should not have been allowed to count. And, you see, my cousin Will, who is the best and most honourable of men and a believer in the White Man's Burden, he felt the plan was so excellent – '

Oliver Stansgate helped himself to a teacake and began to

eat voraciously. 'My dear Miss Paget. So you have grown up with John Stuart Mill on the one hand and Rudyard Kipling on the other. I am fascinated to know which of the two you find finally most alluring.'

Frances said, pouring tea unsteadily, 'Oh, Mill, of course. But then I behave as I have done!'

'I don't find that very astonishing, given the circumstances you told me as we came along. Men like your brother will have a new state to live in in twenty years and of course they won't have to behave as he has done to soothe their savage breasts. This war will put an end to Kipling, I can promise you that. I shouldn't be surprised if it put an end to the monarchy too. We can't tramp about the globe full of missionary zeal after this. Apart from anything else, the opportunities for trade which we have so enjoyed as the Empire grew are being heavily tainted with greed at the moment. The morals of the mining camp, you might say, make the air smell not quite so sweet. How can one honour a fellow like that diamond dealer Beit, and how can one disentangle his name from our doings in South Africa? Miss Paget, you must eat. Look, I have almost devoured the plateful and you are still toying delicately with a morsel. May I have more tea?'

'What you say only makes my own position weaker. I should not have encouraged Matthew to go, I should have protested at least to Will – '

'For the comfort of a clear conscience? It wouldn't have been for much more.'

'I suppose I could not have stopped either of them – '

'Of course not. All men of strong character are Doubting Thomases. Taking other people's word for experience is poor stuff. How do you not know that they will not come back much finer men from the experience? Men with a decided view of how this country should conduct itself in the future. After all, the course of the war is not affected by whether two more young men do or do not fight. But it may be just the lesson they both need. Are you in love with your cousin?'

'No.'

'But he is with you.'

'How can you tell?'

'I should expect him to be. Have I entirely drained my teapot?'

Frances lifted the lid and peered in. 'Half an inch – '

He pushed his cup across the table.

She said, pouring tea, 'You really don't think we are a superior caste, we English, do you?'

'No.'

'I think part of me still does.'

'I am not at all surprised. You are a child of some of the most confident years of all time, perhaps only exceeded by the fifties. But you are going to see great changes. I was born in Canada and I think that might have given me a slightly more objective view of Mother England. Also I am sceptical by nature and probably twice your age.'

'You have been very kind to me.'

'I was intrigued, you know. Most women cry in their bedrooms and I could not imagine why you had chosen a public hall.'

'It wasn't really choice.'

He looked at her for a moment. 'If I came to Oxford I should of course require a guide. I know nothing of architecture at all. Would you undertake to instruct me?'

'If I promise not to cry?'

'That would clearly be an advantage.'

Frances stood up.

'I return to Oxford in the middle of January and tonight I am going back to Salisbury. I must go and catch a train.'

'Of course.'

He rose too and held out his hand. 'Thank you,' he said, 'for a most unexpected interlude.'

8

Enlisting had disappointed Matthew. Talking to people on
board ship, some of whom, journalists, adventurers, young
men on the run from the professions, were bent upon the
same goal as himself, had convinced him that what he sought
was a mounted infantry regiment of irregulars and he had
fully expected, even looked forward to, a certain amount of
opposition in getting into the regiment of his choice. But it
was easy, like everything else had been – the voyage out,
finding a billet in Cape Town, getting to know his way about.
He had explained himself to a recruiting sergeant, provided
details of himself of only a very sketchy kind, been asked
almost nothing of his background or how he came to be in
Cape Town at all, and found himself signing on in a matter of
minutes. He felt a little swindled.

He had selected the South African Light Horse for the
most arbitrary of reasons. He had been lounging about one
day with a group of young men whom he had met in a bar the
previous night and they had been swapping tales of the
various regiments and boasting lazily of where their talents
would be best exploited. And one had said, 'Leave the
SALH alone, whatever you do. They'll even take muleteers.'

'They what?' Matthew said.

'There's a squadron of the SALH almost entirely made up
of muleteers.' The speaker paused and then said with derision, 'From Texas.'

Matthew's mind was instantly made up. Any regiment
which encompassed a band of mule drivers from Texas
appealed to him powerfully and immediately. He took himself off almost directly to Rosebank where the South African
Light Horse was encamped outside Cape Town and before
nightfall found himself enlisted as a trooper, equipped with a
Boer slouch hat with the left side pinned up, khaki tunic and

breeches, boots, puttees, and a Lee Metford rifle of uncertain vintage. Home became part of a white bell tent among rows of identical tents, meals issued from a camp kitchen in which food was cooked in deep aluminium canisters in the open, and his identity dwindled to that of Trooper Paget of C Squad. It was briefly exhilarating, then very dull indeed. Training seemed to him monotonous to a degree and to allow for none of the ingenuity he had learned on the hunting field once he had mastered pulling his rifle from its leather bucket in the front of his saddle and firing as he rode. His hair was cut remorselessly by the camp barber, his own clothes removed entirely and replaced by khaki drill laundered as hard as boards, and a sizable portion of each day was spent in cleaning his rifle, a task he was detailed to perform with another man, one of them holding the gun, the other pulling through it a cleaning wad tied to a length of string.

The only aspect, and it was an important one, of the whole business that aroused him was his fellow troopers. He discovered that there was only a handful of English volunteers in his squad and not many more in the entire regiment. It was composed, almost exclusively, of Uitlander refugees from Johannesburg, a tough and independent-minded bunch of men, paid by Wernher–Beit in the main and led by officers who had seen the Jameson Raid and did not care to see such a thing ever happen again. If Matthew thought he had seen entrenched attitudes in England, the men of the South African Light Horse made him think again. His first instinct was to run, followed by the swift realization that for the first time in his life he could not, and the inflexible discipline of that drew from him a reluctant admiration. He was in the regiment and he must stay. The fact was sobering and in its way impressive.

Dozing in the sun beneath the tilted brim of his hat during moments of leisure, Matthew had ample time to reflect upon the situation. He could see quite well that the manner in which he had conducted his life was one which had suited him admirably up to now, a kind of plunging recklessness and indulgence in every ebb and flow of his inclinations. He could not actually recall an occasion – apart from the ritual chastisements of his educational career which had affected him about as much as if he had been pelted with corks by way of punishment – when he had had to abide by a decision of any authoritative body, let alone a decision of his own. He had eluded discipline by being impervious to it. But, of course, such discipline as he had known had been administered by academics and the application of his wits had often saved him from it.

Not so now. He was with seven hundred men of a physical toughness and mental ruthlessness he had never encountered before. His commanding officer, Colonel Villiers, had actually ridden with Jameson in the raid and, if anything, the feelings about the Boers that had carried him from Pitsani to Johannesburg were even more decided now. Most of the men, it seemed to Matthew, shared his view. They were not so much interested in the Empire as in South Africa and their own part in her future. They treated Matthew with a rough tolerance, forgiving him a good deal for his competence on horseback but displaying an indifference which could flare at once into intolerance of any opinion but their own. In their view the Boers had to be driven from the land, into the sea, it seemed, if necessary, but certainly at the very most to be the subject race in the country that they had laboured in so long.

The regiment had, like its brother regiment, the Imperial Light Horse, its own views on strategy and policy. No one, it seemed, not even General Buller himself, was going to interfere with this staunch independence and Matthew was forced to admit that he had, in many ways, met his match. He had enlisted, he had discovered his fellow soldiers to be more intransigent in their views than anyone he had ever met, and this being a regiment, not a university college, he could do nothing about it. He was obliged to serve a term of at least six months and the only alternative was desertion and the firing squad. Life became a black and white matter of sleep and wakefulness, food and drink, exercise and regular duties, and all of it in the company of men who were not, unlike Will, prepared to discuss their opinions. Deeds for them spoke louder than any words and the deeds were motivated by such powerful and simple feelings as revenge.

114

Matthew, caught up in this inescapable situation, was forced, for the first time in his life, to endure.

In the last week of November, Matthew, his horse and his regiment embarked for Durban by sea. The railways that ran north from the ports of Cape Province – Port Elizabeth, Port Alfred and East London – all turned inland behind the mountains of the Stormberg and Winterberg ranges, and were of no use in transporting troops to the scene of the most pressing matter in hand, the relief of Sir George White and his Field Force, locked up in Ladysmith. It was instead several days' journey around the blunt tip of South Africa by sea to Durban and then a railway line would take them inland to the Tugela river. The sea journey bore little resemblance to Matthew's idle weeks between Southampton and the Cape; gone were the basket chairs on the upper deck and the elaborate games and gargantuan meals; instead Matthew found a ship packed to overflowing with troops, where the decks were almost impassable for bodies and the horses were crammed into the hold, two to a stall in canvas slings bolted to the timbers of the deck above.

He learned to snatch sleep when he could and to be hungry enough to find a soldier's diet of beef and bread appetizing. The green southeastern coast of the Cape slid interminably by and he played poker rather than watch it, with Louis Durlacher, whose parents had come from the industrial bleakness of northern France when newly married thirty years before, and Gilbert Wildun, orphaned on a Belgian farm at the age of six and sent out to an uncle in Johannesburg with a change of clothes, two horseshoe-shaped spiced black sausages, and a label round his neck. They spoke the nasal English of the goldfields and owed no allegiance to either Paris or Brussels. Louis had once almost been punched in the Fountain Bar in Johannesburg by Hendon Bashford and enjoyed the story of the croquet hoops.

'He was three sheets in the wind all right,' Louis said. 'Two mates of mine had to hold him up so I could knock him down.'

It was how most of Louis's stories ended. No matter what the discussion was about, no matter with whom, no matter what the outcome, it was an inevitable part of every incident in Louis's life that it should conclude with his saying nonchalantly, 'So, of course, I had to hit him.' He hit Matthew on the third night of their acquaintance after a disagreement over their poker stakes, and when Matthew, boiling with rage, hit him back, Louis was only gratified. 'Give as good as you get, man. Better if you can. You'll get by fine.'

Gilbert was surly and resilient. His opinion of the relations who had dispatched him into the unknown like a parcel twenty years before he now used as fuel for his feelings about the Boers. They were farmers, so was the half-brother who had not wanted an extra child, an extra mouth on the farm in Flanders. He had become a mine manager and he was not stopping there. 'When this is all over, I'll go back to Jo'burg. I can get more out of my men than any manager on the Rand, and I'll get it.'

If he lost at poker, which was seldom, he doubled the stakes and won his money back, and when Matthew, bankrupted completely, asked for a loan, Gilbert agreed but charged him interest.

'You'll learn,' he said to Matthew. 'What this country teaches you is survival. Stay on top or go under. And no damned Boer is putting me under.'

Durban had wonderful beaches, half obliterated by the squalor of all the disembarking transport ships. It was very hot, a steaming, heavy heat, and the sky arched overhead in a dome of hot blue enamel. They spent most of a day in the railway yard, dozing on their packs, eating the watery flesh of the prickly pears that grew around the edge and spitting mouthfuls of seeds into the dust. At nightfall they were loaded in, the horses, reluctant after the sea voyage to travel by means other than their own four legs, having to be shoved into the slatted trucks that would carry them up the line to Chieveley and Frere. There was a last-minute rifle drill and inspection of ammunition, then an issue of bottles of soda water, and into the train, truck after truck, all converted cattle wagons still strongly redolent of their previous occupants, climbed fifteen hundred men of the volunteer regiments.

The train crept through the night at a pace suitable to a

funeral cortege. Packed in their trucks, the men smoked and grumbled and dozed, while outside the night was still and hot and black, scattered occasionally with a hail of glittering red as sparks blew back from the huge double-tendered locomotive ahead, specifically designed to deal with the vast distances of Africa or India. Matthew, crammed against a wooden wall whose splinters caught painfully in his clothing, thought of very little. His mouth tasted of stale cigarettes and smuts, his skin felt tight and gritty, and his eyes were too sore to close. Everything smelled of smoke and sweat. People said, 'Move your bloody boots,' and fell sideways in brief slumber and snored and were shaken awake to swear softly again in a dull monotone that matched the rhythm of the wheels rolling northwards through Pinetown and Clermont, Camperdown and Ashburton, Pietermaritzburg and Howick, on and on, mile after mile, to the sudden dawn at the Mooi river turning the Drakensberg mountains beyond hyacinth-blue and rose-gold.

'That's Natal,' Louis said. 'They raided the English farms down here. Bloody Boers. We'll wipe Majuba out – '

Between the slats of the wagon, Matthew peered at the sunlit landscape. Even with such narrowed vision he could see that it was huge, great undulating waves of green and dun land rolling away to a range of mountains like a castle wall to the west. It excited him suddenly, all that space, filled him with an abrupt exhilaration. It was almost as if that splendid country, throwing up its red and grey rocks, was heaving and galloping along beside the train, as if the land had a life of its own, a huge energy generated just by being so big, so free.

'Bloody hell,' Gilbert said, 'it must be over a hundred – '

'Old Buller's brought his bathroom – '

'And his bubbly.'

Someone said, 'Botha's been drafted in. In command of the Boers.'

Matthew took his eyes from the entrancing landscape. Botha was something of a boy wonder. True, at thirty-seven he could hardly be called a boy, but when all his fellow generals were grey-bearded patriarchs, ‹thirty-seven

117

seemed boyish enough. He had distinguished himself at Talana Hill, at the Battle of Ladysmith, and now, having penned the English into Ladysmith, he was waiting on the north bank of the Tugela.

Gilbert knew the Tugela, his uncle had attempted to buy a farm at Bergville. 'It'll be a problem to cross, man. I'll tell you that for nothing. It's wide, it's got rocky sides and it comes down out of the Berg like something you never saw. When the Tugela's in flood you can't hear yourself speak. Kopjes all over the shop to the north. Botha'll be dug in there already, he's had plenty of time.'

'Bloody Boers – '

Matthew looked away again at the strip of Natal careering past his vision. Whose country was it? It had belonged to the Zulus sixty years before, the Zulus under their chief Dingaan whom the Boers had beaten to a pulp at the Battle of Blood River. And then the Boers had farmed there in the rolling lands among the rivers below the mountains and had left it to trek north and west, away from the liberal reforms pressed upon them, away to their own life by their own creed. The English had always loved Natal, the governers had scattered it with their own names, Sir Harry and Lady Smith, Sir Benjamin D'Urban, Sir Bartle Frere, places that were for the most part no more than unremarkable clusters of corrugated iron houses along the railway line, but English in spirit, English in sympathy, anti-Boer. Zulu warriors, English administrators, Dutch farmers, and now me, Matthew thought, rolling over Natal towards heaven knows what, I only know I'm waiting for something, waiting perhaps for a sign . . .

'It's a three-pronged attack,' Matthew's commanding officer said, 'over the Tugela and then straight on to Lady-smith. Two prongs you can forget about – they're sending the Irish out to the west, the infantry up the middle with the naval guns, and we are to take that hill to the right, to the east – '

If it had been hot in the train, the plain to the south of the Tugela was like an inferno. The mountains of the Drakens-berg had swung west out of view and before them, to the north, where the midday sun blazed like a brass shield, the ochre veld, tufted with wiry grass bleached the colour of their own uniforms, rolled to the Tugela river. There was nothing to break the landscape but the scruffy little dorp of Colenso, a handful of huts around the railway line, and the low kopjes beyond it, blurred in the heat, and to the right the hill the Zulus had called Hlangwane. There the Boers had dug their trenches, but the lie of the land was such that if they could be dislodged, the British would be in a position to overlook the main body of the Boer army, General Botha and his commandos waiting on the north bank of the river.

'Who's CO?'

They looked at each other.

'Dundonald. Lord Dundonald.'

Matthew had seen him exercising a horse in camp down the line at Frere, wonderfully handsome, an earl, ex-commander of a camel corps that had attempted to relieve Gordon in Khartoum, commanding for the moment this strange and single-minded collection of irregular mounted infantry of which Matthew found himself a part. It was from him that a disturbing piece of news had filtered down among the Mounted Brigade, the first item of news to drag Matthew back to the world that had been his before Cape Town. Lord Methuen, on the Western Front, had had a serious reverse at a place called Magersfontein and three-quarters of above a thousand men killed there had been of the Highland Brigade, the brigade that included Will's regiment. Matthew had fallen like a wild thing upon the casualty lists. No Captain Marriott reported killed, but one reported both missing and wounded. There was nothing further he could do, no other source of information he could tap. He must wait and obey while the whole adventure gathered pace; he was caught up in something he couldn't stop, whatever he thought of it.

'This,' Louis said, 'is where the fun begins. This, man, is what I've bloody come for.'

'Ladysmith by Christmas – '

'Colenso by sunset – '

Out there in the darkness the Boers waited, and under the hooves of his horse Matthew could feel Africa waiting like a giant beast asleep.

'Botha's got eight thousand,' Louis said at his stirrup, 'eight thousand riflemen.'

Gilbert, on his other side, looked at them both in triumph. 'So what, man. We have eighteen – '

The sun was already high and hot when they came to the foot of Hlangwane. Between the brigade and the Boer trenches on the southern flank of the hill stretched a huge rippling field of mealies, their cobs still half-ripened, yellow-green and rustling in a sheaf of leaves. The order was to dismount, and to creep round and through the corn on foot in pairs and small groups, carrying no more than a rifle, ammunition and one water bottle per man. As they climbed off their horses, a jerking thudding boom began to their left, the guns of the Royal Artillery brought up to the river and pounding the Boers dug in on the farther side. Matthew, crawling through the stiff stalks of the mealies, over the dug red earth speckled with white stones, found that his rifle was slippery in his grasp and that sweat was running freely down his face as if a tap had been turned on, a sensation at once cooling and faintly oily. In front of him the soles of Gilbert's boots moved onwards in a steady rhythm, behind him he could hear men panting in harsh gasps. His fingernails were full of earth, his knuckles begrimed with red dust. When the firing broke out from the hill above and a sharp rain of bullets began to patter among the papery leaves of the mealies, he halted where he was in amazement, motionless on all fours, head bent. His eyes fixed upon a gleaming oval of blue metal embedded in the earth just in front on him, metal that a split second before had not been there.

The order came hissing back to lie flat. Matthew lowered himself to the earth and turned his head sideways, pillowing his cheek on the gritty back of his hand. He could hear the big naval guns to the west and shouts from close at hand, but most sounds were drowned by the fire from the hill above, the crackling of rifles in the hot still air. There were times during the hours he lay there when he must have dozed. He woke with a start once or twice, his back aching, his mouth sour and dry, his neck stiff and raw from the sun. He felt no fear, only a giant boredom and frustration, born of seeing nothing, knowing nothing, hearing nothing but the thump of artillery half a mile away and close at hand, the steady soft swearing of his comrades. The contents of his water bottle were gone at a draught, he was too improvident to husband it, and then he lay and dreamed of waterfalls and cataracts and thunderstorms while the mealies rustled over him, casting little blocks of moving shadow like ghostly butterflies. The thought of Will came to him unbidden and nagged like the rifle fire spitting all around.

'Hell,' Matthew said. 'Hell and damnation. Bloody, bloody war . . . '

9

When Christiaan took leave to go and see to the farm, he left Gaspar in the commando. The first time he had gone on leave, they had ridden home together, skirting Ladysmith to the west, riding all night, to show Bettie that her boy was now a man and in possession of a whole skin. She had cried a good deal when she saw him and old Aunt Johanna had cried too, forgetting her city ways and throwing up her apron and sobbing 'Aie, aie, aie . . . ' into it. Gaspar, for all he had pretended not to, had liked the crying. It made him look down at his calloused hands and touch his new fluff of beard with a keen pleasure. Alecia had not wept one tear at the sight of him and he scowled at her. She seemed very strange in two months, taller, more remote, with an appraising look in her eyes that he knew his father would not take for one moment. And quite right too.

They had spent two nights at the farm in an orgy of solicitude and food. His parents had retired to their room each night at an hour early even for them, and Gaspar had felt a pang of jealousy that his father and comrade should become so quickly a man and husband again and so he vented his spite upon his aunt and made her cry afresh, taunting her that Hendon was an English-lover and a traitor to his blood.

Alecia said, 'On the Modder river, on the Cartwright farm, the women are nursing the wounded of both sides. They don't believe in this war.'

Gaspar stared at her and spat a stream of tobacco juice into the hearth place. 'If I get down there, I shall rape each one.'

He watched them both steadily, reaching for the squat tumbler in which his father had given him two fingers of gin now that he was a soldier, a comrade.

Alecia was just before him, pushing the glass out of reach. 'You have had enough.' She looked at him and her upper lip lifted. 'Rape! You wouldn't know how to begin.'

It had, all things considered, been a relief to get back to the commando. He had liked his clean comfortable bed, he had liked the meals and the spoiling and the feel of newly laundered shirts, but his swagger had sensed itself subtly undermined somehow. He had swung himself up into his saddle with a feeling of swinging back up into something altogether more manageable. So when, a few days after the new year, the new century, had begun and Christiaan had said he must go home and see how things were ripening, how the harvest did, Gaspar had hoped very much that he would prefer to go alone. As luck would have it, he was saved by Daniel Opperman. No commandant in the Boer army could refuse to allow a man home, it was an essential part of the democratic principles on which the army was based that each burgher fought of his own free will, but Red Daniel did not like to see his commando even one rifle short.

'Your place is here!' he shouted at Christiaan. 'How are we to stop the English crossing the Tugela if you all go home to cut mealies?'

Gaspar said, 'Leave me on commando, father. Then it is not so bad. Take my mother news of how well I am. You do not need to take me.'

Red Daniel had jabbed him in the chest with a strong forefinger. 'There! At least your son has a sense of duty. Go home to your old woman then. But be quick about it.' He leaned forward, his face so close to Christiaan's that their beards brushed harshly together. He said softly, smiling, against Christiaan's ear, 'And give her one from me. Heh?'

Gaspar's tent comrades were very good to him after his father had gone. He was the youngest by five or six years and they looked after him with a solicitude his mother couldn't have bettered. Even the Field Cornet, a surly old countryman unused to dealing with other human beings of any kind except the black labourers on his farm, took to sending him off to his own wagon for snatches of sleep during the day, commanding him to use the spare clothing he found in it as bedding. His comrades made him presents of rusks and strips of game biltong, strong and spiced, made from the guinea fowl that ran in flocks across the veld, speckled black and white, big as small turkeys. In the next tent in the laager was a woman, the small tough young wife of Frans Aggenbach, as good a shot as her husband and an English-hater to beat them all, and she developed a particular fondness for Gaspar. She made him mealie porridge over the camp fire and stewed him a jam of amatunguli, wild plum, to spread on his rusk. She mended his shirts and trimmed his hair and told him he would soon have a beard as fine as any in the commando. When she went out shooting game, she took him with her, drilling him remorselessly, setting up cairns of stones as English soldiers.

'Count down three buttons on their tunics, a handspan right, and fire. Don't waste time. Shoot only to kill.'

The laager was out to the west of Ladysmith, below a hill named Spion Kop.

'In 1835,' Leah Aggenbach said to him, 'my grandfather stood up there and looked down upon Natal, he and many, many other voortrekkers. And then the English came − '

The kop stood high and sharp between the laager and the river, a knoll covered in aloes to the east, a ragged chain of lower hills running west. The top was a small space, someone said, not more than half a dozen acres, and the climb to the summit a stiff pull from the northern side of a good two thousand feet. Opperman made them run up the lower slopes for fitness drill and sent patrols to the top to watch the English, over thirty thousand of them, milling about their camp life away to the east on the far side of the Tugela. They wouldn't attack as far west as Spion Kop, Opperman said. Why should they? What would be the point of taking a hill so far to the south and west of Ladysmith?

There were perhaps eight thousand men in the laager, waiting for the next British move. Red Daniel kept his commando moving, drilling, exercising, telling them each man must do the work of ten.

'I tell you why. It is the best joke of the war. The English general, old Buller, has sent a message to London saying that eighty thousand Boers are waiting for him on the north bank of the Tugela. What he doesn't know is that we have not eighty thousand Boers altogether in the nation, men, women and children, and he will not know. When General Botha calls us and we go, each man of the Carolina Commando will make old Buller think it is ten times as bad as he feared.'

In the third week of January, men began to pour into the laager, thousands and thousands of burghers, many of them city-soft men from the slums of Pretoria.

'Botha has called them,' the Field Cornet said to Gaspar. 'He must double his numbers. The English are going to cross the Tugela.'

'Not here – '

'Right here, boy.'

That night Opperman sent Gaspar on the first patrol of his life. With five others he climbed the northern face of Spion Kop and found below the summit, stretching all the way to Aloe Knoll, a line of burghers digging trenches. Following these round as far to the east as they could go, they came in the first glimmerings of dawn to a view down to the river and the sight of six English soldiers, naked in the Tugela, pushing the old ferry at Potgeiter's Drift from the northern to the southern bank. On the bank stood twenty more, dressed in the bush shirts and slouch hats of the volunteer regiments, Lee Metfords at the ready to give them cover. As the six scrambled ashore, Gaspar could see in the strengthening light that one of them had hair as red as Opperman's.

It was plain the English meant business. Quite apart from the matter of the ferry, there was more than enough activity on the dark bushy slopes of Mount Alice on the opposite bank of the river to show that there were plenty of soldiers there, maybe even old Buller himself, his headquarters moved from the safety of the railway line. There were moving masses of khaki by the second ford over the river, Trichardt's Drift, some way to the west, and here and there on the higher slopes the sunlight caught dull flashes of metal, the gleaming length of those terrible naval guns that could smash a whole hillside to pieces, let alone the men on it.

There was a twisted lump in Gaspar's stomach, a lump that heaved and turned low in him as he looked. What at first sight was dun veld was in reality dust-covered men, soldier after soldier after soldier, ten thousand more than General Botha could hope to have even if he raised all the reinforcements he wanted. And those men were all professional soldiers, drilled and trained, while half the burghers in the laager back there were yellowbellies from the city who would need gin to get them going at all and Commandant Opperman's whip to keep them at it. Some of them could hardly ride. He looked up at the hill behind him, empty and innocent in the clear morning sunlight, the line of the crest broken only by a clump of aloes here and there, rearing their spiky heads into the blue January sky. It was going to be hot.

When the firing began, Gaspar was told to stay back. His unit lay to the rear of the front line of commandos from the Free State and the Transvaal and was not to move into action until the battle was actually engaged. It was not a comfortable day. From where he was, Gaspar could see the summit of the kop blurred with blots of black smoke and flung earth from the heavy shells pounding out across the river. Shrapnel began to fly about like ragged black birds and, as the light strengthened, rifle fire spat and crackled, the sharpness of the sound muffled by the hill. He found it impossible to sit still, impossible to concentrate, impossible to feel hungry or thirsty, but fidgeted about restlessly, biting his nails, a childhood habit Bettie had tried to cure him of by dipping his fingers in a bitter lotion brewed from the juice of aloes.

'Is there battle? Has battle begun?'

Frans Aggenbach went on cleaning his Mauser. 'No. No orders to fire back yet. We are saving our ammunition.'

At midday the Field Cornet took him closer to the front line. 'You give us all the fidgets, boy. Better you see what is coming to us all.'

For the most part, the burghers lay in their trenches, saving their fire. Even their artillery was silent. But the two hundred guns thundering away from the south were not simply making a noise. Shells came spinning over the crest of the kop and exploded among the Boers below, leaving a beastly trail of mutilation such as Gaspar had never imagined. Before his eyes, men were quite literally blown to pieces or had arms and legs torn away as if they had been no more than stuffed dolls.

He cried out, 'Why don't we fire back? Why don't we fight?'

'All in good time. When the English attack, we will fight. They are trying to frighten us now. They are trying to drive us back – '

'But they are killing us! Look what they do! They are killing us!'

'And we, boy, will kill them.'

At sunset the bombardment sputtered out. With the other men of his corporalship, Gaspar sat round the camp fire while supper cooked and the light died rosy and soft over the jagged peaks of the Drakensberg hills. Lying in his tent later, he could hear the rain begin softly on the canvas by his head, cooling the air, bringing the strong rich smell of the earth into his nostrils. He slept at last, lulled by the steady tattoo.

Walter Rissik woke him at dawn, shaking him by the shoulder and banging a tin mug of coffee down by his head.

'Wake up! Get up, get up! The English have taken the kop in the night! Listen, listen to the fire!'

There was no time even to consider whether he was afraid. He had slept in his clothes and was awake in seconds, gulping the scalding coffee, soaking his rusk in it. He could hear the firing already, and above that the shouting nearer at hand of his corporal bellowing at the black mule drivers to saddle the horses. Bettie had made him a many-pocketed canvas waistcoat for ammunition and when he had filled it from the box on the wagon he felt as if he could not breathe, as if his lungs were flattened by the weight he carried. His pony was brought to him and he was in the saddle and off with the others in a single movement and thudding across the veld towards Spion Kop.

The northern face of the kop was dotted with climbing Boers. There must have been almost a thousand of them swarming up the steep hillside while English rifle fire spattered down among them from the top. As they reached the summit, Gaspar saw a fringe of English soldiers rise from their cover and the Boers began to give answering fire and he could see falling men against the skyline and then the line was pressed back over the rim of the hill and lost to view.

'Dismount,' Frans Aggenbach said to him.

'Dismount?'

'Yes. We follow up the attack.'

He flung himself off his pony and began to run, stumbling a little, up the stony hillside. The paths between the boulders were choked with dead and wounded men, their blood clotted dark on their clothes. A little way below the summit he was met by Commandant Opperman, rifle in right hand, whip in left.

'Round to the left!' he shouted. 'They are still holding the top! I want you to harass their flank!'

What had looked like the summit from below was in fact a ledge running round the kop some thirty feet from the top. Working his way round with the others towards the knoll he had had pointed out to him, Gaspar could see that the British had built themselves a low stone wall across the summit and from behind this were pouring a steady stream of rifle fire into the faces of the Boers not twenty yards away. In the glimpses he dared take, he could see the odd face, the odd tunic, as one raised himself just a little for better aim.

'The third button,' Leah had said to him, 'and a handspan to the right. Aim for that.' He saw one fall, crumpling forward over the stone wall and then a hail of fire crackled all around him and Walter Rissik's hand, hard on his spine, jabbed him down among the rocks.

'Keep low. Follow me.'

They crawled forward behind the boulders, among the casualties hideous in their damage. From behind them on a high spur almost a mile away, the artillery of the Transvaal commandos began to boom and crash, sending shells high over their heads into the English army packed on the plateau. From behind the boulder where he had finally taken shelter, Gaspar began to fire, steadily and relentlessly as he had been taught, wedging his rifle in a cleft in the stone, taking careful aim. The sun climbed high into the hot blue dome of the sky. There was no food and no water. On the broken body of the man who lay on the far side of Gaspar's boulder, the flies began to gather in sticky black clots, buzzing loathsomely.

When he paused for a moment to reload and shift his

aching shoulders, Gaspar could see that for many of his comrades it was already too much. A trickle of men had begun to creep back down the hillside and, if it had not been for Red Daniel roaring among them with his whip cracking as loud as any rifle, the trickle would have become a flood. To stand there in the blazing heat, without water, under heavy fire from above, on a rocky hillside strewn with the bodies of comrades was too much to ask of any man.

'And we are not soldiers!' Gaspar said to Walter. 'We are farmers. We are farmers with rifles.'

Walter jerked his head to the north. 'Look.'

Massing on the plain behind them, in the laagers where they had swallowed that snatched breakfast a few hours ago, horsemen were gathering in great numbers.

'The reinforcements!'

They never came. The hours dragged on, the firing never stopped, the stench of the dead rose sickeningly into the hot air. Gaspar lay against his boulder, dazed with heat and thirst and weariness, firing whenever an English helmet showed itself, but inaccurately now, his hands shaking almost too much even to load his rifle. His eyes were blurred with dust, his tongue thick with it. He wanted keenly to crawl away from that place, down from that awful bloody ledge, back down to something cool and dark and wet and quiet. If that whirling ranting figure with the rhino-hide whip had not been between him and the plain below, he would have done it. As it was he could do nothing. He imagined the English up there, grinning at the devastation they were causing, surveying that stricken hillside and the deserters stumbling down the slope to safety with the exultation of victors.

'My first battle. And we have to lose it – '

There had never been so long a day since the beginning of time. The strain was like a physical pain, drawing and sapping at his self-control like a knife turning slowly and inexorably in a wound. Towards dusk, when the boulder he had sheltered under all day had cooled sufficiently, he laid his cheek on it and shut his eyes and his consciousness dropped abruptly down into a nightmare loud with rifle fire.

It was Daniel Opperman who shook him awake. 'Come

with me. There are more than twenty of us. Come this way.'

His stiff limbs would hardly move. He said through dry lips, 'Walter? Frans?'

'Dead,' Opperman said shortly. He stopped and put strong hands under Gaspar's arms. 'So many of my commando.' He pulled Gaspar to his feet, slapping his rifle into his hands. 'This way.'

On the ledge to the east, a couple of dozen men lay crouched behind rocky cover. The light was fading, long fingers of shadow running over the rocks and bodies, and a blessed breath of cool air had sprung up. Gaspar could not fire. He lay against a rock, fumbling and fiddling to load, his fingers as nerveless as if they had belonged to someone else. Beside him, Red Daniel rose to his feet. He stopped his clumsy rattling and looked up. Opperman beckoned to him to stand too and then raised his rifle to shoulder height.

In the twilight, from the slopes that ran southeastwards to Potgeiter's Drift, a figure was climbing. It was impossible to make out his details, only his outline showed that he was tall and hatless and carried a pistol in his right hand. From the direction he was coming from and the fact that the English above him on his left did not fire, it could be deduced that he was indeed an Englishman and the closest Englishman Gaspar had ever seen.

'Take him,' Daniel said. 'He's yours. A trophy for your sister.'

'I'm not loaded. I can't – '

Opperman's rifle, heavier than his own, was thrust into his hands. He raised it, shaking, to squint along the barrels. In the darkness it would be difficult to see the buttons . . .

Red Daniel's hand shot out and slapped the barrel down, sending the bullet spitting into the earth. The man jerked his head up and peered forward into the dimness. There was a pause and then he called, in an unmistakably English accent, 'Werda?'

Red Daniel began to laugh. To Gaspar's amazement, he climbed over the rocks in front of them and strode towards the stranger. A yard away he stopped and pulled off his hat, still laughing. Gaspar and several of the men around him climbed gingerly behind him, stepping cautiously over the rough ground until they were within six feet of their commandant. Then they saw the reason for the wasted shot, the laughter. Both men were laughing now, facing each other, a yard apart, indistinguishable from anyone else in their dust and dirt except that both heads were crowned with flaming-red hair.

It was only after that that Opperman would let them retreat. The moment, with its curious light-hearted hint of comradeship in spite of everything, had somehow broken the strain of the day, had brought home to him that no one, however determined, could fight on in darkness and broken country. It was over sixteen hours after Gaspar had first climbed the hillside that he was allowed to descend it, horrible now with the fallen, towards the pony that stood where he had tethered it as hungry and thirsty as he was himself. There was a stream nearby; already full of splashing men and horses, and Gaspar plunged in with them, towing his pony, hurling water into his frantic mouth and over his head and neck.

Fifteen minutes later, he found panic back in the laager. His commando, stretched to breaking point all day, could take no more. Daylight would bring the English pouring over the Tugela and sweeping on to Ladysmith, and not one exhausted disheartened Boer wished to see it. The first wagons were already creaking out of camp towards the north and men were riding with it, cramming food into their mouths as they rode. Gaspar turned his pony's head to join them, too infected with discouragement to do more than stumble where he was led, too tired and sick at heart to care.

They had not gone more than a hundred yards before a horseman came plunging in amongst them, shouting at the wagons to stop. Gaspar could not see him in the darkness but could hear him shouting harshly, his voice commanding them all to silence.

'Will you desert now, brothers? Will you turn away and leave our land in this hour of danger? Think of the shame that will be upon you, walk with you all your lives, if you turn your backs on the Tugela. The English have taken one kop, one kop only. The line is still ours, the line that keeps them south of the river. They have only made one gap in that line, one gap only. They are so timid that if we just trust and believe, they will weaken and give in. In the name of God, in the name of our dear country, for the sake of our women and our children and our farms, I beg you to turn. I beg you, for all we hold dear, to turn back, to go back to your positions either side of the Spion Kop gap and wait there for the English. Do not fail our country and our God, my brothers, do not fail to hold on to what is so dear to us. May God bless and keep you all.'

Gaspar sat numb in his saddle, his throat full. Within minutes, the great wagons were turning, the men were pulling at their horses' heads, pulling them round to the south, towards the carnage they had left by the Tugela. A hand took Gaspar's bridle in the darkness and he felt his pony double in its tracks. Beside him Daniel Opperman said, 'That was General Botha, boy. Our general. He will spend all night at this task. I tell you, he will ride all night from commando to commando and by morning every man will be back at his post. You will see.'

Gaspar slept fitfully that night at the foot of the kop, his head on his saddle. None of his tent mates had survived to sleep near him, only the old Field Cornet was a familiar figure, snoring beside him, his huge beard heaving with each breath. The dew woke them all, falling chill and thick as the night wore on, and they made coffee over an open fire and waited for the sky to lighten and a new day's horror to begin. Gaspar, gazing upwards with a sort of dread at the ledge where he seemed to have spent half his life, clutched suddenly at the sleeve of the man crouched beside him. 'Look! Look up there! Oh, look!'

The commando was on its feet in a bound, cheering like madmen. On the summit of the hill, outlined sharp and clear against the pale dawn, two Boers were waving their hats and rifles in an ecstasy of triumph.

'The English have gone!' Opperman shouted. 'They are not holding the hill! The hill is ours, still ours!'

Casting their mugs down, every man went for the hill at a run, scrambling breathlessly to the top, hardly heeding, in their exultation, the bodies that littered their path. It seemed like a dream to Gaspar to scramble over the ledge and plunge onward towards the English trenches, empty now and silent in the dawn of a new day. He ran forwards, shouting in delight, and without considering leaped the shallow wall the English had built and found himself in a carnage more awful than anything he had seen among his own people.

The English lay dead in heaps, in piles, bodies on bodies, two and three deep, hideously mutilated by the Boer guns. It was hardly to be believed. The long shallow trench was a scattered jumble of limbs and torn khaki, helmets, weapons, and wounds unspeakable to look on. Gaspar turned sweating and sick, stumbling back over the wall he had jumped with such high spirits, and vomited violently on the far side.

Someone put a hand on his shoulder. 'Look down there.'

He straightened slowly, shivering, his eyes following the line of the pointing finger. Below, in the strengthening sun, lay the gleaming curving line of the Tugela, and across it, at the drift places, the English were plodding back to the south, long columns of men and guns and horses, retreating even from the places they had gained. He looked at it in amazement, at the huge military machine withdrawing in clouds of pale dust to Colenso, and then he turned to the man beside him. His voice was filled with awe.

'So we won!'

Part Three

10

War or no war, Adelaide could feel nothing but exuberance at the sight of Cape Town. She had never seen anywhere so lush in her life before, never encountered a place where nature was so absolutely lavish that waste became irrelevant. The mountains, the green vineyards, the crops in the rich earth, the Dutch houses painted the pale colours of ice cream, the flowers wreathing balconies, spilling over garden walls, the huge bright shell of the sky, all of it made her feel that she was in some delightful limbo, well out of the way of reality. Her spirits had risen steadily as they steamed south away from England and her impressive but grim hospital training and the disordered inefficiency of her father's house in Oxford. It was astonishing not to be physically exhausted, to be able to spend hours strolling on deck under skies which really had no knowledge of winter at all, to read and think in an idle and desultory manner. It was, in reality, that voyage, the first holiday of Adelaide's life and it culminated in the sight of Cape Town from the sea and a quayside where baskets of grapes and apples were dotted among military stores and pieces of artillery wrapped in sacking.

And then, of course, somewhere up there to the north, there was Matthew. Adelaide had no expectation of seeing him and absolutely no shred of hope that it would make the smallest difference to him if she did. She had never spoken openly about her feelings for him to anyone, but she had thought about them a good deal and had acknowledged to herself that, except in the most practical sense, she could actually be of no use to him at all. If he had been the kind of man for whom a steady and supportive love is the fuel for every endeavour, things might have been different. But Adelaide knew that Matthew was not that sort of man. Quite what sort he was, she was not even decided, but she was sure that when he had finished with flinging himself about the world and its ideas, he would be an impressive human being. And at that point, he would need a wife of a very different sort to Adelaide. Her feelings for Matthew had given her about as much pleasure as steady toothache, apart from the brief weeks when his enthusiasm had exceeded her own, but they seemed to be as much a part of her as breathing. She did not know where he was in this great country that rolled northwards, but even the feeling that he had docked at Cape Town as she was now doing was some tiny grain of comfort. She could find out about him and send news of him home to Frances, and the thought of such positive action ahead of her gave her a feeling that was very close to hope.

The hospital to which Adelaide arranged herself to be assigned was unrecognizable as such after the barrack-like buildings of St Thomas's. It was in a house that was no less than a mansion, designed over a hundred years before by Louis-Michel Thibault, and its owner, a magnificent and terrifying matriarch named Mrs Smit, had withdrawn to a family farm outside the city and left her house to be a hospital for the British. It had been assumed, somewhat naturally, by the military authorities that the house of so towering an imperialist as Mrs Smit would be used only for officers, and accordingly the first officer casualties of the Western Front were brought in and laid on army cots under the complicated plasterwork of the high ceilings. In the third week of December, Mrs Smit had swept in, sparkling with wrath and hundreds of thousands of pounds' worth of Smit diamonds.

'This is to be a hospital for the Empire. The Empire may be designed by men such as my dear friend, Lord Milner, but it is built by the effort of the British soldier. For every officer here, I want to see a private soldier too.' She paused and glared about her.

Beside her, someone pointed out respectfully that the sepoy was also a British private soldier and that he was of a curious colour . . .

Mrs Smit said superbly, with no indication that she had heard a word, 'This is to be my hospital. The Smit Hospital for Servants of the Empire. All shall come to my doors, from

138

the general to the drummer boy. Providing, of course, that they are white.'

It made for awful difficulties. Dr Trevor, in charge of the hospital and a military surgeon of thirty years' experience, said the Smit mansion was just the kind of kindness they could do without. 'It's the Pharisee praying in public. Good works must be seen to be done. She leaves us with the hideous responsibility of her damn great house and never for one moment does it occur to her that no general on the face of this earth will share a latrine with a private and that the privates will pilfer the door, furniture and anything else that isn't bolted to the floor. I'm strongly tempted to ignore the old bat completely.'

'Compromise, sir?'

'Such as – '

'A few hand-picked privates as window dressing, sir. We can wheel them on if Mrs Smit comes again. And leave the officers where they are. At least the worst damage they inflict is cigar burns.'

'Wait till they're better. Too smashed up to do anything at the moment, poor brutes. But give them another month or so – '

It was, for Will Marriott, an interminable month. He had been put in a bed at the end of a wide polished corridor, beneath a window just too high for him to see out. When he first came to the Smit house, he was in such pain and fever that he could not have cared where they put him or what they did with him, and when some of the agony subsided, it seemed like making an unnecessary fuss to ask to be put somewhere more congenial. They did at least take away the screen that had made a tiny room of his corridor end, so that he could see the nurses going to and fro and, after a while, limping, stooping figures in pyjamas, stumbling about with sticks and crutches.

He still had his leg though he couldn't see it would ever be any use for anything much. The huge raw wound in the front of his thigh, through which his broken bone had grinned like sharks' teeth, had been roughly stitched at the field hospital behind the lines at Magersfontein. It had worried Will in case they had not troubled to set the bone before they began sewing him up, but he was so dazed by pain and shock that he could not be sure of what he said and what he simply thought. In any case, unconsciousness had rushed at him unbidden every so often, and when he came round he had had to begin his train of thought from the beginning each time.

But whatever they did up there in that ghastly tent full of flies and buckets of lopped-off limbs like some grisly painting of hell, they did it well and cleanly. He had been propped up in the train at the Modder river station, wedged between others equally damaged, and within hours had been on his way to Cape Town, hot, sick and wretched, obsessed with the possibility of gangrene. They had reached Cape Town in a cool dawn and had been lifted down into canvas chairs and stretchers and it was only then, looking at the clean well-fed faces around him, that Will remembered fully.

'We lost,' he said to the orderly who was pushing him through the crowd to a waiting horse ambulance, 'didn't we? At Magersfontein. We didn't see them and they shot us down –'

'That's right, sir,' the orderly said cheerfully. 'Black Week, they're calling it now, Stormberg, Magersfontein and Colenso.'

Will ran his hand over his chin. 'I haven't shaved – '

'Wouldn't worry about that, sir. Sight of your face wouldn't help you much, neither. Hospital will fix you up.'

Dr Trevor had talked of stitching the wound again but had not done it. It was dressed twice daily and, to begin with, Will could not look at it. He had nightmares frequently, shouting orders and trying to get out of bed and crawl to the foot of the kopje again, so that they had to strap him into bed for several nights and dose him heavily. When he could sit up, he demanded paper and wrote to Frances, reams and reams of explanation and description and regret, wildly repetitive. He wrote most days, propped sideways against his pillows in his comfortless corner, resting his paper on a Bible printed in Dutch.

I never thought we should have so little chance. I never dreamed they wouldn't give us a moment to reply, I never thought they would open up on us like that before we were even halfway ready. I didn't see anything, except the fire. I haven't even seen

140

a Boer. I've been away from Cape Town for only a month, I've been in three engagements and I'm out of it. I don't know what to do with myself, I don't know where to go. It was all such a muddle you know, the Highlanders leaping down the hill with the Boers behind them and we trying to push our way up and nobody knowing what the orders were or even, after Wauchope was killed, who they were coming from. I'm lying at the end of a passage and I can see blue sky out of a high window above me and sometimes a bird. I can't write what I think about the war but I wish you were here to talk to. Everything's gone to pieces, my Highlanders, you, Matthew, me. It was all over before I could grasp it. The month I was away seems like two minutes and all my life. And now I've lain here as long. Please write. I must think about something else. Please write.

When Adelaide found him he had fallen abruptly asleep, slumped helplessly sideways, his face squashed against the wall. She looked at him for a moment, considering him in relation to Frances, and then she reverted to being a nurse and shook him awake to bang his pillows and settle him into them.

'You're new,' Will said.

'Quite right. Off the boat three days ago. I was sent up to Groote Schuur but you were not there so I hunted about Cape Town until I found you.'

Will regarded her. 'Found me – '

'Yes. I am Adelaide Munro. You don't know me but I was instructed to find you by Frances Paget.'

He flung an arm up against his eyes and said from under it, 'You wouldn't be real, would you?'

She put a firm capable hand over his free one. 'Feel.'

'Then do you think you could say what you have just said again?'

'My father, Adolphus Munro, was Matthew's tutor at Oxford. Through Matthew I met Frances. I was training to be a nurse in London and, through the Peace Society, met Emily Hobhouse by whose good offices I am here. With instructions to look you up. Which I have.' She looked about her. 'What on earth have they put you here for?'

'I don't know. The wards are pretty full. And I think I shouted a bit at night.'

'If I was stuck in a passage, I should shout in the day too. I shall do some shouting for you. Are you in pain?'

'Not so much. Now and then – '

She said, 'You are rather smaller than I imagined you would be.'

He smiled ruefully. 'Compared with Matthew – '

'I wasn't thinking of Matthew. I was thinking of Frances.'

He looked down. 'How is she?'

'Extremely well. I will tell you all I know in measured doses. Like medicine. And bring you a letter.'

'A letter!'

'Have you any news of Matthew?'

'None. I've asked and asked. But when you are stuck in a confounded bed – '

Adelaide glanced up at the maddening square of blue sky above them. 'What was the point of putting a window up there? Only fit for giraffes. I shall make inquiries about Matthew.'

'Miss Munro, you can have no idea of how glad I am you have come.'

'I am not quite used to it yet,' she said. 'It's so beautiful here and I never saw such sunshine. But the casualties are awful, they keep pouring in – ' She stopped and then said, 'Did you know about Spion Kop? Two days ago.'

Will nodded. 'Lost fifteen hundred – '

Adelaide sat down on the edge of his bed. 'Highly irregular to do this, mind you. I shall be sent home straight away if anyone finds me. Tell me, do you know nothing of Matthew at all?'

'Only what his plans were. Not if he carried them out. I had left for the Western Front before he landed. I left messages of course, but you never know if he got them or, if he did, did anything about them.'

'I must do some investigating. What a war. Black Week or not, England thinks it is winning and I get out here and it seems to be reverse after reverse and the casualties quite appalling. No wonder I don't believe in it as a way of settling problems.'

'Miss Munro?'

She looked at him. His face was very white around the dark curve of his moustache.

'Will you fetch the letter from Frances?'

*

142

Things were very different after that. He was moved into a corner room with windows facing south and west, shared only by a major of the Gordon Highlanders and two of Rimington's Guides. The major had lost an arm and an eye and spent all day setting up targets at the foot of his bed and firing paper pellets at them with his remaining arm.

'Damned nuisance. Right arm, left eye. Can't see why the buggers couldn't clean me out on one side. Always was a right hand, right eye man.'

One of the Guides had a deep flesh wound in the stomach that had to be persistently drained and dressed. He was a huge man with a frame like a giant, and lay limp and still all day, his eyes closed, his skin like wax. He should have been somewhere quiet and out of the way, with others as ill as he was, but the hospital was overcharged and the organization was buckling under the onslaught. The other Guide had lost a foot. He was a skinny, tough man who had grown up in Natal and he complained that his nonexistent foot gave him more pain than when it was attached to him. 'Can't understand it. Bloody awful it is now. Couldn't sleep a wink last night. And the bleeding thing isn't even there – '

The sun reached Will's bed in the mid-morning and lay there until mid-afternoon, and from his pillow he could see into Mrs Smit's celebrated garden where bougainvillea rioted in half a dozen colours and flamboyant trees brandished their orange sweeps of blossom. Adelaide brought him books and newspapers and he kept the letters from Frances under his pillow.

> You cannot imagine what we feel to know Adelaide will see you [she wrote in the latest]. There really is no way to express our relief – nor any way for me to tell you what I feel about your being wounded. I keep thinking of you playing croquet in Salisbury, bicycling, running upstairs, and I hate to think of you doing all those things stiffly, impeded by this horrible thing that has happened to you. Of course I am filled with pride at your gallantry but I wish it did not have such a price. Will they decorate you? You must deserve it.

He liked the descriptions of Oxford in her letters. It was an infinite comfort to think of the stately safety of somewhere like Oxford when you lay in a room with three other men none of whom would ever be complete again. He liked thinking of the slow dark January river and Frances walking beside it in the red knitted hat and muffler her mother deplored because the colour fought so with her hair; he liked picturing the wide blond curve of the High Street and Frances flying down it on her bicycle with books in the basket in front of her; he liked almost best of all the half-humorous, half-despairing description she had given of her room.

> Oh, Will, so self-consciously student-ish! You would hate it. I rather think that I do, though not for the same reasons. I thought all the colours would look wonderful together, like a garden does, but they don't. They just look like the living image of a headache. You and Matthew stand about in it looking disapproving. You're on my worktable, in uniform, and you have never had to look at such a mess in your life before. I can't tell you how reproachful you are. Matthew thinks it is just what he would expect of a woman student. Oh, I do long to hear from him! It is nearly two months since he went away.

There was no word from Salisbury of the reaction to Matthew's escapade.

'They do not know,' Adelaide said shortly in reply to his muttered question. 'At least they didn't when I left.'

'She *must* – '

'Write and tell her so.'

After a few days in the sunny corner room among the major's flying paper pellets, Will was lifted into a wheelchair and taken down into the garden. He was left under a flamboyant tree on the edge of a huge sweep of lawn with a view of the strange flat-topped ridges of mountain rising behind the house. He looked about him, at the other figures dotted about the grass.

'Why must you leave me here? Can't you take me closer to someone else?'

The nurse, a plump fair woman whose impressive bosom was the subject of much comment on the wards, looked arch. 'Wait until you see what I've got for you – '

Daisy Bashford came lightly across the lawn trailing lilac

144

gauze flounces and spinning a ruffled parasol. It took her a long time to reach Will on account of having to stop here and there at other chairs and Will could hear her laughing and saying, 'You shan't keep me, wicked man!' When she eventually reached Will and stood before him, soft as a fondant and smiling her sleepy kitten's smile, he could not say anything at all.

'Naughty Captain Marriott. Who is going to dance with me now?'

'I shall. I'm to try sticks tomorrow.'

An orderly came running with a chair, one of Mrs Smit's French chairs released as a special favour from Dr Trevor's office.

'Awful men,' Daisy said, settling herself. 'Look at them all staring.'

'You do make rather a change from nurses.'

'I should hope so!'

'Daisy – '

She looked at him sideways and swung her skirts so that he could see glimpses of satin shoes and neat ankles.

'You're a brick to come and see me.'

'I should have come before. But I'm such a coward about wounds and things. And I've been so busy – '

'Parties, parties, parties?'

She gave a tiny yawn. 'What wouldn't I do for sleep!'

'What is Hendon up to?'

She giggled. 'Busy, too. He'll have to go up to Johannesburg soon or we'll be begging in the streets. Wars seem to make things such a price.' She leaned forward, bringing her parasol down so that she and Will were screened from view behind it. 'When you danced with me that night, Grace Taggart was so furious, you can't think. One dance was all very well, she said, but five in a row was the limit. *And* she saw us go onto the balcony – '

On the balcony of the Mount Nelson Hotel, pressed against some jasmine that grew between the French windows, Will had kissed Daisy. Thinking about it afterwards, which he had done with considerable pleasure, he wondered if, actually, Daisy had kissed him. Whoever it was who had begun it, it had all been wonderfully easy and her little pink mouth had at once opened enthusiastically under his and he had felt her tongue, firm and pointed, against his own. They had stayed out there quite a long time, Daisy's arms round his neck and her fingers in his hair and his hands running over the satiny skin of her shoulders, kissing and kissing, and then a colonel of the Seaforths had come out quite close to them with someone else's wife and the balcony had suddenly seemed rather crowded.

Will said, hoping he wasn't colouring, 'Did she disapprove?'

'No, silly! She was jealous. Jealous as a green-eyed cat. She thinks you are one of the best-looking men in Cape Town. She wanted to come today but I wouldn't let her.'

'You wouldn't – ?'

Daisy put her face so close to his that he could have counted the thick brown lashes fringing her round blue eyes. 'What do you take me for?'

He said, 'You really mustn't flirt so outrageously with a man in a wheelchair. It isn't fair.'

'Who cares about being fair? It's fun.' She swung the parasol upright again and surveyed the figures on the lawn. 'Poor dears. How many of them will dance again?'

'Daisy. When I am upright again, will you dance with me?'

'Oh, yes – as long as you don't take too long – '

'With an incentive, you know, I might be bouncing about in no time.'

'What's an incentive?'

'A prize to make it all worthwhile.'

She pointed to her mouth and pouted and giggled. 'Like that?'

'Absolutely like that.'

'You are wicked. It must mean you are getting better. I must go.'

'Don't. I feel better every minute you stay.'

'I must say, Will Marriott, you have the smoothest tongue. Think what those dragon nurses would say if they knew what we were talking about.'

He smiled at her. 'Can you talk about anything else, Daisy?'

146

She gave him a small toss of her head. 'Don't you like how I talk?'

'Very much.'

She got up slowly and stood so that he could look at her while she shook out her skirts and balanced her parasol on the opposite shoulder.

'Will you come again? Soon?'

'I can't say – '

'Please, Daisy.'

'Shall I bring Grace?'

'I'd rather not.'

'Hendon sent you his best wishes,' she said carelessly.

'Thank him and say I hope my nest egg is flourishing in his capable hands.'

Daisy made a face. 'Don't talk to me about money. It's too awful.' She looked round the lawn, then stooped to kiss Will lightly on the mouth. 'Goodbye then. And let's hope all the dragons were watching that from the windows.'

Will sat on in the garden until the shadows were long fingers across the lawn and the sky was as pale as a bird's egg. Two nurses had attempted to take him in and he had begged to be left, so they had collected everyone else and he was alone and strangely happy in the twilight. He found that for the first time since he was wounded he wanted to try his legs again, he wanted to be free of this cocoon of convalescence and indolence and back in the life that had been broken off for him. He wanted to prove himself – reassure himself – that his dreams of England and Empire had not foundered in a welter of red dust and blood on Magersfontein Kopje, that he only felt as he had this last month because he had never been wounded before, hadn't known what to expect. When Adelaide came out in the dusk to wheel him into the house, he was almost humming.

'I am to attribute this lightness of heart, I suppose, to that pretty goose who was here this afternoon.'

'Very pretty – '

'And very silly.'

'Doesn't matter,' Will said, 'when she's as pretty as that.'

Adelaide sat down on Mrs Smit's French chair. 'Doesn't matter?'

'Not with that sort of girl.'

'You mean that that sort of girl is for looking at and touching, I suppose?'

'I wouldn't put it so bluntly, but yes.'

'I can't help putting things bluntly. It's how my mind works. Heaven knows I've tried to see things less straightforwardly but it really is quite impossible unless it comes to you naturally. Try as I might, I can *always* see the wood for the trees.'

'Adelaide,' Will said with admiration, 'you are splendid.'

'Oh, my dear, don't you tell me so too. I'm getting more splendid by the minute, I can feel it. I have almost reorganized this hospital in two weeks and Dr Trevor says I am so capable I might almost be a man. I am, of course, prostrated by such a compliment. Don't laugh, Will. It isn't kind. And I saw you being kissed this afternoon and I think a dozen officers of the British Army would gladly have murdered you in jealous rage. I stood at that top window up there and thought, fortunate Miss Bashford.'

'What can you mean? Her only piece of good fortune is her face – '

'You see,' Adelaide said, 'I am not particularly attractive to men. I am too brisk. It isn't alluring.' She paused and then continued calmly. 'I am reasonably handsome but I don't think men ever want to kiss me.'

Will leaned forward. 'At this moment, I do. Very much. Will you let me?'

She regarded him for a while in the dim blue light and then she said with the same reasonableness, 'No, I don't think so.'

'Why? Why not? Would you think it improper?'

'No. Not at all. The truth is I am afraid of liking too much something that I shouldn't be offered again.'

Will sighed and then he said, 'I think that's all absolute rot and I am very disappointed.'

Adelaide stood up. 'If it soothes your vanity, so am I. But I always have taken thought for the morrow, I can't help it. It's time I took you in.'

She grasped the handles of his chair firmly and began to push him towards the house, leaving Mrs Smit's Second Empire chair standing empty beneath the flamboyant tree.

11

'There are two significant pieces of news,' the Archdeacon said, holding *The Times* at such an angle against the light that no one could read it but himself. 'The first is that Ladysmith has at last been relieved. Of that we can be quite sure. The first of Buller's columns entered the town on 28 February. The second piece of news I can only guess at. And that is that our son Matthew was presumably involved in the relief.'

Harriet began to cry very quietly, crushing herself into the corner of her chair as if to make her crying the more unobtrusive. Frances watched her miserably. She had been summoned home, a fortnight before the end of the Lent term, because her father had said that as one of the prime causes of her mother's nervous condition she was duty bound to do something about it.

'I didn't want you to come!' Harriet had cried, rocking herself back and forth in her armchair. 'I asked him not to send for you! I wanted you to finish your term.'

'But I feel so guilty – '

'My dear, we all do. In our various ways. Except perhaps your f—. It's part of this whole horrible war business.'

'I should have told you at once about Matthew. I should not have let him be gone over two months and you not knowing he had gone in the opposite direction. Of course I am guilty. And so sorry. For you, I mean. I don't think Father minds much, in fact he seemed quite jubilant – '

'Please!'

She had eventually broken the news on Christmas Eve. It was about as ill-chosen a moment as she could have selected, with the burden of Christmas services on the Archdeacon making a war in his opinion seem a trivial thing by comparison, but Aunt Beatrice had been there and her chill disapproving composure had been more than Frances could bear.

She had sat at dinner on Christmas Eve and listened to the three adults talking, going round and round the subjects of Matthew and Will like circling birds, and then, unable to hold out any longer, she had blurted out the news about Matthew as clumsily as a child confessing a peccadillo and after that put her head down and cried like anything among the tangerine peel and nutshells on her plate.

There was suddenly a tremendous amount of noise, quite apart from her sobbing, and she had had to sit upright and say it all over again, very slowly, and then again, even more distinctly, and then, as a crowning awfulness to the whole saga, confess that she had not heard from Matthew since he sailed. The Archdeacon took her into his study and talked at her for a very long time indeed and then he led her into the drawing room and said the same things all over again in front of her mother and her aunt. Her mother said nothing, only looked frightened and stricken, but when Frances went over to kiss her goodnight Harriet said softly, 'You should have told us sooner. You know you should. But really Matthew should have told us himself. It was very wrong of him to make you bear the burden of his scrape.'

Aunt Beatrice's cheek, when Frances stooped to kiss it, was as cool and smooth as an egg. She did not attempt to kiss her father, but ran upstairs in a great hurry and locked her bedroom door behind her and wished powerfully for Oxford and Celia and Rose, and funny, fascinating Mr Stansgate who had sent her a Christmas card from the offices of the *Speaker* and with it a bottle of champagne and a pineapple.

That was over two months ago. Christmas, of course, had been quite ruined, despite her mother's efforts to console her that she was not, after all, the most undutiful and unloving of daughters. By the New Year, the Archdeacon had assumed the mantle of suffering so effectively that he was obviously enjoying it, and on the Sunday before Frances returned to Oxford he preached on the effectiveness of prayer, concluding by saying that they must all join together in praying for the cause of right in South Africa, since they were already joined together by a bond of endurance, the strain caused by anxiety over their fighting sons.

'It was exactly as I thought,' she said to Rose, heated in her recollection of her father's behaviour. 'He loved to wear his injury in public but at last he had to give way to his private delight that Matthew was doing what was orthodox. I expect he is now discreetly boasting about it.'

She had not enjoyed her second term as much as her first. Distressing, confused letters came from Will, in hospital at the Cape, all the more alarming because of the frequent black blocks of censorship on every page; the January weather in Oxford was wet and wild, and riding a bicycle was the least attractive form of transport; the war news in general was gloomy; and most of her work seemed pedantic and unexciting. She caught a chill and went to her multi-coloured bed for a week, and reread Will's patchwork letters far too often and was frightened by them. She tried to write cheerful, gossipy letters back as an antidote, but that seemed heartless, so she took to writing long descriptions of Oxford and the weather to him in the hope that such things were more comfortable to a man in a state of shock after his first severe wound. When Adelaide wrote and said that she had found him and that he was in a very pleasant place and would certainly walk again, Frances had felt almost sick with relief. And on the same day as Adelaide's letter, by the afternoon post, had come another letter, this time from Oliver Stansgate, saying he would be in Oxford on the following Saturday and would exchange a very good luncheon for a guided tour of the colleges.

For three days she had been extremely happy. She wrote at length, with relaxed cheerfulness, to Will, bought a new blouse of cream spotted voile with a high frilled collar, almost bought a new hat, and was oblivious to the rain. Saturday morning had dawned grey but dry, with a sharp little wind whipping round corners, and she had gone down to breakfast with a light heart to find a telegram from London in which Oliver regretted that he would have to postpone his visit to Oxford. He wrote to her later, a very nice letter, and said journalists made entertaining but unpunctual friends and that he did not expect to be forgiven, only guided at some future time. Two days after that he sent her a little basket of hothouse apricots and she and Celia ate them over their Latin translation and wondered why he always sent things to eat and drink.

And then in the middle of February, Adelaide wrote again.

Matthew is found. I am only sorry it has taken so long, but as of today – to be exact, yesterday, when I heard – he is alive and well and a trooper with the South African Light Horse. They are a volunteer mounted infantry regiment, chiefly raised among the foreigners who came down from Johannesburg when the war began. He sailed for Durban in November and was involved – and quite unharmed – in all the battles at Colenso and on Spion Kop. He must now be in the throes of the newest attempt to relieve Ladysmith. I have all this from a fellow trooper, a taciturn man called Gilbert Wildun, who was wounded at Colenso and shipped back here to convalesce. It wasn't very difficult to find someone from Matthew's regiment once I had discovered what that was, which I did by going to all the recruiting sergeants of the volunteer regiments. So I have written to Matthew himself at all sorts of places and begged him to write to you himself. And I have told him about Will, though I suspect he must know it is likely Will was wounded. He is walking quite well, though he looks a little venerable doing it!

Frances celebrated with Celia and Rose by opening the champagne Oliver Stansgate had sent her at Christmas. They drank it from teacups and then they put on their hats and went out to the post office to telegraph to Salisbury. Archdeacon Paget responded by summoning Frances home. Her mother, he said, was very alarmed to think of the danger Matthew was in and Frances' place was most certainly by her side. He wrote by the same post to the college principal asking that Frances should be released in these exceptional family circumstances and it was only loyalty to her mother that prevented Frances, in her interview with the principal, from begging her to refuse the Archdeacon's request. She packed her belongings in a mood of great gloom.

She bought a copy of the *Speaker* at Oxford station to read on the train journey, and found the leader was a discussion of the anti-British press so rife in France and Germany and contained a novel suggestion that the Russians might choose this vulnerable moment to swoop down and carry off India.

From the tone of it, she did not think Oliver had written it, but then she turned the page and found an article which said that the current attitude in the Continental press was a revelation of how much England had made herself detested in the previous fifty years. It was a great chance for the nations of Europe to let their loathing of English success, their hatred of English superiority and hypocrisy and liberalism, have its head.

> We regret very bitterly [the leader concluded] that our actions in South Africa have laid us so wide open to these violent accusations on the Continent. But we must reap where we have sown, and all will not be lost if we take a revolutionary lesson from the harvest.

Underneath the leader was a headline, 'Massingham Dismissed!' The article read:

> Liberalism no longer has the courage of its convictions. The worse we fare in this unhappy war, the more unpopular any criticism of it becomes. Massingham has been dismissed as editor of the *Daily Chronicle*, a victory for blind and misplaced patriotism, a defeat for farsighted and liberal justice.

It sounded more like Oliver, but for all that, she found she did not want to read on. She was beginning to be unable to think about the war at all, it seemed to have got more out of hand than had ever seemed possible. Rose had gone up to London to meet her father for two days and had come down with reports that the capital was brimming with patriotic tears at the sight of thousands and thousands of volunteers off to South Africa with Lord Roberts, who had replaced General Buller as Commander-in-Chief. She said that she had been walking down Bond Street with her father and half a dozen young men in uniform had gone by, laughing and joking, and when she looked round, everyone seemed to be weeping, all the people on the pavements were reduced to tears at the sight of them. She had said all London was like that, and that when they went to the theatre, any man in uniform was allowed in for nothing. Mr Hemming-Hemming had declared it was the worst kind of sentimentality over the worst kind of waste of human life and Rose said she was thankful to get to Oxford again. They were expecting twenty thousand volunteers and the rest of the population was in patriotic floods.

That was disturbing enough. The savagery of feeling on the Continent was an added pain. Frances might not support the war in any way, yet she could not bring herself to feel indifferent to her nation's being so detested and, on top of that, acknowledge that it might be behaving with sickening emotional folly. The society girls with tear-filled eyes behind their veils were displaying a travesty of what Will believed in – and what Oliver did not. They both might think a bright future lay ahead, but Will saw it in terms of England's beneficient work in the world, Oliver in terms of England's role being entirely different from any she had played before and with none of the race nationalism that had taken such deep root.

Frances closed her eyes. How appallingly easy the war had been to start, how appallingly complicated and mis-directed it had become. In England it was all argument and talk and theories and emotion; in South Africa it was hideous scuffles in the red dust and heat and thirst, and Will's leg ripped open like something in a butcher's shop. Gentle, humorous, decent Will. What an engaging combination, Will and Adelaide, Will so gallant, Adelaide so businesslike. How pathetic to have to learn to walk again, what a humilia-tion, added to everything else.

There was nothing to do at home when she got there. Poor Harriet, at last able to visualize Matthew somewhere, was certainly much alarmed by what she imagined but wanted little succour. Life with the Archdeacon had taught her to do largely without it. She gardened in the cold spring earth, clearing weeds from the new green spikes of bulbs, and spent long hours in the cathedral and in the church school where she read poetry to the children. Frances went for solitary walks along the river in the wind, and wrote to Rose and Celia, to Adelaide and Will, and Matthew, and felt that they were all going round and round and round, trapped on some endless circuit like mice in a wheel.

*

The relief of Ladysmith caused massive jubilation. Frances and Harriet made banners with huge white letters appliquéd onto backgrounds of red and blue serge and hung them from the windows. An enormous bonfire was lit and all Salisbury surged out into the streets and caroused with torches and beer mugs and flags. The army had kept doggedly on and on at the Tugela and at last they had forced their way across and crept on to Ladysmith, halted here and there, massively afflicted with dysentery and exhaustion, ceaselessly sniped at. They lost five hundred men at Harts Hill, almost all from the Irish Brigade, but had plodded staunchly on, day after day, to a curious armistice on a Sunday morning when British and Boer had actually met under white flags while the wounded and dead were collected. They had shaken hands with each other and handed out tobacco, but there did not seem to have been anything to say, and when the armistice was over it all began again and the British inched northwards, capturing forty prisoners after a bayonet charge – an impressive bag – and battering their way on with shells and lyddite.

The first columns riding into Ladysmith saw the Boers streaming away to the north, fleeing fast as they always did once they had turned their backs. And so poor hungry Ladysmith, with its rows of sick lying at Intombi, helpless with enteric, was relieved. The rescuing army rode across the plain at a gallop and with it, said *The Times*, were two squadrons of the Imperial Light Horse and the Carbineers and, it seemed, 'several troopers of the South African Light Horse who had been given permission to break through the rear guard and enter the towns'.

Frances tried to picture Matthew. It was quite easy to do so physically, after she had found newspaper photographs of troopers from another mounted infantry regiment, but what his state of mind could be was almost impossible to imagine. He had now fought on the British side for over three months, so even Matthew must have made up his mind to something, unless he was just wallowing in the fighting itself, and she did not like to think of that as a possibility. It was fruitless to worry about it. One simply had to wait, as usual, wait and wait.

'Of course,' Harriet said after breakfast, when the Archdeacon had gone out and they had devoured the newspaper together several times over, 'women have always waited. All the wives of Crusaders and wives of soldiers in the Civil War, and the wives of fishermen and miners and sailors and explorers. If you think about it, much of life is just waiting. Waiting and praying. Except for the few in this war who can go out and be nurses, what else can we possibly do?'

Oxford in April was a welcome sight. The new green visible through gateways and over walls gave a lightness to the city, and the rain, when it came, was soft and harmless stuff, lying like dew on new leaves and grass. Rose had reached St Hilda's before her and left primroses in a green glass on her worktable and there was white lilac beginning below her window and a great deal of chattering in the downpipe head outside it where a swift had chosen to raise its family. Best of all, there was a letter from Matthew. He had written it from Ladysmith in early March, sitting, he said, on the hill in the town which was crowned by the house Sir George White had used as his headquarters.

It's a handsome house [he wrote] but it's about the only handsome thing here. Ladysmith is two streets of tin-roofed shacks and a railway station. That doesn't matter much because the countryside around it is grand, like all I've seen. You cannot imagine how much space there is, how free you feel. Tell Mother I haven't had a scratch. It's good to be here where there are some people to talk to, they have had a rough time. The news of Will is better than I had hoped. I was glad to get it. How doth your emancipation progress?

She read it several times. There were descriptions of Ladysmith, of a dinner with the correspondent Winston Churchill who was in the same regiment, of a hunting expedition in the hills around, of the relief of new clothes after eighteen days in the same ones without being able to change, and no clue at all as to what he was thinking or of his reaction to this adventure he had cast himself into. He sounded cheerful and entirely noncommittal. It was more like the sort of letter Will used to write before Magersfontein. Frances folded it up, curiously disheartened and dissatisfied, and posted it on to her mother.

On 1 May, she went out at dawn with Rose and Celia to hear the choir sing from the top of Magdalen Tower. The high clear sound came floating through the dim air like some heavenly message and was both soothing and uplifting. When they turned away at last to cross the river back to college and breakfast, Frances found Oliver Stansgate lifting his hat to her.

'Ah. I am gratified by your astonishment. I slept at the Mitre, which I would not particularly recommend, and I thought I should find you here if I could stir from my pillow at five. It was all part of an express design, you see.'

'But you never told me you were coming!'

'I hardly knew myself. It was an impulse and, I must confess, a man I need to see at Brasenose. It was only last night that the waiter at the Mitre told me of this touching and presumably medieval ceremony and I felt sure I should find you here.'

'Not only me, you see, but Miss Miller and Miss Hemming-Hemming.'

He took off his hat again. 'What astonishing luck. I never much wanted to be an undergraduate but I now see I may have been mistaken.'

He escorted them back to St Hilda's and invited Frances to tea. 'I shall have exhausted the man from Brasenose by then and you will come as the greatest relief. He is a don who supposes himself to be a political commentator and he has bombarded us with his opinions for months. Some of them are rather good and to our taste and so I thought I should meet the fellow and see what he is like. Will I have to beard your principal to get you released? Give her my card – or do you think that will only prove how unsuitable an escort I am?'

They met in Fullers where he had found a window table, won the waitress over, and ordered an immense amount of food.

'I did wonder,' Frances said, gazing at the plates of scones and muffins, 'though it seems ungrateful to carp at any kind of present, why you always send me food.'

'It is the highest compliment I can pay you. There is nothing I would rather receive myself so I naturally suppose those I like and admire will feel the same. What news of your errant brother?'

'Odd. I don't know what to make of him at all. He is alive and well so far as we know and has fought for six months with the South African Light Horse and was involved in the relief of Ladysmith. He has written once, at last, and told us nothing we could not have gleaned from newspapers.'

'And what about his republicanism?'

'I simply don't know. His letter said nothing about his opinions or feelings at all.'

'How disappointing. I had high hopes of him, you know. A rare type, an educated man with intellectual sympathy for the enemy fighting in the front line. As a journalist, I have to admit that he is not only interesting but also might have been very useful. I insist you eat a muffin while they are hot. I hope you weren't as careless about the apricots.'

She smiled at him. 'Certainly not.'

'And the cousin?'

'Will? Badly wounded at Magersfontein but recovering. He can walk again.'

Oliver poured tea into both their cups. 'That was a beastly battle. The endurance and obedience of men is something that I shall never cease to marvel at. And what about you?'

'Me?'

'Do you suppose I came to Oxford entirely for Dr Fairfax? I want to know very much how you are doing, what you are doing, about those young women you were with this morning. You see, men may go out and rape and pillage and build empires, but it is women who are the essential substructure to all that activity. And, as I believe I said to you before, things will not be the same after this war.'

She put her hands up to her face. 'How long will it go on? How much longer?'

'I am afraid that I don't think we are even halfway through. At least another year, perhaps two even.'

'No, oh, no – '

'My dear, there is so much to do. It is a vast country to subdue and I regret to say the Government is bent upon

158

doing just that. And the Boers, with their particular tactics and tenacity, can go on for months and months and months. I think they hate the war a good deal more than we do because, after all, we are in the main professional soldiers but they are only fighting because they have to defend their very lives. But they are very stubborn people, tremendously independent. They won't give up unless something cataclysmic happens.'

'Or,' Frances said, cradling her teacup, 'we think of something particularly horrible and effective to do to them.'

'I should hope it would never come to that. I wish you would eat.'

'I don't seem able to when I am thinking.'

'How very classical. The Greeks thought like that. Or was it love that was incompatible with greed? If so, I am a living proof that that is nonsense, or perhaps I should just have made a most unsatisfactory Greek. I can see what is the matter with you. You feel you should be out in Cape Town binding up the wounded.'

'Yes,' Frances said.

'I am sure I am not the first to tell you how gravely mistaken you are.'

'No, you are not. I have a friend who *is* binding up the wounded and before she left she told me I was much better employed here.'

'What a sensible woman. What did she say?'

'That we should need teachers very much when the war was over.'

'And I should take it further than that. I should point out to you that your generation of young women, educated and perhaps even professional, will be the mothers of the first generation born without the stifling opinions of the last century, free of all the smugness of imperialism. Imperialism started as an energetic and free-spirited business but it has sadly changed. You see, you will rock the cradle of the future.'

'The semi-socialist cradle?'

He laughed. 'Even that.'

'The old order changeth – '

'The new will be magnificent. It may take some time as

these things do, as soon as we have a government that will spend far less money on these outward trappings of power and far more on its own people.'

Frances sighed. 'It always comes back to money.'

'Such is the nature of man.'

'But when I listen to Will, even though I may not agree with him, he doesn't talk about money.'

'Because he has it.'

'So you believe people would be improved by having more of it? If it was more generally spread about?'

'Roughly speaking, yes. Poverty is not an ennobling condition.'

'Have you ever known it?'

'Not personally. Not grinding poverty, that is. Will you walk me down through the Meadows to the river on this evening of the first of May?'

The white college barges, like so many wedding cakes, were moored along the bank of the river. Eights Week would soon bring, war or no war, a flock of sisters and female cousins to Oxford and the towpaths would be thronged with hats and sunshades.

'We students will despise them heartily, of course,' Frances said. 'I mean, we really are honour-bound to, aren't we? They will have ravishing clothes and we have our wonderful brains.'

'It is perfectly possible to have both.'

'Not at St Hilda's. Your clothes are the outward and visible sign of your inner and earnest purpose.'

Oliver took her hand and drew it inside his arm. 'I think you should start a sartorial revolution.'

He stopped to contemplate a moorhen and her babies in a shaft of light on the water. 'Will you come to London soon?'

'I haven't really thought about it – '

'I shall think about it for you. Come soon. Do you like music?'

'Very much, though I am not musically well educated.'

'Mozart, then. I shall find some Mozart to take you to. Will you come?'

She nodded.

'And if I take you out to dinner will you eat?'

'Oh, of course – '

The path took them along beside the river in the dappled light. There were few other strollers, a trio of undergraduates, an old man in an ancient caped greatcoat, some nursemaids and children and a yapping terrier. They walked slowly and Oliver told her about his childhood in Quebec and how his mother had died when he and his brothers were under eight and how his father had given up his shipyard on the St Lawrence and brought the boys back to his own parents in Kent. His father had left them there and gone up to Greenock where he had shipbuilding connections and the three boys had been left to a strange early-Victorian upbringing in which they floundered at first with their French-Canadian ways. Oliver had won a scholarship to Westminster and had gone straight from school to Fleet Street, refusing even to consider his grandfather's college at Cambridge. His father was still alive, a substantial shipbuilder on the Clyde with a huge grey stone house on Park Terrace above the park in Glasgow, and a new, now middle-aged wife, and two more sons.

'And your brothers?'

'One works for a tea-shipping company and one is a stockbroker.'

'And do you ever see your father?'

'Not recently. He has a huge yacht which I was invited to visit two years ago. I endured two days of my allotted week. My stepmother is extremely uncongenial and the yacht was worse.'

The path eventually left the river and became a walled walk to the end of Magdalen bridge. Halfway along it, Oliver stopped and turned Frances to face him. 'I should like very much to give you the courage of your convictions.'

She said, 'I think I almost had it myself a year ago – '

'Then I must restore it. I shall write to you. You will come to London.' He picked up her hand and kissed it. 'And now, with the greatest reluctance, I shall take you home.'

12

Beatrice seldom wrote to Will. She disliked communication when there was nothing particular to say and her own life yielded up very little that was not domestic detail, which she knew he would abhor as much as his father had done. She had written, of course, when he was wounded, and she had written when Matthew was found, but in between she had written very little. It seemed easier and more to the point to send parcels, slippers and socks and books and the Egyptian cigarettes he liked. But when Frances asked if she might use the Hans Place house to change there before an evening concert and dinner, and to be collected there by a man, Beatrice felt another letter was clearly due.

She had been at pains in an earlier letter to stress the unfeeling unfemininity of Frances' behaviour. This last request only served to emphasize that. She was proposing to spend the evening with a man her parents had never met and who was, inquiry revealed, a journalist of very unpatriotic leanings, whom she had met quite casually at a public meeting. It was ridiculously improper, but as poor exhausted Harriet had seemed unable to rouse herself to any objection and the Archdeacon had said that he washed his hands of his children's wayward behaviour, there had been nothing for it but to order the house opened and the water heated. After all, preventing Frances from changing in comfort was not going to stop her seeing this Stansgate man. And seen him she had, leaving the bathroom at Hans Place strewn with damp towels and a bedroom littered with discarded clothes and hairpins. The housekeeper reported that she was not home until almost midnight.

After that, there was very little to say. Frances had written gratefully and said how London was still gripped with war fever, but of course she, Beatrice, saw little of that out here in the country where nothing seemed to make much difference. The roses were quite wonderful if only the deer would not keep devouring them and she had been appointed to the committee of the local orphanage which was absolutely the last thing she wanted. She had fondly supposed that allowing people to sit in her dining room once a week and knit khaki socks and roll bandages was more than enough for her share of good works . . .

Will read her letter twice through and put it in the wastepaper basket. Then he fished it out and read it once more, and tore it up and went out to the garden. He had been moved, since he became more mobile, from the Smit house to another, smaller house near the Mount Nelson Hotel which was being used as a convalescent home for officers. It was ideally suited for this, being almost entirely on one floor, built in a hollow square around a garden courtyard. Everyone there had lost a limb or had a damaged one, and from there some went home – to be fêted like kings it was said – and some went back to the front.

Will had graduated from crutches to two sticks to one. His thigh would always be hideous to look at, but there seemed a cheerful possibility that it would function perfectly adequately in time.

'Your symmetry is spoiled, I'm afraid,' Dr Trevor had said. 'But, in the long run, I don't think your mobility will be.'

He had spent long and patient hours as the South African summer cooled into winter swinging himself around the garden at the Smit house. He had sought out Gilbert Wildun, shot through the chest and shoulder, and talked to him about Matthew.

'He's got a charmed life,' Wildun said. 'So many of our squad got it at Colenso. Louis Durlacher was shot clean through the head, and look at me. Matthew came right through it, red head and all. He looks like a heliograph in the sun.'

When Will was moved to complete his convalescence at the du Plessis house, he was given a room of his own. There were two other young captains from the Irish Brigade in the same wing and a major from Will's own regiment. All four of them talked of going back to the front.

'Can't lose, not now. Roberts has come – '

'And Bloemfontein's fallen.'

'After what's happened, I want to be there at the finish, I don't want to watch it from Cape Town.'

The major had a wife and three children waiting for him on the shores of Loch Long. The eldest boy was due to start at Eton in the autumn and John Matheson fretted that he would not be home to see his son before he left. 'I can't leave it all to his mother. There are things I can't expect her to tell him, that I wouldn't want her to. I shall have to write and I'm so awkward on paper. Poor old fellow. It's the first time I can be of use to him in his life and here I am, thousands of miles away and helpless.'

The captain from the Iniskillings had a fiancée in County Limerick. He was perfectly sure she was behaving badly in his absence because she always had and he had known her all his life. 'She's the damnedest flirt and the best horse-woman in all Ireland and I've never wanted to marry anyone else. I write to her and tell her I'll horsewhip her when I get home and she writes back that I'll have to catch her first. Irish women! You have to be Irish yourself to stand it.'

Both he and Harry Fermor of the Dublin Fusiliers teased Will enviously about Daisy. The stronger he got, the more regular were her visits, and once he was installed in the du Plessis house, she came frequently.

'So easy, you see! Luncheon at the Mount Nelson and then here and then not too far back to the maison Taggart to rest and change before dinner.'

She sat most afternoons on the verandah of the garden courtyard and sometimes she brought Grace Taggart and other friends and the du Plessis house became known as the best spot in Cape Town to convalesce in. They played cards and silly paper games, and someone found a guitar and John Matheson played sad Highland songs and Daisy said he mustn't as they made her want to cry. She was queen of the afternoon gatherings but she made sure Will was chief court-ier. She also brought all the gossip from the Mount Nelson, who owed whom for what cards, who had seduced whom, who had been asked to leave for really unpardonable behaviour.

One afternoon, she did not come, but Hendon did. He had grown sleek and rather stout since Will had seen him in London almost eighteen months before and had taken to parting his hair in the middle and curling his moustache.

'Good God,' Will said, 'you look like a French barber.'

Hendon shrugged. 'It's all the rage, you know.'

He wandered about Will's room for a bit, picking up books, fingering things, then he settled himself in the only armchair. 'Should have come to see you before, I suppose. Glad you made it.'

'Thank you.'

'Been so damnably busy. Business in peacetime is one thing, but in war time it's quite another. Twice as much work for even half the result.'

'I don't see how you can do any at all in wartime.'

Hendon looked at him. 'That's it. Can't do much.' He cleared his throat. 'Daisy looking after you?'

Will said nothing.

Hendon got up and went over to the window. 'Gather Matthew is alive and kicking.'

'Yes, I'm thankful to say.'

'You should have heard him in Oxford, ranting at me that there would never be a war. I never thought he would fight.'

Will said, 'He seems to be doing it rather well.'

'Awkward blighter. Well, glad you're on the mend. Going back to the line are you?'

'I hope so. Hendon – '

'Yes?'

'It's – well, it's a bit difficult for me to ask, but what about my money?'

Hendon looked at him.

Will said, 'I know things have been upside down because of the war but you can't have forgotten. I gave you £2000 to invest in Eckstein's. I just wanted to know what was happening.'

'Just what is happening to everyone else's investment, old boy. Ticking over till this stupid business is cleared up. No news, good news.'

'You did invest it, then?'

'Of course. What do you take me for?'

165

'Sorry,' Will said. 'It's just that as I hadn't heard – '

An orderly came in with Will's mail. It was a letter from his mother which he put by his bed to read later.

'Actually,' Hendon said, 'I rather wanted to ask a favour.'

'Well?'

'I expect you know a bunch of officers are holding a ball at the Mount Nelson to celebrate Mafeking and Ladysmith's being relieved and all that? Well, fact is, I want to be on the committee. I *ought* to be on the committee. I'm the person in this town who knows where to get things and, damn it, this is South Africa and I'm a South African. I've approached the committee and they aren't keen, but they say they will consider me if I have the recommendation of a few British officers. What do you say?'

'Heavens,' Will said, 'same old Hendon. Why such a fuss? It's only a party.'

'It's a British party. And it's not a fuss. It matters to me. Will you put in a word?'

'If you want me to. What do I have to say?'

'You just write to Major Doulton and say you recommend me to be on the committee for the Mafeking Ball. Will you do it today?'

'Hendon, is something up? I can imagine you aren't much of a one for the sickroom, but it seems a little odd to call on me after six months and ask about a party – '

Hendon said, 'I told you. It matters to me. I might want to go back to England.'

'Are you sure?'

'What is it costing you? A little letter – '

'All right,' Will said, 'all right. But I warn you. I'm coming to that dance, gammy leg and all, and it had better be damn good.'

It was when Hendon had gone that he read his mother's letter. He knew exactly why she had written it and that somehow made what she had written harder to bear. What sort of girl she wanted for him, other than a very close copy of herself, he could not guess, but he knew and had known for a long time that she did not want Frances. The trouble with her letter was that it did not alienate him from Frances as much as it did from her. It gave him a tremendous amount of pain but inspired none of the anger and distaste Beatrice had intended. He limped about the garden for a long time until it was too cold to stay out any later and then he went back to his room and paced unevenly about that and knew that he was wretchedly unhappy and jealous to boot.

A week later, Matthew arrived in Cape Town. He came completely unannounced, Will just finding him one afternoon, sitting on the verandah of the du Plessis house, his chin propped on one hand, apparently staring into space. He got up when he heard Will coming and watched him limp along the verandah and when he reached him, he said, 'Thank God, you can move.'

Will said, 'I've been moving for months.'

'I should have come before. I've got some leave – '

'I'm so bloody glad to see you.'

'I've nearly deserted a few times. Once when you were wounded.'

'Not a very good reason – '

'When have I needed a good reason for doing something?'

Will laughed. 'True. Come to my room. I have a pretty girl who brings me bottles of Cape brandy. Do you remember the dreaded Hendon Bashford? He's here but so is his sister.'

'Lord. Does she resemble him?'

'In no way that I can see.'

In Will's room, Matthew flung himself across the bed.

'Soda in your brandy?'

'Please. Will?'

'Yes.'

'Are you going back?'

'Yes. As soon as I can. Expect to be passed fit any day. I feel as if I've been an invalid since the beginning of time.' He crossed the room and put a toothglass full of brandy and soda by Matthew's head. 'What about you?'

'I'll go back,' Matthew said. 'But not for ever.'

'I wouldn't expect you to become a regular soldier – '

'I don't mean that.'

'Well?'

'When the war is over, I think I shall stay here.'

Will sat down abruptly, splashing brandy over his hand. 'Stay in South Africa?'

'Yes.'

'Matthew, why? What are you talking about?'

Matthew propped himself on one elbow. 'It's Africa. I never thought a country could get into one's blood, particularly not under these conditions. I've been hotter and dirtier and more tired and thirsty here than I have ever been anywhere and still I love it. No, love is the wrong word. I need it. It satisfies me, I like being in it, doing things in it. I had to swim the Tugela before Spion Kop to bring a ferry back and it was like swimming in milky coffee. I didn't want to get out. I don't want to get out of Africa.'

Will said, 'But the Boers – '

'Funny thing. I don't know about them. I know partly what they are fighting for now, and I'm with them all the way. They're a deceitful, narrow-minded, unprogressive lot, just as I always thought, but I like their tough independence, I like the democracy of their army, their way of life, I like their determination, the way they fight. I almost met one – '

He stopped and took a gulp of his drink. 'It was most peculiar. I've sometimes wondered since if I dreamed it. We nearly went mad at Spion Kop you know, hanging about all day while everyone else shot each other to bits on the top and in the late afternoon I couldn't bear it and managed to badger an officer into coming up a bit of the way with me and a few others. We climbed up through the most awful carnage, you must have heard, and then somehow we got split up, I think it was a whole lot of poor exhausted fellows coming down that got mixed up with us, and I went on alone, up towards a knoll covered with aloes. They were still all firing away to my left and I thought I would just go on and see what I could see from the top and suddenly there was a huge man in front of me, armed with nothing but a whip, and a boy with a Mauser behind him, green with exhaustion, and a few more. I can tell you, Will, I thought that was my last moment. I didn't even bother to cock my pistol. And then the big fellow pulled off his hat and began to roar with laughter and point at my head, and I remembered I wasn't wearing a hat and even in the fading light you could see his hair was as red as mine. And I began to laugh too and so did the boy and we stood there like idiots while everyone was still blazing

168

away above us and then the Boer waved me away, almost saw me down the hill, and when I looked back up they all had vanished over the crest.'

'Extraordinary story.'

'Isn't it. I think about it a lot.'

'What about your regiment?'

'I'm used to it now. I wanted to get the hell out at first, I can tell you. They must be, in their own way, as intransigent as the Boers.'

'But you'll go back?'

Matthew swung his legs off the bed and sat cradling the toothglass between his knees. 'For the moment. Until I can see the next step.'

'Was Africa a step?'

'Yes. Will, do you feel just as you did before all this began?'

'In a sadder way, exactly. If I had been a hardened professional before I began I probably shouldn't even feel sad.'

'That battle – '

'You saw Spion Kop.'

Matthew looked up. 'Will, I know everyone at home thinks I have yet again behaved disgracefully because I didn't write. I couldn't write, I didn't want to, it wasn't – oh, it doesn't matter now. I have written now but I'm not going to say any of the things I've said to you until I know exactly what I'm going to do. I suppose if you want to tell Frances – '

'No.' Will said, 'I shouldn't think I will.'

'How is she?'

'Very well, I think. Going to Mozart concerts with a pro-Boer journalist.'

'You wouldn't expect her to choose an anti-Boer pro-war one, would you?'

'Between you and me,' Will said unhappily, 'I had rather she didn't choose any journalist at all.'

'Poor old boy.'

'More brandy?'

Matthew held out his glass. 'Well, what next?'

'It looks as though Roberts will have Johannesburg and

Pretoria in the bag fairly soon. Then I suppose we round up all the Boer generals, export old Kruger somewhere, annex the Transvaal all over again. If we do, what happens to you? Will you turn into a farmer overnight?'

'I might,' Matthew said. He looked at Will's leg. 'Does that give you trouble?'

'At night sometimes. It's a mess to look at but it mended.'

'I wish you could see Natal. And parts of the Transvaal. It's so difficult to describe what I feel. The land is like an animal somehow, a huge, raw, vigorous red animal. It doesn't even smell like anything in England.'

'Nor, I'm told, do the Boers at close quarters.'

Matthew grinned. 'They have pretty ways. They drink gin and chew tobacco. I wonder if their women do the same? They sound a dauntless lot, the Boer women.'

Will poured soda into his glass. 'Matthew, Adelaide Munro is still in Cape Town. She's nursing but also collecting information for the South African Conciliation Committee. She's been wonderful to me. Do you – shall I tell her that you are here?'

'I don't know,' Matthew said.

'You should see her. She really is remarkable.'

'I know that.'

Will said slowly, 'Somehow it's very difficult to remember about ordinary life when a war is going on, but when a war is going on, if there wasn't ordinary life to think of, I believe most of us would go mad. Adelaide somehow manages to carry sanity and ordinary life around with her. She knows exactly what you feel. She is quite disarmingly frank, you know. Shall I ask her here?'

'She wrote to me, you know. She shamed me into writing home.'

'Then it's only courtesy to see her.'

'I'd – like to.'

'How long will you stay?'

Matthew shrugged. 'Two or three days.' He looked up. 'I came to see you.'

'I know,' Will said.

13

Throughout May, Alecia waited for the end to come. When Bloemfontein fell and reports reached the Transvaal of jolly British and Boer cooperation in the capital of the Free State, it had seemed to her that it was all over. Bloemfontein and Pretoria were the two hearts of the two republics and if the one went, the other was sure to follow. She heard that the British had taken over the Boers' old *Express* newspaper and were publishing a new one, called the *Friend*, on its presses, and that many Englishmen of literary distinction were contributing to it. She wanted to see a copy, if only to prove to herself how well she could read it.

Reading had become so necessary to her that she no longer kept it a close secret. She had even had a book in her apron pocket throughout the week in January when her father had been at home, and had read snatched paragraphs under his nose, but he had been so obsessed with the farm, so determined to reassert himself as its master, particularly with her mother, that he had hardly noticed her at all. When he went back to Ladysmith to rejoin his commando, Alecia read openly, and as burdens mounted at the Van Heerden farm, it was only reading and the presence of books dotted about in their hiding places that saw her through the long and gruelling days.

At the end of March a wagon from Dreyersdal came rolling into the yard. It had been sent on Bettie's father's orders and contained three of the grandchildren for whom Dreyersdal was home.

'It is only right,' old Jan Dreyer had said to his daughters-in-law, 'that with my sons away at the war and the work on the farm falling upon you, that my daughter Bettie, who has no little ones at her skirts, should help you. I ask you, what else is a Christian family for? You will find the work easier with less children about. Send the ones who make the most work, the little ones. Send them to the Van Heerden farm.'

Two girls and a boy jumped down from the wagon and stood in the dust waiting for a welcome. To Bettie they were an imposition and a nuisance, to Johanna a welcome relief. They were small enough not to find her exasperating and vacillating, big enough to pull on their own boots and run errands. Alecia watched them obediently spooning up their mealie porridge at meals and thought what victims they were, uprooted from their own mothers and dumped down, like so many parcels, at the demand of war. They had the broad flat faces of all the Dreyers, snub-featured, with straight thick yellow hair and the round blue eyes Johanna had passed on to Daisy. Gaspar looked a Dreyer but Christiaan van Heerden had given his daughter his own dark curly hair and strong sharp features. Alecia had hated her brownness until she started upon Jane Austen and came to Elizabeth Bennett. Lizzy had proved a great consolation.

The children, good though they were, made a deal of extra work. Bettie's temper was very short these days, exacerbated by anxiety over Gaspar and Christiaan, impatience with her sister, and overwork. For Christiaan to be satisfied, it seemed the farm must be in better order when he returned to it than when he had left it. Kaffirs, as everyone knew, were as idle as you let them be, and Christiaan had taken on some Zulus who unnerved Bettie because Zulus were so prone to side with the British. She kept them working so hard that they would have no energy left to side with anyone, and she paid no one, to force them to stay on the farm.

Alecia ran the house, kept the accounts, looked after the laundry, the poultry, and the domestic servants. The day began at five and ended sixteen hours later, seven relentless days a week. Without Christiaan, even the unswervingly biblical Sunday had to be given up in large part to work. Some days she only read a page, in single scattered sentences; mostly she read at night, by the light of the tallow candles she had dipped herself that autumn.

When Ladysmith fell, Gaspar had come home for a few days, thinner and older and tired beyond speaking. He had gone to bed and slept through two nights and a day and

Alecia had washed his clothes, thick farm clothes dense with red dust and patched by himself with squares of rough grey blanket. He didn't boast and swagger this time, but went out onto the farm by himself and came in only to give his mother more orders and eat ravenously. When he left, Alecia filled his saddle bags with coffee and rusks and biltong. She looked up at him when he was mounted, shading her eyes against the strong autumn sun.

'Will we win?'

'Of course. We have to. However long it takes.'

Three days later, in mid-April, Bettie fell. She was in the huge open-sided barn on a ladder, directing the threshing on the barn floor below her, when without any warning she had fallen, ten or twelve feet, heavy and quite unconscious. They brought her into the house on one of the hurdles used for making cattle pens and her face was blanched green-white, with indigo shadows under her eyes and round her mouth. Alecia was boiling linen. She directed her mother to be carried to her bedroom and her aunt, shaking and tearful, to take the children outside. Then she sent old Frans, the black houseboy who had been baptized on his fiftieth birthday, off fifteen miles for a doctor.

Bettie opened her eyes after two hours, but her speech was thick and uncertain. Old Frans returned with the message that the doctor had gone to Pretoria.

'The pain – ' Bettie said indistinctly, 'the pain – '

'Now? You have a pain now?'

Bettie's head rolled slightly on the pillow. 'In the barn. Pain here – '

Her left hand fluttered over her bosom and ribcage. Alecia raised her shoulders and held water to her mouth. Most of it ran down her neck and into the dark stuff of her gown. She attemped to pull herself further upright.

'Must get – must get up – '

'You stay there. You must. I will go out to the barn.'

Bettie fell back and turned her face sideways, crying softly into her pillow, mumbling for Christiaan. She lay there all day, hardly moving, and the children came and stood in the doorway and stared at her. When the doctor came after nightfall, Alecia received him in the parlour among the

173

monumental pieces of mahogany furniture that were so exhausting to polish.

'It is her heart,' Dr Reiff said, 'a small attack. She must not work so hard. She must do light things only, little things in the house.' He looked at Alecia. 'It is not so bad. She has you. You are young and strong.'

It was accepted. There was nothing else to do. Bettie, slack-faced and listless, sat in the kitchen, snapping at the servants and shelling beans with trembling slowness. The farm was now Alecia's responsibility, the hundreds of red acres, the black labourers and their disorganized families, the herd of Afrikander cattle by which her father set such store, the crops, the house and all its duties. Johanna, holding the children to her as if they were some sort of talisman against further ill luck, had asked to know what she might do to help.

'Would you nurse my mother? Would you do that? You are the only one with the patience – '

A message was sent to Christiaan, but it was three weeks before he came. Bloemfontein was flying a Union Jack, he said, and the spirit of the Boers falling back before the onslaught of the huge army Lord Roberts was pushing on to Pretoria was terrible and getting worse. He sat in the kitchen by his wife and held her hand and looked alternately from her spiritless face to the Bible in his hand. He read to her from it. Johanna and the children, working at the table or out in the nearby dairy, could hear his voice, on and on, verse after verse, like a kind of incantation to bring her back to life and health. Alecia knew that her mother's immobility was not so much an aftermath of her attack as a paralysing fear of death as a result of a second one, and how could she confess such a blasphemy to Christiaan of all people? He would lean towards her, whispering, '*In vol moed*, be of good cheer,' and she would gaze back at him without hope.

With her mother drooping in the kitchen and the Boers losing morale out there on the veld, it was hardly surprising that Alecia should wait for a worse calamity to come than Bloemfontein. Christiaan was fidgety, wanting to be simultaneously on the farm and with Gaspar. He had little patience with Alecia but then he never had had. Her quietness made him suspicious. Men came by with messages every so often but they were bad tidings each time; the great British army, swelled by thousands of volunteers after Black Week, was moving steadily towards Johannesburg, tramping relentlessly onwards either side of the railway line and in front of this juggernaut the commandos were giving way, ever more broken up, the firing ever more sporadic. Alecia sometimes imagined that she could feel the earth shuddering away to the southwest, beyond Johannesburg, under all those booted feet, coming nearer and nearer.

On 2 June, Gaspar rode in. He looked as he had done on the last visit but angry too. 'Johannesburg has gone,' he said. 'The British battalions are marching along Commissioner Street. All the Kaffirs are in from the mines, cheering – '

There was a sharp frost that night. They sat round the supper table, together for the first time in nine months, and drank the soup Johanna had made, rich and spiced, thickened with pulses.

'The British gave us two days to leave Johannesburg,' Gaspar said. 'They reached the city two days ago. Today they walked in – '

Christiaan said, 'And then Pretoria. Pretoria! With Pretoria gone, all is gone.'

'No,' Alecia said.

Gaspar raised his head from his soup and looked at her.

'The heart of the volk,' Alecia said, 'is not in the cities. Our heart is out here. In the veld. They can have the cities. We will always keep the veld.'

'They will annex the Transvaal,' Gaspar said.

'But they will not take the farms from us. We will always have those. And if the volk must have the cities, we will win those back too. But they are not what matters.'

'You know nothing of war,' Gaspar said.

She said calmly, 'I know that in the veld you can fight in a way the British cannot deal with. If we keep fighting that way, if they cannot catch our leaders, the war will go on. We will win.'

Christiaan looked at her with suspicion. 'Who have you been talking to?'

'No one. I just think. It's the only thing I have plenty of time for.'

175

Her father pushed his bowl in her direction. 'More soup.'

'Kruger has left Pretoria already,' Gaspar said. 'The army is in a mess such as you never saw. I came some way with them and there was never such confusion. It's hopeless. Even Botha thinks it's hopeless. They are looting all over Pretoria already and then going off home. We are going to surrender.'

Johanna, from vague feelings of unease, began to cry. She did not like to weep in front of her brother-in-law, so she made some excuse about the children and went quickly from the room. Bettie watched her go and then she said, with some faint echo of her old vigour, 'Will they take the farm?'

Gaspar shrugged.

Christiaan stared down into his soup. 'Only the Lord knows that – '

'Will they kill us?'

Alecia looked across at her mother. 'No.'

'How would you know what the English would do?' Gaspar said. 'What do you know of the English?'

Alecia shrugged. She got up and fetched a huge black skillet of fried beef from the stove.

'You are getting a big tongue,' her father said, watching her while she divided out the meat. 'Daniel Opperman said to me it was time you were married. It seems to me he's right.'

Alecia said, 'Mother – '

Bettie gave a small shrug. 'As your father wishes. My sister will look after me.'

'It's no time to talk of marriage,' Gaspar said. 'Later. When we know where we are.'

After supper he came back to the kitchen where Alecia was piling up dishes. Christiaan and Bettie were in the parlour together.

'You have done well on the farm. Has Father told you so?'

'No.'

'We lost one calf – '

'It was a breach,' Alecia said.

Gaspar sat down at the table and leaned his elbow on it. 'I don't want to kill Englishmen any more. I don't want to kill anyone.'

'And let the rooineks have our land?'

'You know nothing. You just stay here and do the farm.'

'That is what you are fighting for.'

He looked up at her out of his round sunburned Dreyer face. 'You can read English,' he said. 'You have English books.'

'How do you know?'

'The little girl, little Martje. She told me.'

Alecia put her hands on her hips. 'So?'

'Why do you want to read English?'

'Because there is more to read in English than there is in Afrikaans. Because I need something to put in my head.'

He gestured around the whitewashed room with its rows of moulds and pans, its shelves of European imported china of which Bettie was so proud, its dangling bunches of herbs and corn cobs. 'You have all this.'

'This uses my hands. Not much of my head.'

'You said you loved the farm. You said the veld was the heart of the volk.'

'I meant it. I want both, all three, head, heart, hands. And I want the English to go back to their own farms.'

'But you can speak their language!'

'Maybe some of them can speak ours.'

Gaspar stood up. 'Ours is the language of God. We are His people. What if I tell Father that you have English books?'

'Tell him.'

'You wouldn't care?'

'Take away the books,' Alecia said. 'You won't understand one word. But I know the language now and you can't take that away.'

'Where did you get the books?'

Alecia came round the table so that she was facing him. 'From Daisy. Her father gave them to her but she didn't want them, only dresses.'

'But Daisy hated you – '

'So she gave me things she hated.'

Gaspar grinned. 'Would you like to have been on commando?'

She nodded. 'But not now, not after Mother.'

'Perhaps your English will be useful after all, after they take Pretoria.'

'No,' Alecia said. 'that won't happen. We won't give up so easily. We can't. There is so much to fight for.'

Gaspar crossed to the door and paused, his hand on the latch. 'What did Dr Reiff say about Mother?'

'That she must be very careful. She mustn't tire herself.'

'And she will be all right? If she is careful?'

Alecia paused. 'He didn't say,' she said.

It was a week later that Daniel Opperman came to the Van Heerden farm. He came with a handful of men of his commando and they sat around the kitchen table while Alecia made coffee.

'It's to begin again,' Opperman said.

'They rode through Pretoria four days ago!'

'I tell you,' Opperman said, leaning forward, 'they made a blunder. They gave us two days to leave Johannesburg so we got away all our guns and all the gold in the Mint and in the Standard Bank. Smuts got it. So we have money. And we have the veld. De Wet has sanction to go back to guerrilla strategy. We are going south, behind the British army, and we will cut off their communications. Break the telegraph, blow up the railway, the bridges. We will isolate them up here so no supplies can get to them.' He looked round at them all, smiling. 'You see?'

'De Wet,' Christiaan said.

Opperman nodded. He touched the whip coiled round his waist. 'I am not the only man to encourage faint heart with a sjambok.'

Christiaan glanced across at his son. 'You ready, boy?'

'At once!'

The men round the table laughed.

'It is the answer,' Opperman said. 'Guerrilla warfare. We are going into country we know, the farms will feed us, give us news. The British think they have won now that they have saved the mines on the Rand. But we have a lesson to teach them. The second part of the war is only just beginning.'

'But have we enough men?'

Opperman looked round the table. 'Well now. We have seven here. And De Wet has a few more. Maybe two thousand, maybe more –'

'But the English have twenty thousand!'

'We will have food and supplies and we will pick our time

to fight. We can move fast. They are tied to the railway, they cannot move quickly.' He stood up. 'Botha keeps seven thousand men in the Transvaal army. He will fight a more regular war. The English will not know which to choose.'

The others stood up with him, exuding a powerful stench of tobacco as they rose.

From her chair Bettie watched Gaspar. She beckoned to Alecia. 'Let me fill his saddle bags,' she said. 'Bring them here and let me do it.'

Only a few days later, she was dead. Johanna found her sprawled across her bed in her voluminous nightgown where she had knelt to pray. In one hand she was clutching Christiaan's old Bible, the other was clenched in a fist. They lifted her solid body and turned her so that she was lying on the bed and drew over her face the white linen bedspread with drawn threadwork round the hem that had been part of her trousseau over twenty years before. On her bosom Alecia laid her father's Bible and crossed her hands upon it. Then she blew out the candle and left the room in darkness until Dr Reiff should come.

Johanna came to her bedside a little while later, and they sat together holding each other while Johanna wept and told stories of their childhood at Dreyersdal. Two deaths in so short a time, first Jim, now Bettie, two deaths of people who had made up her world. Alecia held her and listened and was filled with an anguish she had no idea in the world how to manage. When the morning came and Dr Reiff, she found herself mistress of everything at the Van Heerden farm, in every way her father's deputy. She went around the barns and the house in a mood of great loneliness, looking at and touching familiar things as if for the first time.

'You will manage,' Dr Reiff said. 'You can keep things going for your father.'

'Yes.'

'Child, I am sorry. I am sorry it should be this way. But the Lord giveth and the Lord taketh away. Think if you can of what He has given.' He looked round at the sweep of land running gently away from them and put his hand on Alecia's. 'You would not want the English to take this away . . .'

179

14

War, Will considered, standing in the doorway of the ballroom at the Mount Nelson Hotel, had many faces, most of them ones that were most astonishing. It had surprised him, hanging about the Modder river and then tramping towards Kimberley, how obsessive everyone, of every rank, had become about a dry place to sleep and perhaps half a hoarded biscuit; the grand scheme gave way completely before the details. And here was another peculiar thing. A large room, tremendously decorated with garlands and flowers, full of lavishly dressed people all bent upon having the time of their lives, while twenty thousand men seven hundred miles to the north slept out on the veld and dreamed of the day they could take their boots off.

Across the room, Will could see Hendon Bashford, in a white collar so tall he appeared to be standing on tiptoe. Hendon had been an appalling nuisance about this ball, badgering and pestering until Will approached the chairman of the ball committee, a colonel of the Seaforths whom he had known slightly in camp at the Modder river, and made sure Hendon was included.

Colonel Barclay had been a little surprised. 'But the fellow's a bounder!'

'I know he is, sir. But quite a useful bounder and being seen to be accepted seems to be tremendously important to him.'

'I'll chuck him out, mind you, the moment he puts a foot wrong – '

'Oh yes, sir. Absolutely.'

Hendon had swaggered a good deal after that. But he had secured excellent champagne at only 50s. a dozen quart bottles, not mention gallon casks of Cape sherry and brandy at two-thirds the price that the hotel was asking. He then proved embarrassing by wanting to invite a whole lot of extremely unsuitable gold and diamond dealers and of course he had to be snubbed, which he took with all the lack of grace expected of him. And now here he was tonight, with an alarmingly wild-looking party, in an evening suit edged with the kind of black braid Will associated with lamp-shades.

In his party, of course, was Daisy. She wore a dress of pale-green silk gauze, cut extremely low, out of which her shoulders and bosom rose as smooth and plump as a pile of satin pillows. Will watched her for some time while she dipped and swayed and chattered and then he turned away because watching her made him need to swallow a lot. She had cried a good deal that afternoon when Will had told her he was going back to the front, to fight under Lord Roberts and assist in putting an end to this war. Will had not been at all sure what the tears had really been about, since for every. Captain Marriott who went to fight there were two others at least to take his place, but he had rather liked her crying all the same and been more than a little put out when a captain from the Inniskillings had paused beside them to say in an audible whisper, 'The Soldier's Farewell, I see – '

He leaned against the wall and watched the dancers. Matthew had said that no one could believe the effect that the first sight of a woman in six months could have upon a man. He had gone off to see Adelaide and, in a garden on his way to the Smit house, had seen two little girls playing with a ball under the trees, girls of perhaps eight or nine in sunbonnets and white frilled pinafores over their print dresses.

'I just stood and gazed,' Matthew said. 'I couldn't move. I held on to the railings and stared at them like an imbecile until a governess came out and herded them away behind the house. Heavens, the things you take for granted – '

And here, before Will, was a roomful of them, the last roomful perhaps for a long time. All that silk and satin and powdered flesh – not something you could hoard up and take with you; it was more something that perhaps you hardly knew how much you missed until, like Matthew, you saw it again and remembered. None of which, most unfortunately, was true of Frances. He could remember fewer of the precise details of how she looked than he would have liked, but the impact of her personality was as powerful upon him as if he had left her nine minutes, not nine months before. He was not at all clear what he had written to her after he was wounded but he knew that he would not write the same sort of thing now and he wished she did not know how broken he had been, not so much because she would ever exploit that knowledge, but more for the sake of his self-esteem. Since his mother's letter his self-esteem, with regard to Frances, had had a very hard time of it indeed.

He looked about for Daisy. She was dancing, of course, head thrown back, eyes half closed, lying back against some fellow's arm. She was an unprincipled flirt but she certainly took one's mind off things. Matthew had found it quite impossible to see any charm in her at all.

'At least I knew, when I saw Adelaide, what I had been about once. You wouldn't, for a moment, confuse Adelaide with anyone else! But this little bit of nonsense – Frances would rap your knuckles for classic subaltern behaviour.'

Daisy, for her part, had found Matthew immensely attractive and had been entirely disconcerted to find that she had no effect on him at all. The only other man in the whole of her life who remained impervious to her was her brother and she expected that. After all, she had never seen Hendon behave to a woman any other way. But this boorish cousin of Will's was quite another matter and she took care to let Will know that Matthew's behaviour was of absolutely no consequence to her whatever.

Will took his shoulder from the wall and went off in search of a diversion other than that of watching Daisy behave badly. A supper room had been set out in the manner of an English conservatory, with a lot of white trelliswork and trailing plants, and there were already several elderly guests settled happily at tables and stuffing. Above their heads, among the green and white tracery of the décor, hung scarlet banners with 'Mafeking!' embroidered on them in gold thread and on every table was a menu with a small photograph of Baden-Powell at the top in the place where a regimental crest would have been. There were rooms set aside for cards and sitting out, and the billiard room was thick with cigar smoke and crammed with refugees from the dance floor. In the hall of the hotel, someone had set up an imitation of the Mafeking dug-out of Lady Sarah Wilson, complete with white panelling and Matabele spears, and a group of men and girls had crowded in to sit at Lady Sarah's table, laid for Christmas lunch, and squeal at the novelty. There were portraits of Baden-Powell everywhere and photographs of Mafeking had been pinned on the hotel noticeboards and decorated with trails of ivy. It looked an awful hole. The Africans called it 'The Place of Stones' and stones were about all it seemed to possess apart from the railway line.

Daisy found him contemplating a photograph of Dixon's Hotel, Mafeking, taken the previous October as the last coach left the town before the siege began. Dixon's Hotel, with its blank exterior walls and verandah of corrugated iron, looked particularly unprepossessing.

'I don't know why you should think *I* should come and look for *you*.'

Will turned round towards her and smiled. 'The Baralong tribe gave Mafeking its name. It means the place of stones. It really ought to be spelled a Mafikeng,' he said.

She pouted at him. 'I'm a girl of my word, you see. I said you should have the first dance when your leg was mended with me. And here I am.'

'I'm flattered you should remember.'

'So you should be. And I don't want to hear about boring old Mafeking. I want to dance.'

He offered her his arm. 'I won't promise anything very agile or graceful – '

'I've had such a time!' Daisy said. 'One wicked man after another.'

'That's what war is all about. Isn't it?'

She turned round eyes upon him. 'Are you trying to spoil the party?'

'Certainly not. I'm teasing you.'

He put his arm around her warm firm waist and swung her onto the floor. 'One, two, three, one, two, three – whoops! I say, Daisy, not so fast – one, two, three, one, two – I say, I do beg your pardon – Daisy, slow down a little, give a fellow a chance – '

'It's your last chance,' Daisy said, replacing her smile with a piteous expression. 'Tonight, and then you will be gone and then what happens to me?'

'Exactly what always happens to you.'

'Will – '

'Yes.'

She leaned forward and moved her left hand inwards from his shoulder so that her fingertips rested against his neck above the collar of his tunic. 'Shall I tell you something?'

'Please do.'

'I only went to visit you at the Smit house because Hendon said I should. I didn't really want to. Does that make you very cross?'

He looked down at her, saying nothing.

'I know it was horrid of me. But I'll tell you something more. I went the first time because I was told to. But I went the second time because I wanted to. And the third and the fourth and all the others. So, you see, you needn't really be cross after all. Need you?'

He still said nothing. He was looking down at her as she turned in his arms to the rhythm of the military band upon the stage and it suddenly occurred to him that he could seduce her, that she would let him, even like him to. He had never before danced with a girl and deliberately entertained the idea of taking her to bed but, if you thought about it objectively, that was exactly what Daisy was designed for, intended for. The whole essence of her, her clothes, her manner, her movements, her behaviour – it all brought just one thing to mind. Perhaps she already had had lovers, perhaps bedrooms and Daisy Bashford were not strangers to each other. That didn't matter, maybe was even an advantage. And this was, of course, the perfect place to do such a thing. The Mount Nelson Hotel, forbidden to all well-brought-up girls, home of intrigue and stealthy nocturnal tiptoeings. So easy to get a room here and take Daisy to it . . .

He slid his arm a little farther round her smooth waist and felt her sink against him at once.

'Oh, Will – '

He bent his head a little and his mouth grazed across her forehead.

'So you aren't cross? About Hendon making me come?'

He said a little thickly, 'Of course not. He told me he wasn't much good at sickbeds.'

'Oh, it wasn't that, naughty Hendon. It was the money. He was afraid you would find out and be angry.'

They went on turning and turning, Daisy's hand on Will's neck, his arm more and more firmly around her waist, her hair and the flowers in it brushing lightly across his mouth and chin.

'What money?' he said from far away.

'Oh,' Daisy said, 'you know. That he was going to invest for you. Boring old money. I hate it. You are naughty, Will. Everyone is staring – '

He lifted his head and looked down at her. 'What has Hendon done with my money?'

She raised her left hand and ran her fingers along his jaw.

'Don't do that,' Will said. 'And tell me what Hendon did not want me to find out.'

'If you're cross – '

He lifted the hand he held in his left and kissed it. 'Please, Daisy.'

She shrugged. 'I don't know. Not really. I think he – we – sort of borrowed it. Until the war is over. That's all. Then he's going to invest it as he said he would.'

There was a pause. They went on turning but Will's arm slipped from her until he was holding her waist lightly with his hand. He gave Daisy a small smile. 'So Hendon thought that if I became sufficiently infatuated with you I shouldn't think to ask, and if I *did* ask I would not, because of your being his sister, do anything unpleasant about it.'

She nodded. 'It's just as I told you. I didn't want to go and then I was glad I had. I think you are a much wickeder dancer with a wound than without one.'

'Daisy,' Will said, 'Hendon has £2000 of mine. And the same, if not more, from several other fellows I know. He is behaving, your famous brother, like a blackguard.'

Tears welled at once in Daisy's eyes. She took her arm off

185

Will's shoulder and hunted for a handkerchief. 'There's no need to be horrid.'

'Daisy. I'm not – being horrid. But I do think, if what you tell me is true, that Hendon has behaved dishonourably to say the least and that you should not have abetted him. Can't you see that?'

'But I need things!' Daisy wailed. 'There wasn't any money coming from Johannesburg and I couldn't get any more credit. Don't you see?'

Will dropped his arms and began to steer her from the dance floor. 'What I see, Daisy, is that I probably paid for this green confection. Which I should have done with pleasure if you had asked me honestly. But the way you have done it is despicable.'

Daisy began to cry in earnest. People went waltzing by on the dance floor, staring in open fascination and amusement.

Daisy said unsteadily, 'I don't see what's so wrong. We didn't steal it, we're only using it until we can get some of our own.'

'Listen,' Will said with mild exasperation, 'it's the way you have done it that's so wrong. It's underhand. It's dishonest. I would gladly have lent – *given* – you money if you had asked me. But you didn't. You went behind my back and the backs of several others, I imagine. There are at least two other men whom Hendon knew in England here tonight and I don't think they would be best pleased to know what I know.'

Daisy clutched at him. 'Are you going to tell Hendon? That I told you? Oh, don't, Will, please, don't, don't!'

He put a hand under her elbow. 'Of course I shan't mention you. But I must speak to him.'

'Not here, not now!'

'Daisy, I leave tomorrow.'

'You'll spoil everything!'

'I couldn't do that. You and Hendon have done it already.'

She said sullenly, head bent, 'I'd never have told you if I thought you would take it like this. But I didn't think you would mind. I thought you were rich. I thought you liked dancing with me.'

'I did.'

She looked up at him and understood his expression. 'All because of some stupid old money.'

'No, Daisy. No. All because of some deceitful behaviour. Now dry your eyes. And then I shall take you back to your party.'

The small room at the back of the hotel where a dozen officers had been playing bridge had been turned into an impromptu courtroom. Chairs had been grouped in one corner to form a makeshift dock and the bridge tables put together to make a bench behind which was ranged a row of chairs. There was nothing on the tables except glasses and several bottles of Cape brandy. The remaining chairs had been put in a line for the jury and one table, upended in the centre of the room, served as a witness box.

In the dock, his hands lashed together with his own white evening tie, stood Hendon Bashford. He had been very drunk when Will and three officers had dragged him out of the supper room, but the drink seemed to have drained out of him with his bravado, and he stood white-faced and visibly wretched. His collar flew up either side of his head like grotesque wings where the studs had been wrenched away in getting his tie off, and every time he moved, his collar ends waved like antennae.

In the judge's chair sat John Matheson, cradling a glass of brandy. He was flanked by a couple of officers, and behind him stood several more, having given or waiting to give evidence. The jury was composed of twelve others, all undoubtedly good men and true but also all undoubtedly British and friends of the witnesses. Will stood in the witness box with his arms folded. The curtains had been drawn, a chairback had been wedged under the doorhandle, and the only light was a fringed effect on a brass pulley above Hendon's head. Beneath it he stood out starkly in black and white.

'Say that again,' John Matheson said, tipping his brandy gently round the bulge of his glass, 'slower.'

'I understood,' Will said, looking at Hendon, 'that Mr Bashford had assumed his late father's directorship at Eckstein's — '

'I never said that,' Hendon muttered.

'You did. You told me that your father's death had left a directorship vacant and that it was the influence of that position that enabled you – '

'Address the bench, Marriott.'

' – that enabled Mr Bashford to be in an astute position when it came to investment in gold shares. He informed me, as other witnesses have already testified, that Eckstein's were going in for deep mining, needed the capital, and would find rich seams. I even went to the trouble of asking about Eckstein's in London, and when I found that they were a subsidiary of Wernher–Beit I was sure that my money would be well invested.'

'And you trusted Mr Bashford?'

'Yes.'

'Can't think why,' someone said. 'He's a blackguard.'

'Thrown out of every house in England!'

'And Scotland.'

One of the jury said, 'Anyone who treated my sister as Bashford did deserve to be tarred and feathered.'

John Matheson regarded his victim. 'I'll think about it.'

Hendon shouted, 'It's not fair! None of this! You have been looking for a chance to do me down for years! You hate me because I'm a businessman, because I'm successful, because I'm an Englishman too.'

John Matheson stood up. 'You are most certainly not an Englishman. You are an unprincipled half-caste. No gentleman would hire you to polish his boots. You are not fit company for anything but vermin.' He turned to the group behind him. 'Look, Bashford. Six men to whom you owe money. One more over there. I must say, you are a sickening sight. I shouldn't be at all surprised if you were a Boer-lover too. You've got Boer blood, peasant blood – '

Hendon began to shout. The jury leaped up onto their chairs chanting, 'Bloody traitor! Boer-lover!' and the group of men came out from behind the tables to stand round Hendon in his circle of light. John Matheson thundered on the table before him with a brandy bottle to silence the uproar.

Hendon was almost in tears. 'I don't stand a chance! You

188

are all against me! It doesn't matter what I say, you wouldn't believe me! You tricked me in here and now you're behaving like a bunch of low-class bully boys.'

A fist shot out and missed Hendon's mouth by inches.

'Steady, old boy.'

'I hate the Boers,' Hendon said, 'I hate them! I know them better than you ever will and I hate them! I was going to pay all the money back, I can now, now that Johannesburg is freed, you can have it all back tomorrow, as soon as I can arrange it, I promise you.'

'Shut up, Bashford,' one of the witnesses said. 'Snivelling won't help.'

Hendon looked across at Will, his exhausted face crumpling into a sneer. 'What about my sister then? Not too much of a gentleman to want to take advantage of her then?' he shouted at the room. 'I'm not good enough for your sisters but my sister is quite good enough to serve your low purposes!'

An officer leaned forward until his moustache almost brushed Hendon's own. 'Spot on, Bashford. Absolutely right.'

Will, head bent, said nothing. He put his hands out and leaned upon the upturned table legs. Hendon might have been equally prepared to use Daisy for his own particular ends as Will had been willing to, for other ends, but at this moment Will found that he did not want to say so. The brandy bottle that had been passed up and down the jury was handed to him and he took a grateful swallow.

'Well,' John Matheson said, looking round him, 'verdict?'

'Guilty!'

'Bring him over here.'

Hendon was dragged from his corner and held up between two officers in front of the bench.

John Matheson was writing rapidly on a sheet of the hotel writing paper. 'You have to put your signature to two things, Bashford. You have to agree to reimburse all those named here, together with the sums you owe them, before a week is out. And you have to agree that any activity that took place in this room tonight was no more than a joke.'

'Yes,' Hendon said eagerly, 'yes, yes –'

'We don't want to see you around in Cape Town any more, Bashford. We don't want you in this hotel, or at any place frequented by officers and gentlemen. Stick to your own kind, Bashford, unless you want a repetition of tonight.' He pushed the paper forward. 'Now. Sign.'

Hendon held out his lashed hands piteously. Someone took out a pocket knife and cut his tie through with a single slash that made him wince. He stooped over the table and wrote his name with a shaking hand.

'And there.'

The room smelt of smoke and sweat. Will watched Hendon's bent back and reflected how exhausted anger left one, how dispirited, possessed only by a kind of emotional hangover.

John Matheson picked up the piece of paper, folded it and buttoned it into a pocket in his mess-jacket. 'I hope, Bashford, that this is the last time I ever set eyes on you.'

They began to cheer all round him.

'Hear, hear!'

'Amen to that!'

John Matheson looked round. 'I think we should go back to the ball. Leave Bashford here to reflect upon his sins. I could do with a distraction.'

There was a hearty stampede for the door, leaving only Will and three others, all witnesses, alone with Hendon. One of them leaned across the table over which Hendon still stooped and grasped his shirt front, jerking him upright.

'Got away lightly, eh, Bashford?'

'Leave him,' Will said, 'Leave him.'

Hendon spun round. 'You say that now! But who put them all on my tail! Who started this farce? High and mighty Captain Marriott, that's who. I'll tell you something, you and your double standards, pawing Daisy all night then running for help from the bullies, acting whiter than white! I tell you, I wish I'd done more in England. I wish I'd got every one of your sisters and wives and cousins – '

What followed had a kind of stately dignity about it. Hendon, gagged with Will's white silk handkerchief through which blood from the blow on his mouth was seeping, was led out of the hotel and into the garden, bathed in sharp

190

winter moonlight. He was taken to the pond – celebrated for the size of its goldfish – stripped entirely and slowly pressed down into the water. All this was done in complete silence except for the groans from behind the handkerchief. When he was thoroughly soaked, Hendon was pulled out again and his clothes were thrown into the water instead. The four officers then laid Hendon out upon the grass, and while three of them knelt upon him, Will untied the handkerchief and with a pocket knife neatly shaved off a precise half of his moustache. Sobbing and incoherent, Hendon was lifted to his feet, marched briskly to the garden gate and thrust through it, naked, running wet and grotesquely shaved, to make his way around sleeping Cape Town. After a short deliberation, his clothes were left floating among the goldfish, and Will and his companions, linking arms and singing, ran back across the lawn to the lights and the party.

15

That summer, Frances planned a walking tour. She and Celia and Rose would stay with Rose's people and explore Hadrian's Wall. They would do so with books in their pockets, in all weathers, and walk at least ten miles a day. They bought rubber capes and stout boots and blackthorn sticks and small pocket-sized copies of poets and playwrights and promised each other a reunion at the Hemming-Hemmings' house in early September to begin this enterprise. Buoyed up at the thought of it, Frances went home to Salisbury with a light heart.

It was very necessary to have a project to look forward to. The war did not seem to be going anywhere. General Buller was doing better and two thousand British prisoners had been released, but De Wet had escaped, creating a host of new problems which seemed to indicate that things were becoming unpleasant in quite a new way. It appeared that the Boers, despite losing both Johannesburg and Pretoria, had not given in as they had been expected to, but had taken to the veld that they knew so well and were harassing the British very successfully in small guerrilla groups. The British, tied to the railway lines for supplies as usual, were too easy a target. The Boers, on the other hand, fed and sheltered and kept well informed by the farms out in the country, showed every sign of being able to wear the enemy down for as long as they chose. The solution as devised by the British was to make life more difficult for the Boers, to force them out into the open to fight in a way the British could handle. The Boers' source of supply, both food and information, must be cut off. Farms must not be in a position to help them. Farms must be burned.

Frances had attended an impassioned lecture at the Peace Society, delivered by Emily Hobhouse. A new society had been launched, the South African Women and Children's Distress Fund, and Miss Hobhouse was on the general committee. She was there at the Peace Society to fan flames of outrage and raise money, and she brandished at her audience a sheaf of untidy papers.

'And what are these? Reports, letters, from my team of nurses and colleagues who are in South Africa and who send me first-hand knowledge of the unspeakable suffering caused by this wanton destruction. No military aim should be so careless of innocent lives, no army should be allowed to make such victims in pursuit of its squalid purpose. I beg you, in the name of all that is Christian and liberal, to help us in helping these wretched creatures, turned out upon the veld without food or shelter to watch all that they have worked for put to the torch.'

Frances thought inevitably of Adelaide. Her last letter, dated mid-July, had been curious and unsatisfactory, as if she were holding something back. No doubt it was the effect of censorship. She wrote that she had actually seen Matthew and that he was wonderfully fit and well – 'his face and hands are so brown that he has the appearance of wearing a brown leather mask and gauntlets. Most striking with his hair!' – but there had been no mention of Will beyond a brief remark that his rejoining his regiment might be delayed a little while. Of the farm-burning, then only in its infancy as applying to a handful of farms around Bethlehem in the new British-named Orange River Colony, she wrote with indignation and awe for the behaviour of the Boer women.

I am told that at least at one farm the women sat placidly and watched the flames, so confident that this was all merely a small part of assured victory for their own people, that they could take even something so shocking with equanimity. The British officers here say Sister Boer is as obstinate and stupid as Brother Boer, but I think the women believe in their cause in a way we are too complicated and sophisticated to understand. I will let you know more very soon for I am to go to Johannesburg at the end of the month to help organize a fever hospital. Typhoid has really got a grip in Natal and the Transvaal and, between ourselves, I shall be thankful for the change. There is getting to be too much of the lady's white hand about nursing in Cape Town!

Frances had shown the letter to Oliver and he had said that Adelaide sounded just the sort of woman he needed. 'Excellent good sense but plenty of imagination too. Perhaps I shall ask her to contribute articles to the *Speaker*. Would you not rather approve of that? Articles from a female observer.'

'She wrote often to the *Daily Chronicle* when she was growing up. She had to pretend to be a man.'

'Absurd – '

Oliver had come to Oxford regularly all that summer term. Sometimes he took all three girls out in a punt – which he handled with surprising skill – and sometimes he took Frances out alone and lectured her on the need for a fruitful life. 'There is a time coming when you will be able to do anything you please. You will be able to work and raise families and vote, all in one lifetime. But I will warn you of two things. A large number of men will detest your freedom and your capabilities, it will shock and alarm them very much. And the second thing is that you are all, all you free women, doomed to be very tired and at times very confused in your loyalties.'

She learned very little, during these walks along the river and through the meadows at Headington and Marston, about what his life was like when he was not at his office or in Oxford. He lived, she deduced, in a sort of bachelor chummery which she had built up in her imagination as an extended smoking room full of ponderous leather chairs and Turkey carpets and tottering piles of books and papers. He said 'we' when speaking of domestic arrangements but was never explicit. He seemed to eat in clubs and chop houses and other people's dining rooms, always alluding to remarks made by someone he sat next to the week before. He went to meetings endlessly and worked a good deal at night – 'I'm the original man in the green eyeshade' – and once let slip that he was writing a book on the dying fall of the Empire.

'No one will publish it until either I or Queen Victoria is dead. Probably both. And then it will become a standard work at all the universities and I shall get neither the money nor the public acclaim.'

Of his own money he never spoke. He wore good clothes but mostly the same ones and he was generous to Frances but did not spoil her. He gave her meals and books and wine and fruit, but never flowers. 'I don't believe in anything ephemeral that I cannot consume.'

'Turks eat rose petals – '

'I am not a Turk. And in any case they cheat and fossilize them in sugar.'

Rose said that he was a mixture of Henry Tilney and Mr Knightley in the exterior of John Bull. 'And are you in love with him, do you suppose?'

Frances hesitated, to delay having to say yes. 'I suppose so – '

'You mean yes. I think he is an excellent choice. I am longing to be in love for the first time if only to get the first time over with. Do you imagine that he is in love with you?'

'No,' Frances said truthfully.

'Are you sure? He is here almost every week bearing startling new novels and chocolate truffles. It all looks lover-like to me.'

'But not when he talks. We never talk of anything intimate. He asks me about my family and Matthew and Will and what I mean to do, but not what I feel about things. And I have no idea what he feels about anything except public issues, anything intimate. Particularly not about me.'

'Bravely ask him.'

'No, thank you,' Frances said. 'I wouldn't dare. It might drive him away for ever and that I couldn't bear.'

The nearest that they could get to talking of love at all was to talk of Will. Oliver was intrigued by the idea of Will because he declared that he seemed such a perfect carbon copy of conventional young English manhood. 'Reasonable education, good regiment, noble ideals, sufficient money, and in love with a pretty cousin since childhood. Perfect, really.'

Will had not written in weeks. She knew only that he had been moved to a convalescent home and that he was sure of rejoining his regiment soon. And, of course, after that solitary letter, Matthew had not written at all. Thank heaven for Oxford, for work, for Rose and Celia, thank heaven for Oliver.

There is almost no way [her mother had written that term] to beguile waiting. You *think* that you are fooling it, you *think* you have escaped its thrall by hurling yourself from one activity to another, but it has infinite patience and it is always lying in wait for you. There's a new painting someone was telling me of, by Mr Liston Shaw, showing a woman standing lost in thought in a garden with an unwound skein of wool hanging forgotten from her hand. It's called *The Boer War*. Oh, so true, so true!

She had asked Oliver what he was waiting for.

'The New World, of course. And to be the most influential newspaper editor in London.'

But he didn't ask her in return. She hardly knew herself. Some days she was waiting for time to pass, some days she knew that luxury would lie in not having to wonder if Matthew – and now presumably Will, back at the front – were still alive, some days – rare days – were happy and busy enough to forget the war for a sweet brief interlude. That wasn't easy, if only because most of the shops in Oxford were decorated with Union Jacks and photographs of Baden-Powell and Lord Roberts and General Buller. Salisbury, when she reached it for the first month of the vacation, was the same and even the tea caddies in the grocer's where her mother had an account were decorated with flags and 'Mafeking!' in embossed golden letters.

Her mother was very thin. Harriet and Beatrice were neither of them tall women but they were well proportioned and gave an impression of height. Harriet was now stooping a little and her cheeks had sunk beneath the cheekbones. The Archdeacon, rosy and firm and upright, was a considerable contrast.

'Your dear mother is quite naturally much affected by anxiety. It would not be becoming in her to allow pride in her son's serving his country to outweigh the tender feelings of a mother.'

'Matthew is not serving his country,' Frances said, 'you may be quite sure of that. He is fighting for the fun of it. You are very mistaken to attempt to dress it up as anything nobler.'

'Ah,' said the Archdeacon kindly, 'the opinions of one who lacks both maturity and judgement. I beg you will see that your mother wants for nothing.'

'What I want,' Harriet said later, as they laid lavender out in the midday sun on trays to dry, 'is to have Matthew home, with a profession and a wife and a family. And dear Will too. But I know very well that that is not what Matthew wants himself and therefore I cannot really want it for him. It is so difficult not to project one's own desires into other people's lives, or at least not to feel guilty at doing so.' She straightened and put her hands to her back. 'There now. My safety pin is showing again. I don't suppose such a misfortune ever befalls the Bishop's wife but how else am I to keep blouse and skirt together?'

Frances ran her hand over the grey-blue, scented stalks. 'Mother. How old were you when you were married?'

'Twenty-two. Your father was curate at Iwerne Minster and we had waited three years for his mother's consent. She was very formidable, old Mrs Paget, and regrettably rich so that she had to be humoured. Your father was very nice looking, always stood so well. I used to like looking at him standing on the chancel steps, so grave and so confident. I did not in the least intend to marry a parson. I thought I should like to marry someone rather bohemian like a painter or a writer, and then I could become his muse. I went to stay with some distant cousins near Fordingbridge and there was your father on the lawn playing croquet. But, my dear, you know it all.'

'I rather wanted to hear it again.'

Harriet sat down on the low wall of the terrace where the lavender was drying. 'I played with another partner against your father at croquet and we won. I think that is what made him notice me. He was all in clerical black and made the others seem very young. My dear, shall you become too modern to marry?'

Frances shook her head, laughing. 'Not a bit of it!'

'You know who I have always hoped it would be.'

'Will may have – changed in South Africa. And, in any case, you know my feelings for him – '

'You see? There I am again. Trying to make my desires into other people's. Marry as you will, dearest child, only just make entirely sure that you are happy. I could bear anything but your unhappiness.'

197

Frances stooped to kiss her forehead. 'I forbid you to worry about that. Or about me at all. I can't stop you worrying about Matthew – I do myself so I am hardly in a position to object to your doing it. But you must have great peace of mind when you think of me.'

Rose wrote enthusiastically from the north. The weather was marvellous and showed every sign of holding, she had obtained the copy of Bacon's essays that Frances wanted and she was raring to begin.

> My sisters all pester to come with us and so far I am holding out. They are quite charming every one, but owing to darling Papa's enlightened method of bringing us up, they are dreadfully vociferous and articulate. I do not think there is a single topic upon which they have not all got a decided opinion and I think they would exhaust us and trip us up by running round us in circles. I want to get you up here, into all the air and heather and sunlight and away from all your worries. Two of my cousins have gone with the City of London Volunteers, and even though I do not know them very well, the thought of them preys upon my mind and makes me understand what is in yours. How horrible it all sounds – and getting worse. I looked down into the dale below us yesterday and imagined a whole lot of Boers tramping through it and setting fire to the farms. If they did, I should rush down screaming and throttle them with my bare hands. So imagine a Boer wife and her children out there in those red hills watching jolly British Tommies reducing her life to ashes –

Two days before Frances was due to travel north, Oliver Stansgate called. She found him in the shaded drawing room with her mother, eating cucumber sandwiches and talking through them.

'I have really come to apologize,' he said, standing up, 'though I am well aware that I am shutting the stable door after the horse has bolted. I have taken you to concerts and out to dinner and tea and out for walks and hazardous journeys in punts, and because you are a new woman, I entirely omitted to introduce myself to your parents first. So here I am.'

'Better late than never at all, as Nanny would have said.'

'And I say it too,' Harriet said, pouring tea.

'I gather I am just in time. You are going striding along Hadrian's Wall in company with Rose and Celia – '

'I told you,' Frances said, 'weeks ago. You helped us to choose sticks.'

'And subsequently forgot all about it. Such is the press of life. Will you keep a journal?'

'No. It's to be all fresh air and exercise and stimulating reading.'

'But you might consider writing an article for me on it when you get back?'

Frances turned to him, glowing. 'Oh! Oh, yes!'

He smiled. 'I am so glad. Everyone knows that male undergraduates go off on reading parties to the Alps and stride about in great boots shouting quotations from Descartes and Cicero to each other. But imagine the draw of an article written about the female version.'

'I – I should love to – '

'And I should love you to. What excellent sandwiches. Do I detect a gesture of nutmeg?'

Harriet held out the plate. 'You do. And our own cucumbers. They are horribly prolific this year. Speaking of food, I do hope, Mr Stansgate, that you will stay for dinner?'

He shook his head. 'You are most kind, but sadly I cannot. I cross to France early tomorrow to gather up a little Gallic loathing of England at first hand. And then Italy and Spain and Germany. I expect to be gone a month. I came really to say goodbye, perhaps for ever since I shall undoubtedly be lynched by a mob which discovers, despite the beautiful fluency of my French and Italian, that I am an Englishman. I intend to publish my findings in a series of articles this autumn and unpleasant reading they may well make, so you see, Frances, how much the paper will need some light relief from you.'

'If you patronize me,' Frances said, 'I shall not write one word.'

He leaned towards her, smiling. 'And if you do not write one word, I shall not be able to pay you. Your first professional earnings. He looked towards Harriet. 'Do I require the Archdeacon's permission for this transaction?'

'I think,' Harriet said, 'that knowing about it could only disturb the Archdeacon's peace of mind.'

He seemed, despite refusing dinner, to be reluctant to go. He lingered in the drawing room, rose slowly, paused in the doorway, stood still talking in the hall, gazing upwards admiringly at the seventeenth-century staircase. At last he turned and bid Harriet goodbye and took Frances' hand in his. 'I shall send you postcards and tell you of all the wonderful meals I am eating so you will get a great many from France and not so many from Spain. I hope your reading party is as much fun and as much of a holiday as it deserves to be. And I will see you in October.'

'With my article?'

'I shall not open the door to you without it.'

She said quickly, 'Which door?'

'The office? It might amuse you to see it.' He let her hand go, gently. 'Goodbye, Frances. Goodbye.'

From the windows beside the front door, the windows from which her mother spied for arriving guests, Frances watched him walk across the Close. He crossed the road and made straight for the cathedral rising grey and perfect out of its smooth ocean of surrounding grass. He stood there for some minutes, shading his eyes and gazing upwards to the summit of the spire, and then he shook himself, like a dog shaking off water and, without looking back, began to walk briskly in the direction of the station.

At Hexham station Rose was waiting two days later as Frances' train pulled in. She was waving a huge straw hat with ears of barley thrust into the band and she was accompanied by two girls, unmistakably her sisters.

'Oh! You can't think how glad I am that you are here! Celia came yesterday and now we are all complete. This is Anna and this is May and you must not let them persuade you into letting them walk with us. They are maddening to walk with, always darting and shrieking. Papa! Papa, here she is! She has come!'

The legendary Mr Hemming-Hemming, believer in women's education and suffrage, was a tall fair man in a crumpled linen suit. He shook hands cordially with Frances, dealt with her luggage, and shepherded his flock out to the carriage. In his jacket pocket, Frances observed, was a folded copy of the *Speaker*.

'Rose and I argue about which way you should walk,' he said. 'I want you to go west because I want you to see St Oswald's Chapel and the camp near Carraw and Crag Lough. Rose thinks it is more appealing to walk towards the sea but then you will end up in Newcastle.'

'It doesn't matter,' Anna said, 'since they are going to read all the way.'

'Not all the way – '

'So difficult to choose between a lovely landscape and a lovely book. You will be torn in two.'

'Not Frances. She is very decided.'

'So am I. But not for very long at once. There is nothing I love more than a new idea.'

'Look! Look, a sparrowhawk – '

'Oh, poor mouse – '

'Perhaps it's a rat. Then you would not mind so much. Frances, is it your brother who thought he might be a republican?'

'It is.'

'I am quite definitely a republican.'

'For this week, little May?'

'I have been quite consistent for longer than that. And you have a sneaking sympathy, Papa, otherwise you would not have that paper in your pocket.'

'I have more than a sneaking sympathy for the Boers,' Mr Hemming-Hemming said, 'and for poor Tommy Atkins out there fighting them too. Miss Paget, look over to your right. That is Beaufront Castle.'

'Beaufront,' one of the children murmured, 'Beaufront. Does it have a beau back too?'

'Don't be facetious.'

'That was witty, not facetious. I could be facetious, if I tried – '

'We will go through Sandhoe, you see, Frances, and then the house is on the hillside facing south towards Corbridge. You will love it. Celia did at once. It was like a glass of champagne, she said, after soggy old Oxford.'

Craghead House had been built twenty years before on a wide terrace in the hills sloping down to the Tyne. It was large and solid and friendly, with a gravel sweep before it and hills climbing behind. Geraniums in pots marched up the steps to the front door and round the square hall to the foot of the stairs. Doors were open everywhere, inside and out, giving glimpses of rooms and dogs on sofas and pictures hung as closely together as if they were stamps in a stamp collection. From somewhere came the sound of a piano and from farther still through long glass doors opening onto a lawn, clearly raised voices.

Mr Hemming-Hemming smiled at Frances. 'Croquet, I think – '

She looked upwards. The staircase climbed in a wide hollow rectangle up to a glass dome far above. Over the stair and landing rails people had hung garments and linen and an Oriental rug. A door slammed somewhere and a child with a ginger cat in her arms came carefully down the staircase to the hall.

'Are you Miss Frances Paget?'

'I am.'

'I am Camilla Hemming-Hemming. I have just been helping Mamma to finish your room. Please come up and meet her.'

She turned and began to climb the stair again and then she paused, looking down at the cat.

'This is Disraeli,' she said. 'We named him for obvious reasons. He also is intelligent but very vain and he distinctly needs a corset.'

The next week was an idyll for Frances. She felt as if she had broken out of a chrysalis and was flying free – better than that, carefree. Up on the moors with the air blowing round her and nothing to think about except which inn they would stop at for bread and cheese and which sonnet sequence they would read next, it was quite simply another life. So was Craghead House, with its amiable confusion and comfort, returned to each night of the first week while they acclimatized themselves to the moors. Her room looked eastwards and possessed a brass bedstead big enough for three and sufficient armchairs to seat a committee. One of them had been pushed up close to the window and Frances sat in it for some minutes every evening just for the pleasure of doing so. She was there on her second Friday, contemplating the clear sky and the green land and the distant shine of the river when Camilla came in with her mother's telegram.

So much regret to spoil holiday but Will involved in Cape Ragging Case. In today's papers so no secret. He is to be sent home and court-martialled. Please –

'I can tell it's bad news,' Camilla said. 'Mamma looked like that when the pony threw May and rolled on her. Shall I get you something?'

Frances looked down at the telegram and could not read it for shaking. 'Rose, please. Just Rose – '

Part Four

16

'Captain Paget, those are my orders. And you will obey them.'

Matthew said, 'Would it not make as much or more sense just to take away the Boers' horses? I hate this burning – '

His commanding officer, a man who did not care for anyone who rose from the ranks, cut him short. 'Do as you are told, Paget.'

In Matthew's hand was a map of the southeastern Transvaal. On it, marked with crosses and approximately spelled names, were the farms that he and his men were instructed to burn. It was a disgusting business. Lord Roberts had promised safety of property to all Boers who surrendered, yet no discrimination seemed to be exercised as to which farm should be spared. There were rumours that Kitchener was coming down from Egypt to take command, finish off the whole confused, unsatisfactory affair. He was going to find a sorry muddle when he got there.

It was October and the spring sun at midday was already fierce. For three months Matthew had slept rough, riding hard and existing on a diet of biscuit and bully beef, playing the Boers' game of hide-and-seek. He had learned a great deal about the veld, a considerable amount about his enemy, and enough about the British cavalry to know that in the present situation he and the other irregular mounted infantrymen were more use than the *arme blanche* and their lances. Guerrilla warfare suited Matthew admirably. He had grown to feel both respect and affection for his tenacious enemy – while despising those who surrendered – and hardly saw the skirmishing among the harsh red hills as any more than a splendid game between well-matched opponents. He received a flesh wound through his left shoulder from which he recovered rapidly but otherwise found himself in a state of positive health and energy.

Until the orders for farm-burning came. He had seen the results of it all over the Transvaal, the blackened swathes of veld, the piteous heaps of half-burned possessions, the groups of women and children gathered up by British columns and added to their camp sites in a spirit of gruff kindness. They seemed a staunch lot, those Boer families, afraid of very little and prepared to live on less, but unless they were taken into some kind of protection, bands of straying Kaffirs would murder them for no more than the clothes they stood up in. Matthew had spoken to several in the stumbling Afrikaans he had acquired and they had all assured him that when the war was won by the Boers they would go home.

'But to what? It is burned, all burned.'

'Then we build again. We chose it with care. God blessed it. Burn, burn, it makes no difference. We will go back. Our land, our home place – '

'I hate it,' Matthew said to his senior officer. 'It's barbaric and it's impractical. We should learn to fight as they do and do it that way, win that way. If we must – '

'Shut up, Paget.'

It was those remarks that had doubtless earned him his orders. He looked at the troopers mounted behind him, talking and joking, unthinkingly easy in the saddle after almost a year in it, almost unable to recall another way of life. Then he looked at his map. He had been given a circuit of sixty miles and four farmhouses between the Eland and Wilge rivers. None of them was to be left standing.

Burning the second one proved even worse than the first. He behaved the same with each one, ordering his men to carry out all furniture and precious possessions before a torch was put to the building, helping to bury china, even to lower a pretty little German piano into a disused well and cover it with a sheet of corrugated iron. At the first farm there had been two women and three children and an old Kaffir servant with no teeth and the women had screamed with rage and the children had been hysterical with fear at their mothers' anger and the roaring flames. They had ridden away in silence, no jokes, no talking, leaving the pathetic little group sitting sobbing and the screams coming after them through the crackling of the fire.

At the second farm, they had carried out everything they could, even sacks of coffee and mealies and sugar. No one had screamed at them. An old grandmother was there, in a vast white sunbonnet, and her daughter and granddaughters and several little children. They had filed out of the house at Matthew's request and then watched while everything was carried out and arranged ceremoniously on the veld – even, Matthew noticed with a pang, a chamber pot under a bed – and then they had crossed to join their possessions and stood before them, hands folded, silent and watching. The screams had been easier to bear. Matthew ordered up straw bales and set them round the house. The old grandmother called to him. He turned and went towards her.

'The Lord will have His revenge for the innocent.'

She regarded him, tiny triangular blue eyes in the flat brownish moon of her face.

Matthew said, 'Is there anything else I can do for you?'

'Only the Lord can help. Do what you must do and go. We are His chosen people. He will not let us suffer so. He will have His revenge.'

A trooper brought Matthew a lighted taper of twisted straw. He walked slowly round the square white house with it, touching each bale, hearing the crack and hiss as the fire took hold. It leaped up, black smoke billowing, yellow flames streaming into the blue spring sky. He went back to the grandmother and stood before her helplessly.

She waved him away. 'Go. Go. There is nothing for you to do. We are in the Lord's hands, we are His children.'

A little boy, no more than three, had turned and pressed his face silently into his mother's skirts.

'For Christ's bloody sake,' someone said, 'let's get out of here. Can't stand any more of this – '

They camped that night in the middle of nowhere, building a fire in a hollow on the side of a kopje, brewing up some of the strong bitter coffee they had found at the second farm. The night was warm and soft, the stars as brilliant as jewels in the velvety depth of the sky, and Matthew could hardly bear to look up at it and think that because of what he had done that day, a dozen helpless people were also lying beneath it instead of under the whitewashed ceilings they had worked so hard to build.

'It won't be so hard tomorrow – '

'It bloody will be. It will be worse.'

'We should have had a singsong before we buried that piano. It would have cheered us up a bit.'

'You think so?'

'That old madam – '

'Those little kids – '

'Shut up, will you? Bleeding harping on. Orders is orders.'

'I don't mind killing the bastards. But I didn't sign on for this. Don't care who they are, they are still women – '

'Sentimental fool.'

'You enjoyed it, did you?'

'Didn't mind. All part of a day's work – '

'Life goes on – '

'Not if you're hacked to death by niggers because you've nowhere to go.'

'Bloody hell,' someone said loudly, close to Matthew. 'Bloody hell. Will you shut up or shall I do it for you?'

He could smell the cigarettes, see the tips glowing in the thick soft night. The horses were moving gently around their pickets, huge screws that were carried strapped to the saddle and twisted into the red earth at night. He turned restlessly, rolling his head on the saddle he was using for a pillow.

'Can't sleep. Keep thinking.'

'Don't bloody think.'

'Suppose they had been your kids?'

'Tell him to stow it, sir, would you?'

'Silence,' Matthew said wearily, 'All of you. Silence till dawn.'

His dreams were full of flames. Sometimes he thought he could hear crying in the flames but, when he tried to plunge in and discover, he found it was laughter. When he woke and found a pale new sky stretched cleanly over him, he could still smell smoke in his nostrils, hear timbers cracking as they burned. The men were in better spirits at breakfast, chaffing each other and grumbling companionably over their hard biscuit and sugarless coffee.

'Right, sir. Where next?'

Matthew, squinting against the rising sun, pointed to the northwest, towards Pretoria.

'Fifteen miles maybe. Marked as the Van Heerden farm.'

The talk died as they rode. The thorn trees across the open places were bursting into tufts of soft green, and here and there the flat cactus-like leaves of the prickly pears had blossomed into orange flowers. Yellow finches and weaver birds darted round the taller trees and, away to the west, like black blots in the blue sky, a group of vultures circled slowly over some dead thing beneath.

They could see the Van Heerden farm a couple of miles before they came to it. It was low and of grey stone shaped like a T, the windows flanked by heavy shutters of unpainted wood. The doorway was crowned with a pair of springbok horns, and someone had taken the trouble to make a garden in front of it with flowers round a space of grass and orange trees clipped into neat balls. Behind it rose the barns and beyond it, huddled at some distance from the house under a group of trees, was a scattering of Kaffir rondavels, bleached silver-grey by the sun.

They rode up to it in silence. There was no wind, hardly any birdsong, just their horses' hooves soft in the dust. As they approached, two children appeared in the open doorway for an instant and then vanished, calling out, into the darkness behind them.

'For God's sake. Isn't there a farm without children?'

A young woman came out of the doorway and stood regarding them. She was dressed in the usual gown of heavy dark stuff and over it a long white apron, but her face was narrow, the features strongly pronounced, unlike the broad flat faces of yesterday. Matthew leaned from his horse.

'You know who we are,' he said in Afrikaans. 'You know why we have come.'

She looked at him steadily. 'Yes,' she said in English. 'You are English soldiers and you will burn the farm.'

'But you speak English!'

'And you speak Afrikaans.'

Matthew turned and signalled to his men to dismount.

'Will you have coffee?' the girl said.

'Before we burn your house?'

'If you burn it, there will be no coffee afterwards. It will be burned also.'

'You are Miss van Heerden?'

She nodded.

'Miss van Heerden. Should you be offering coffee to the enemy?'

'I am the mistress here.'

Behind her in the doorway materialized a plump, pretty, middle-aged woman, wearing another dark stuff dress but on her head a ruffled lace cap threaded with lilac ribbons. The children were behind her, two – no, three – holding up her skirts against themselves so that only their faces showed, pale moons peering out at the soldiers.

Matthew took off his hat. 'I am Captain Paget. Of the South African Light Horse.'

Alecia nodded again. 'And this is my aunt. And my little cousins. My aunt also speaks English. She taught me.'

Johanna smiled anxiously, her hands fluttering over the round yellow heads at her sides. 'But not well. Not good English – '

'Will your men sit on the grass? We will make coffee.'

'Bloody picnic,' someone said.

Matthew turned sharply. 'Sit down! And behave with at least some of the courtesy that is being shown to you.'

'They speak English as I do,' Alecia said, looking round at the troopers. 'They are South Africans. They all hate the Boers.' She looked across at them. 'I expect it will choke you to drink my coffee?'

They were embarrassed, shuffling on the grass, muttering.

Matthew said, '*I* should be grateful for coffee.'

He waited out there in the sunshine, his shoulder against a tree, his back to the men, smoking rapidly. Everything was mildly uncomfortable, his position, the way his men were behaving, the girl, her disconcerting hospitality, her assurance, what he had to do. He shouldn't be drinking her coffee, the men shouldn't be lounging about on the lawn of a house they were about to destroy, the girl shouldn't be able to be so disarming . . .

She came out with a tin tray of cups and her aunt followed with coffee pots. Behind her the children carried a sugar bowl and fistfuls of spoons. All the men stood up and gathered close round her like the destitute at a soup kitchen and Matthew could only see the top of her dark head and her aunt's lace cap in the press of khaki drill. One of his men brought a cup over to him. 'Sugar, sir?'

'No, thank you.'

The man grinned at him. 'Good coffee, sir.'

'Yes,' he said, 'I am sure it is.'

The aunt was looking at him warily, like a frightened beast. She seemed to be hesitating and then she darted towards him and said hastily, 'Must you? Must you do it? My nephew is so ill.'

'Here? In this house?'

'Yes, yes. Oh, it was so sad. He was wounded out by Krugersdorp and he came home to recover and now a fever has set in.'

The girl set down her tray and came across to them. 'Are you speaking of Gaspar?'

'Yes. Oh, my dear. You must show the Captain – '

'I was intending to show the Captain. Come with me please.'

He had to stoop to enter the house. It was cool and dark inside, smelling faintly of spices and smoke, and when Alecia touched his hand to guide him he was surprised to find hers as hard as a man's.

'This way,' she said.

In a narrow white room, the shutters linked against the glare, Gaspar lay on a wooden bedstead pushed along the wall. He was covered with a woollen blanket and on the wall above him hung a crucifix carved of dark wood. There was a chair and a wooden box and a row of pegs on which his clothes were hung and nothing else except a close faintly rotting human smell.

Alecia stooped over her brother. 'Gaspar.'

He rolled his head on the pillow. She said to him in Afrikaans, 'How are you? How is the pain?'

He muttered something Matthew could not hear. Even from across the room there was enough light to see that his face shone with sweat.

Alecia straightened. 'The wound healed. Then this

began.' She put her hand on her stomach. 'Here. I don't know the word. At first no fever but always pain here and – ' She touched her throat. 'Illness through here. And now this fever – '

'Dysentery?' Matthew said doubtfully. 'I have no opium. Or brandy. That is what he needs.'

'We had a little opium somewhere. But I cannot find it, I have turned out the house to find it – '

Matthew swung round abruptly and tramped back through the house to the sunshine outside. 'How far is it to Johannesburg?'

'Twenty miles. Maybe twenty-five – '

He pulled out his map, unfolded it, and jabbed at the Van Heerden farm with his forefinger. 'Funny thing, but this house simply isn't here. We have followed the map precisely and there is no Van Heerden farm. It does not exist.'

'But, sir – '

'Don't interrupt, Musker. I am not asking you, I am telling you. We have followed the map and there is no farm here to burn. The map is wrong. Do you understand me?'

'Sir.'

'All of you?'

'Sir.'

'Two of you will ride hard for Johannesburg and attempt to get the medicines I will write out for you. You will bring them back here at once.'

Most of the men looked away from him, into their mugs, into the middle distance, intent upon avoiding his eye. Matthew stooped and grasped the two nearest by the collars of their tunics, dragging them to their feet.

'Musker. Tatham. Do you understand what you have to do?'

'I won't do it, sir,' Tatham said.

'It's an order, Tatham.'

'Sir. But I won't help an enemy soldier, sir. I'm not putting a Boer back on his feet. It's the firing squad if I'm found out – '

'And if you were dying of dysentery? You would entirely understand a Boer leaving you to die when it was in his power to help you?'

'A Boer wouldn't lift a finger to help.'

'And you will sink as low?'

'I don't care, sir,' Tatham said angrily. 'I just want to win.'

'We'll win all right,' Matthew said. 'I just pity this poor country when all the fighting is over and it's run by men like you. Wyman. Will you ride with Musker?'

Wyman nodded without enthusiasm.

'Yes, sir.'

Matthew took a notebook out of his pocket and scribbled on it. The men watched him in silence. So did Alecia standing in the doorway, hands folded on her apron. Matthew tore out the page on which he had been writing and put it with a banknote in Musker's hand. 'Fast, Musker. And then come on to us. Destination four.'

Alecia said, behind him, 'I did not mean such help.'

Matthew turned. 'What did you mean, then? All this coffee, this talk, showing me your brother. What did you want?'

'Just that you would not burn this house down. If Gaspar lies in the open, he will die.'

Matthew moved away across the garden to stare at the rolling land. Alecia followed him, watching him while he lit a cigarette.

'When Gaspar first rode away one year ago, he said he would bring me the head of an Englishman.'

'You had better have mine.'

'I do not say thank you well. But I thank you. You must keep your head. It is the first English head I see and now I do not want it.'

Matthew looked down at her. 'Do you hate the English?'

'I hate what they do. Of course! But I envy them too.'

'Envy?'

'I wish my language was English. In English you are so free, the world is so big. In Afrikaans it is so small, all the same ideas, the same words, nothing big, nothing new. I love this farm, this is my home, always I will come back here. But I want to see other things, other places. So it is with my mind. I want to see other things in my mind. So I read. I read English books.' She pulled at something in her apron pocket

215

and handed a volume in marbled covers to Matthew. 'Almost the one I like most, I think. It is Maggie I like. I think I feel sometimes like Maggie.'

The book was *The Mill on the Floss*. On the flyleaf was written 'Daisy Bashford. April 1894. The Valley House, Parktown, Johannesburg, South Africa.'

'She never read it. All the pages were still together when she gave it to me. She is my cousin. My aunt there is her mother.'

'Bashford. Bashford. And did she have a brother?'

Alecia grimaced. 'He went to England. He read nothing, he heard no music, he talked no sense. When he came back here, he has never come to see his mother, never asked if she was safe. His sister is only a fool but he is worse. He is bad.'

'Miss van Heerden – ' Matthew paused. 'Can we sit somewhere?'

'Will your men not think it strange?'

'I don't care,' Matthew said, 'if they do. Do you not care about being seen talking to an Englishman?'

She smiled, showing perfect teeth. 'I don't care, like you. May I have my book?'

She took the volume from him and indicated that he should sit on the low wall that separated the garden from the land beyond.

'Miss van Heerden, I have to tell you that I have met Hendon Bashford. In England a year and a half ago. He was in fact the final reason for my being sent away from my university. He annoyed me and with some others I half drowned him and then pinned him out on the grass to dry with croquet hoops.'

'Croquet – ?'

'A game we play out of doors in the summer. The ball has to be hit through iron hoops about this size – ' He indicated with his hands. 'They fit very well over a man's arm or leg.'

Alecia began to laugh, holding her book against herself and rocking slightly backwards and forwards.

'Miss van Heerden, I wish you would sit down.'

She sat beside him, still laughing. 'How long did he take to dry?'

'Hours, I should think – '

'I like that picture. Why did he make you angry?'

Matthew shrugged. 'Many reasons. It doesn't really matter. It's all in the past – '

'I can imagine the reasons. Hendon is true to nothing. He is not true to his mother, to his country, to any belief. He moves all the time. He only likes money, to be big. I would like to drown him too, only I would have to hang him after on my washing line.' She looked round her. 'He never liked South Africa at all.'

'I love it,' Matthew said emphatically.

She smiled again. 'And you love England?'

He made an equivocal gesture with his hand. 'In a way, very much. But I like the size of this, the energy, the openness, the big skies, the promise of what one might do – '

She looked towards the house and barns. 'Just as we have done.'

She held out her book. 'I see England in these books. All green, wet green, wet, wet, many rivers, London very dirty and full of noise and smoke, mud always, cold, flowers spread like carpets, flowers and flowers, little groups of houses, farms close together, poor people in – ' She paused and said with the emphasis on the wrong syllable, 'fac*to*ries, horses everywhere, old churches, bad streets, ladies driving, Scotland – '

Matthew interrupted, laughing, 'Scotland?'

'*The Heart of Midlothian*,' Alecia said carefully.

'And Dickens?'

'Many. Those I love. And Jane Austen. Not so good, too soft, too small. But I like the words. I have thirty-four books.'

'But how – '

'From Daisy. All from Daisy. She hated to read. English was her own language and she hated to read. I learn – learned – it from her mother and then from books. But I speak it like a Boer, not like you.'

'You are a Boer. And you speak it beautifully.'

She rose from the wall. 'Why are you a soldier?'

'I had too much energy. It was of the wrong kind and I used it for the wrong things.' He stopped and smiled at her. 'To be truthful, they may have been the wrong things for the rest of the world but they were not necessarily wrong for me.'

'Perhaps you are like Rawdon Crawley,' she said. 'He was very wild and when he grew older he became very good. I must go in to my brother.'

'Your parents,' Matthew said suddenly, jerked back to reality by the mention of Gaspar. 'Where are they?'

'My mother is dead,' Alecia said. 'Her heart was weak. My father is with the army. He has gone to seek revenge for her dying.' She looked at Matthew and for a moment her expression wavered. 'He does not know that Gaspar was wounded, that he is ill.'

Matthew got up and grasped her elbow. 'My men will be back before nightfall. All is not lost.'

She nodded. 'No – '

'So extraordinary, that you should be Hendon Bashford's cousin. An amazing coincidence. Of all the farms – '

She began to move away towards the house. She said, tapping her book, 'There are patterns. Always there are patterns. Things are given, things are taken.'

He followed her, asking abruptly, 'How old are you?'

'In one month, nineteen.'

'And you look after all this? The farm, your aunt, your brother, the children – '

'Who else? The herdsmen know the cattle like their own children, mealies are easy to grow. Why should I not do it?'

'In England my sister is still learning. She is older than you and she is training to be a teacher.'

Alecia paused for a moment and looked at him in silence. Then she turned and went into the dark interior of the house.

'Sir?'

He stood abstracted, not really listening.

'Should we be getting on, sir? Musker and Wyman will follow later. The sun's high – '

Matthew nodded. 'Get everyone mounted – '

He went to the house doorway and leaned inside. 'Miss van Heerden!' From a room close by, the aunt came at once, cap ribbons fluttering. 'Mrs Bashford – '

'My niece is occupied, Captain Paget. I – I must thank you – '

'Please not. It was nothing. The medicines will be here before dark.'

'Oh. Oh, how good. I thank you. My niece will I am sure—'

'Will you thank her for her hospitality? And bid her good-bye from me.'

'Of course. Oh, yes—'

He nodded and put on his bush hat. At the edge of the garden his troop was mounted, Tatham holding his horse by the reins. He mounted and sat looking back a moment at the low house and the flowerbed and orange trees and the scattering of tin mugs across the grass.

'Sir?'

'What?'

'Just a question about the next farm. Is it or is it not on the map?'

17

It was difficult for Frances to remember that she had ever entered the house in Salisbury with a light heart. It seemed that every visit had been, of recent years, weighed down by some new disaster that had to be faced and shouldered and carried about to sit destructively at every meal by day and on every pillow by night. First it had been Matthew's refusal to go to Oxford at all, and then his seeming capitulation followed by his unorthodox triumph in his choice of subject. No sooner was he there than he was threatened with being sent down, then the threat became a reality and home he came in disgrace, then war, then he and Will going off and all the trouble and deception of that. Then Will's wound and Matthew's silence. Now this. And this the worst of all.

There was nothing, this time, for her parents or her aunt to say. Beatrice had shut herself up in the country, no doubt in a darkened room, and was deaf and mute. She answered no letters and would write none. Harriet had driven over and been refused admittance. There had been straw all over the gravel of the driveway to muffle the sounds of hooves and wheels as if someone lay dying within the house, and the bell had been shrouded in a cloth bag. Harriet had left a message on the silver tray in the hall where calling cards lay thick and unregarded and had driven sadly home again.

Even the Archdeacon was silent. His gout had pounced again and he spent his days in an armchair in his study, the inflamed foot on a stool, his knees draped with a camelhair blanket. He wore his customary air of supreme and nobly borne injury but this time he did not care to parade it before anyone; shame had swallowed up martyrdom. He declared himself too ill to receive any visitors, but sat and stared into the first fire of autumn or down at the newspapers spread upon his lap which told him that old Kruger had left South

Africa for France, that Lord Kitchener was to command in South Africa in place of Lord Roberts, and that Lord Roberts was to come home as Commander-in-Chief to succeed Lord Wolseley. Punctually at meal times, upon his strict instructions, Harriet alone brought him soup and white rolls and fricassées of chicken and sat, mostly in silence, while he ate them. Where she ate or whether she even ate at all, he did not inquire.

When Frances came, her mother met her in the hall and held her and they both cried a good deal and said very little. With so great a scandal in the house, the maids would be listening, Harriet knew, and in any case she felt there was almost nothing to say that wasn't fruitless lamentation. The newspapers had said it all and a brief, though kindly written, letter from Will's commanding officer had confirmed the facts. Will and some fellow officers, in revenge for misappropriation of some money of theirs by Mr Hendon Bashford, had held a mock court-martial in which Mr Bashford had been found guilty, and in consequence of his guilt had been stripped naked, ducked in a fish pond, had half his moustache shaved off, and been turned out to wander the streets of Cape Town in mid-winter in that condition. When he had recovered himself, he had at once sued his assailants and, as a result of a civil action, had been awarded £2000 worth of damages, costs of £2000, and letters of apology from all the officers concerned. Will and his fellow accused had not been present at the case, being more than halfway back to the battle area in the north. His colonel said that he had personally supervised the public apology and had hoped that it, in addition to the most generous amount of damages paid, would appease Mr Bashford. It was a vain hope. Mr Bashford, it seemed, was not satisfied with that. He declared that the War Office was suppressing proper press coverage of the incident and that he had not had sufficient redress for what he had suffered. He wished, he said, to bring a libel action in England. The War Office, embarrassed by the public attention he was beginning to receive both in South Africa and London, and urged on by Lord Roberts' personal intervention in the matter, was forced to act. The four officers who were the chief culprits were to be brought home and submitted to court-martial at Wellington Barracks for conduct unbecoming to an officer. It was deeply regrettable and everything was being done, the colonel assured them, to keep the affair as quiet and calm as possible. The letter was alarming enough in itself but there was an added element that Will's colonel could not possibly know of. To Harriet's mind – and undoubtedly to that of her husband and sister – it only wanted the press to discover the link between Mr Bashford and Matthew Paget at Oxford for the most unimaginably disagreeable publicity to drown them all.

Will's photograph had gone from the top of the grand piano, Frances observed.

'Where is it?'

'Where is what?'

'Will's photograph.'

'In a drawer – '

'What drawer?'

'My dear, don't speak in this way. Any drawer. What does it matter?'

'A great deal. Which drawer?'

'But I do not want you to get it out. I cannot have it on the piano.'

'I shall not put it on the piano. I shall put it in my room.'

'The maids – '

'Which drawer?'

'Please lower your voice – '

'Which drawer?'

'Your father would never allow it.'

'Mother, mother, mother! Which *drawer*?'

It was the photograph of Will taken eighteen months before, the new second lieutenant in all his finery, staring nobly and unflinchingly out into the future. Frances put him on the mantelpiece of her bedroom beside the one she already possessed of him and the one of Matthew in his gown at Oxford looking like a huge and dishevelled crow.

'Write to me,' she commanded it. 'Write to me and tell me what happened. Tell me the truth.'

'You have only the newspapers,' she said to Harriet. 'You don't know it all. Not the whole story.'

'Enough, enough – '

'Mother, mother! The Bashford man took Will's money! We don't know what for, but he clearly did not use it the way he had promised he would.'

'You must not forget that Mr Bashford has already suffered a gross humiliation at the hands of your own brother. Whatever he did was not as wicked as Will's revenge upon him.'

'You don't *know*! You only know it from his side, from the newspapers' side. Will can't speak, can't tell you. How can you be so bitterly unjust? You have known Will since he was a baby and you know what kind of man he is. Yet you will throw him over on the words of other people, a scoundrel, journalists. You amaze me, you do indeed.'

Harriet said, head bowed, 'Nobody is court-martialled for anything trifling, anything trumped up. It cannot happen. It is too serious. It has ruined Will. It could ruin all of us.'

'But Will was provoked! You *know* Will! He could not lift a finger against anyone without excellent cause and hardly then. You *know* him! How can you speak so?'

'War changes people. Being away from home changes people. Dreadful, vulgar, drunken behaviour – '

'All officers drink together. What would you have them do to ease the tensions? Rape and pillage?'

'Frances, I will not have – '

'And I,' said Frances, bursting into tears, 'will not have any more of this. You think of public disgrace, you think of social reputation, you think of the maids' opinions, but do you ever, ever think of Will?'

She rushed up to her room and wept wildly on her bed for a while and then she got up and flung herself at her desk and wrote to Oliver.

It disgusts me, disgusts me through and through and I cannot think what to do next. My parents are paralysed out of all pity and understanding by the magnitude of their shame and the fear that it will become publicly known that Hendon Bashford was the final reason for Matthew's being sent down from Oxford. I need you here so badly to do public battle for poor Will. I am sure he did maltreat this Bashford man but I am even more sure that he had admirable reason for doing so. 'Conduct unbecoming to an officer'! I would laugh if I wasn't so furious and miserable. Does everyone's sense of proportion as well as justice desert them in time of crisis and leave them caring about nothing beyond how things *look*? My mother! Can you believe it of my mother of all people? But it took just two days of Salisbury's cutting her dead for being the aunt of a man at the centre of a public scandal to terrify her back into every stifling convention she ever shed. I am going to ride my bicycle shouting through the Close tomorrow and I shall wear my bloomers and wave a banner proclaiming Will's innocence. Oh, please leave the Germans and the Italians to think what they will of us and come home!

Rose wrote a letter that was balm to her feelings, staunch in her conviction of the justification of Will's behaviour.

And I must add, at the risk of you thinking me dreadfully frivolous, that there is a tiny funny side to all this sadness. Just picture in your mind a naked man with half a moustache running about Cape Town. Any naked man would do for the purpose though aesthetically one should choose Michelangelo's David rather than President Kruger. Mamma and Papa send you their best love and Papa says you must not forget that his brother is a barrister and an able one at that. You have only to say the word. Can you not come back here? We miss you dreadfully and cannot think what there is for you to do in Salisbury but make yourself unbearably wretched.

She wrote an affectionate refusal at once. At the very least, her staying at home might prevent the ostracism and sense of disgrace at home from becoming any more intense. She took care to be seen in Salisbury every day, to greet the inhabitants of the Close with perfect openness, to attend services in the cathedral. She walked by the river west towards Wilton and east towards Britford and bicycled out to Laverstoke and Old Sarum and Combe Bissett. In between, she sat in her room at her worktable and made savage stabs at holiday work, at French and Latin translations, German verbs, English critical essays, historical assessments, and geographical studies. And she wrote letters, every day, some posted, some torn up and hurled towards the wastepaper basket in screwed-up balls. She wrote to Rose and Celia and Adelaide and Matthew and Oliver. She even wrote to Will, sending it care of the War Office since he was on the high seas in their custody and there seemed to be nowhere else to send it.

I suppose whatever I write to you will be censored so this will arrive as a big black blot, but I do so want you to know that I am not at all ready to believe that you are as much dishonoured as they all say and that even if you are partly to blame, you were wickedly provoked and therefore completely justified. The moment my tame Fleet Street pen returns from the Continent I shall steer him to your defence. You are being used as a whipping boy, I am convinced of it. The War Office think that if you are publicly punished, British standing among the inhabitants of the Cape, whose good opinion they both want and need, will improve enormously. (Watch the censor and his black blots on this part!) The army needs a sacrifice to put it back in popularity after a war that has dragged on far too long, and you will do very nicely. I long to talk to you and I will, by hook or by crook, as soon as you reach London. I think that should be by the end of September at the latest.

Oliver telegraphed as soon as he reached London and found her letter on his desk.

'I am going to London,' she announced to Harriet, who was drooping over her desk and a pile of letters impossible to write on account of Will's situation.

'I wish you would not. I imagine you are to see Mr Stansgate.'

'Is that why you do not wish me to go?'

'I wish you to cease from this horrid and strutting behaviour in public. It is so bitterly disloyal to your father and myself and your Aunt Beatrice.'

'And I see you as bitterly disloyal to Will.'

'My dear, you see everything in black and white. And you choose to disregard entirely that Will is the second member of our family to abuse Mr Bashford grossly and that it is only a matter of time before that knowledge is public. Your present behaviour can only hasten the day and make our eventual disgrace the deeper.'

'Mother, the two issues are quite separate. Can't you see? You are so unjust to Will for the sake of outward seeming.

Matthew deserved to be punished, to be sent down. He admitted it, he bore no grudge. Will did a foolish thing in a high-spirited moment after intense provocation and you cast him from you like a leper.'

'Have you no conception of the seriousness of a court-martial?'

'Of course I have! That is why your shunning of Will is so terrible, so unreasonably cruel!'

'Frances, I do not wish to have this kind of conversation again.'

'Nor I. I cannot imagine what has come over you.'

'I think,' Harriet said with weary dignity, 'that it has been my misfortune to bear two children who can imagine nothing that they do not wish to imagine. I have been too free with you, I have indulged your minds and your independent thinking too much. Beatrice always said so. I begin to believe she may be right. You exhaust me at present, Frances, you are so foolish and wilful and angry. Nothing in our lives has been, however hard to bear, anywhere near the magnitude of this present disaster, thank God, and yet at such a crisis you behave like the worst elements of the suffragette movement. Go to London. Go. I am too tired to keep you here. But go with a little restraint, I beg you. And return tonight before your absence is noted and there are yet more coals of shame to heap upon our heads.'

In the second-class railway carriage she chose was a woman in black and a small boy wearing a tin badge with a profile of Lord Baden-Powell upon it. He also carried a Union Jack and an orange. Frances wondered if the woman was a war widow but somehow she did not have the courage to ask. The woman had a firm pale face and said nothing all the way to London except at Basingstoke station to restrain the boy from peeling his orange and throwing the skin out onto the platform. He contented himself with peeling the fruit intensely, surreptitiously, in tiny pieces and stowing the fragments in his pocket. When Frances caught his eye and smiled, he scowled at her to show that she should not have noticed. He then ate the orange, segment by segment, with enormous nonchalance, hardly moving his jaws.

She took a cab from Waterloo to Fleet Street, rumbling

over Westminster Bridge and along the Embankment. She sat back watching the crowds in the early September sunshine dawdling along the pavements, boaters and wasp waists, children in button boots, and here and there a frock coat and top hat, inescapably wealthier and superior. And then others so very shabby, clothes never good, now very sorry indeed, worn to shine. Why should clothes be such a badge? Why should clothes be so difficult, such a business? She looked down at the innumerable tucks of her blouse, the complicated sections of her jacket and skirt with their carefully patterned loops of braid. So expensive, such a labour to make, to look after, to put on. No wonder half the people out there by the river looked down at heel. Couldn't simpler clothes be made and sold in shops? It would mean a joyful end to those hours of standing and being measured and adjusted and tweaked, all for an end result of being miserably uncomfortable. No man could ever guess the unutterable luxury of removing one's corset . . .

It was no thought with which to arrive at Oliver's office. He said at once, greeting her by taking both hands in his, 'You look wonderfully well. A rosy hue along the cheekbones – '

'Oh!' she cried and blushed deeper. 'I was thinking of clothes – '

'Quite right! It's tremendously important. Do you think I look well? I have had the most fascinating time. Pity the poor fool in any other profession.'

He led her into his office and sat her in a brown leather chair studded with dome-headed nails along the arms and back. The room was like a small library, entirely lined with books and files and dominated by a vast desk on which papers lay in surprising order.

'Aha. You thought I should work in unutterable chaos, did you not? I can see it in your face. Let me demonstrate to the contrary. This pile is my next article and the one beyond it the basis for the one after and so forth. Main feature articles, or possibilities therefor, over here. Green eyeshades here. Inkstand there. The model journalist.'

'You are in the highest spirits,' Frances said. 'You must have enjoyed yourself.'

'I'm only sorry,' he said with unexpected gentleness, 'that you could not.'

'It has almost been harder to endure the aftermath than the fact.'

He said, 'Of course, I have read all about it.'

'I think Will is a victim.'

He stood up. 'I am going to get you a glass of Madeira. We always give it to lady visitors. It is perfectly proper to drink it before luncheon – and afterwards for that matter.'

He returned with two Venetian glasses with a twist of clouded glass in the stems and put one down on a table at her elbow. 'Only pretty visitors get the pretty glasses, however. Victim of what?'

'Of the War Office's need to soothe the South African citizens at the Cape and keep them firmly pro-British. After all, they must be very tired of a war they were told would only last a few months. Probably everyone is getting restive, officers included, and if a small group is punished, that will also serve to discourage any more – ragging.'

'Have you heard from your cousin?' Oliver said, writing.

'No. Not yet. He is due home at any time.'

'And the court martial?'

'Later this month.'

'I must say,' Oliver said, 'this Bashford man sounds particularly disagreeable.'

'Matthew thinks so. He and some others ducked him at Oxford and pegged him out in Tom Quad with croquet hoops. Matthew was sent down next day.'

Oliver said, laughing, 'Just for that?'

'No. That was the final crime. But it haunts my family. That it will come to light and increase the scandal. I don't care two hoots about that but I *should* care if it was all raked up again and used against Will. Rose's uncle is a barrister – '

'I don't think you would find that would avail you much at a court-martial.'

'What will avail me something?'

'Drinking your Madeira.'

She took a sip obediently.

'Frances, I entirely understand and applaud your feelings about your cousin's position. But I think you are worrying too much. So, for that matter, is your estimable mother. In the general scheme of things judicial in this country courts martial do not appear to particular advantage for reasons which will suit your cousin rather than Mr Bashford. They are held by the military, for the military, in military surroundings. Your cousin is an officer and an English gentleman of hitherto irreproachable character. Mr Bashford is none of those things and was even described by a senior colonel in today's *Daily Express* as an "undesirable associate for young officers". I would think the War Office see the whole exercise as a sop to South African wounded vanity as you suggest, but I would not for one moment imagine that they would be prepared to sacrifice four excellent young officers for such a cause. There will be a trial in some barracks, the newspapers will seize upon it as an exciting piece of scandal, and the outcome will be all stains removed from your cousin's character and a certain amount of money from Mr Bashford's pocket. Will can then proceed with being a soldier and Mr Bashford with being a scoundrel, as before.'

'And if it becomes known about Matthew?'

'I cannot see that legally that has anything to do with the matter. If anything, it is further proof of what unsuitable company Mr Bashford indeed is for officers and gentlemen. They only have to see him to want to throw him in a pond. Proof of the pudding. Which reminds me. May I give you luncheon?'

'Oh, I wish you would!'

He nodded, smiling. 'Of course. I will ask about for you to make sure the world knows who the blackguard is. But I think you must stop worrying. It is humiliating for your cousin at the moment but that is all the discomfort it will be for him. As for family shame – '

'Yes?'

'What is it in your mother and your aunt to breed these wild young men? It's the imaginativeness of their wildness that intrigues me so. Duck a man and then peg him neatly out to dry. Strip a man and shave off merely one half of his moustache. Nothing shameful in either case, it seems to me. Silly jokes perhaps, but funny silly jokes.'

'My parents don't feel that way at all. Nor does my aunt.'

'Is the Church particularly censorious of these things, do you suppose?'

Frances smiled. 'Only bishops' wives, I think.'

'Not a daunting number of ladies – '

'Oliver.'

'Yes?'

'I am so grateful to you. I've felt so – helpless. I shall of course go to the War Office just to see what the procedure of a court-martial is, what Will's rights are. All we know is that he is under something called open arrest which seems to leave him free to exercise but not to go anywhere in public. As he's on a ship at present, I can't see that he would be much affected except in his mind and that is what troubles me so much – ' She stopped, gave Oliver a small and almost apologetic smile, and said hurriedly, 'I thought of writing to the newspapers but family recrimination would be too terrible.'

He rose from his desk and held out a hand to help her to her feet. 'How long will it be before you are trained? How long before you can take your first job?'

'Two years.'

'Too long at home, my dear.'

'Yes,' she said, ' I know.'

'A room in Oxford in the vacation? A room in London? Could you afford such a thing?'

'Yes – '

He took his hat off a curling bentwood stand and opened the door for her. 'Talking of money, where is your first essay into journalism for me?'

'It never got done. The holiday was broken off. Will, you know – '

'So you walked nowhere? Read nothing?'

'Oh no! We walked every day for a week and read copiously. And of course the Hemming-Hemmings were there, so generous, so broad-minded. They are a wonderful family.'

'Write about it.'

'But it wasn't a proper walking tour – '

'Make it one.'

'I – should like to try – '

'You will try. If I have to kick you every inch of the way. I want the discussions put in, the opinions, the views on what you were reading. Think of the influence you have! How are men to see that women have minds, I should like to know, unless they display them? Display yours and I will pay you and print it. Or send you back to rewrite it.' He took her hand and drew it through his arm. 'Now then. Enough of your life for the moment. I am going to give you, as practice for my own articles, all my observations upon the life and habits of the European.'

18

'These,' Adelaide said, laying a closely written sheet before her chief medical officer, 'are the figures Miss Hobhouse is taking back to England.'

'Huh,' he said.

Adelaide waited.

'Miss Munro, Lord Kitchener has called Miss Hobhouse that bloody woman. I echo him. Miss Hobhouse is a Quaker, which is a pity, and a neurotic spinster, which is worse.'

'I am a spinster, sir.'

He looked up at her. 'Miss Munro, you and your nerves are strangers to each other. For which the good Lord be praised. What am I to do about these?'

'Read them.'

Dr Trevor cleared his throat. ' "Children in the concentration camps are dying at the rate of 430 out of each thousand per annum. Adults are dying at the rate of 264 out of each thousand. Between June and September of this year 5209 Boer children are known to have died in the British camps." I know all this, Miss Munro.'

'It's scandalous, sir.'

Dr Trevor rose from his chair and went to the window. Under the hard summer sun, lines of newly erected wards of the hastily expanded typhoid fever hospital in Johannesburg stretched away to the distant mountain landscape of mining dumps, their tin roofs shining harshly. Through the open louvres of the window came the faint clatter of utensils being clashed together and the powerful smell of carbolic acid. Rubber sheets, hung out in the sun to dry on long lines between the wards, flapped idly and noisily in the light wind like so many orange sails.

'I know perfectly well that it is scandalous. I also know that it is fiendishly expensive and that we are feeding all these families and leaving their menfolk free to go on fighting unencumbered. But I am only an army medical officer. It is not for me even to question the whole insane scheme. It started as an act of humanity and it is now turned into a nightmare.'

'But you are in charge of the medical officers of the camps in all this area. I went to Hekpoor and Vaalplaas and the conditions in both are deplorable. There are not even latrine trenches dug at Vaalplaas.'

He turned round. 'Are you criticizing my administration, Miss Munro?'

'Yes, sir. I am aware that you have this hospital to run as well as the southern Transvaal district to administer, but the camps must be improved. They must. Those poor women – '

'Poor women be damned. They stand and pat their great bellies and shout that they will produce another generation of Boers to kill the rooineks. They are dirty and superstitious and they pour all manner of abominable home-brewed medicines down their wretched children's throats. If we dig latrine trenches they won't use them and the habits of the open veld are a disaster in a confined space like a camp. Typhoid, dysentery, cholera, all the old enemies, and of course these people, used to a life of isolation, have no resistance to anything. And no desire to change their ways to suit their situation. They are narrow-minded and self-righteous and if it is any consolation to you, Miss Munro, I spend more time thinking about them than I do about almost any other problem.'

'Sir – '

'And it is highly irregular to speak to me in this way. You are matron in this hospital, may I remind you?'

'Yes, sir.'

He sighed and smiled at her. 'Go and write a report for me. On Vaalplaas and Hekpoor to start with. Officially you should not do such a thing but we will blink at that.'

'I would rather,' Adelaide said, imperturbably, 'that you sent even a handful of orderlies from this hospital out to the camps taking with them the opium and the saline solutions that the medical officers so conspicuously lack. They have nothing to give the sick at the moment, nothing except the

233

coffee the Boers brew for themselves in any case. Now, if it were possible perhaps to have some ice for the cholera victims – '

'Miss Munro, you are beginning to enrage me. If I could do without you, I would.'

'You have been of that opinion, sir, since the day we met in Cape Town last January.'

'And I am not a man to change his mind.' He picked up Emily Hobhouse's report and held it out to her. 'I spent twenty years in India, Miss Munro, and have seen more men die of cholera than I care to remember. I don't want to be told how to treat it and I don't want one more damned Boer child to die of it than I can help. And I don't want Emily Hobhouse mentioned in my hearing again. Is that quite clear?'

'Perfectly, sir.'

'Go on, then,' he said, 'go away.'

She had been almost three months in the Transvaal. Her status as a volunteer nurse on behalf of the committees working for peace in London had vanished beneath the onslaught of her own competence, and when she had been offered the chance to work with Dr Trevor in Johannesburg, it had seemed to her foolish to refuse. To nurse men as a volunteer and a pacifist and then to refuse to nurse the same ones as part of a military medical team was to Adelaide splitting hairs. It was the men that suffered, not her principles; principles were the spur that got one up and going, but they were not an end in themselves. The spectacle of war had, if anything, made her more firmly a pacifist than before, but she would not for a moment sit and nurse her pacifism rather than be constructively involved in the situation she detested so. In any case, she liked nursing. She had admitted to herself, she liked bodies, she liked the restoration of health and the self-respect that came with it, she liked mending things. She had discovered at the Cape among the officers and up in Johannesburg among the men that she also liked soldiers. They had a dispassionate attitude, in the main, towards their own suffering and this she found immensely attractive; it summoned up whole wells of sympathy in her.

When she looked back and thought of those whispered hours she had spent in her mother's shaded bedroom, her brothers tiptoeing past the door with their boots in their hands, she was astonished that she had borne it all with such patience; she could not do so now.

The new typhoid hospital in Johannesburg, set up after the disastrous medical record during the siege of Ladysmith, when men had died like flies, was a scheme after her own heart. It might be unprepossessing to look at, with its lines of grim corrugated-iron wards lined up with mathematical regularity on the red earth, but it served its purpose. It was possible, given the size of the laundry facilities, to keep both the place and the patients clean, and a team of Zulus stood all day in a jungle atmosphere in the washhouses boiling mountains of linen in strong solutions of carbolic acid. Boiling was the order of the day. Everything was boiled – bedclothes, milk, water, utensils, instruments.

'When you boil me,' a patient had said to Adelaide recently, 'mind you do it thorough.'

She had left Cape Town to come north almost as Will had left it to sail home. She felt that she had been less than forthright, less than strictly honest, in her letters to Frances, but she had not believed that it was proper for her to alarm the family over Will's situation until there was definite news. Cape Town had resounded with the scandal, it was perfectly true, and Adelaide had been profoundly thankful that Will, halfway to Durban, had not been present for the libel action Hendon Bashford had brought against him so vociferously. She was shocked to hear that each of the accused officers was to pay £500 in damages and that they had been found liable for costs in addition. But she had assumed thankfully that that was to be the end of it and that this dreadful Bashford man would retreat back into the society of Cape Town commerce where he rightfully belonged.

It was with the utmost dismay that she heard that the case was, in Hendon Bashford's eyes, only just beginning. There were strident accusations in the *Cape Times*, as well as in other far less reputable newspapers, that the press had been ordered by the British military authorities to subdue the affair, and that Mr Bashford was of the opinion that his name and reputation had to be cleared in London as well as Cape Town before he could begin to see himself as even inadequately compensated for the injury done to him. The whole business came to the ears of Lord Roberts, who declared that, for the sake of his country and his army's reputation, he could not turn a blind eye. What seemed at first to be only unpleasant rumoured mutterings about a court-martial became a reality. Will, in Durban and only a train ride from rejoining his regiment, was summoned back to Cape Town. As an officer, he was placed under open arrest, but Adelaide, despite much beseeching, was not permitted to see him, not being a relation. She wrote an ambiguous letter to Frances that she was subsequently ashamed of, and was ordered north to Johannesburg.

Once there, news from London was sporadic. In her heart of hearts, Adelaide could not believe that any military court, composed of men of a like way of thinking and behaving as the four officers on trial, could find against them and for such a man as Hendon Bashford. On the other hand, if Lord Roberts thought that a larger reputation than that of the four officers was at stake, four officers were a comparatively small sacrifice. Whatever the outcome, there was nothing that Adelaide, in charge of a nursing and orderly staff of over three hundred, could do about it. Frances would tell her when there was something to tell. In the meantime, the enteric victims lay miserably in their new hot tin wards, hundred upon hundred, and out there in the veld, beyond the mine dumps and the prosperous green suburbs, the wives and children of the enemy were herded together in the camps that were causing such public outrage. There was plenty to do in the Transvaal without worrying about Will.

It was by chance that Matthew found his way to Adelaide. Some five days or so after he had ridden away from the Van Heerden farm, he had gone back, a bottle of iodine compound in his pocket for Gaspar. He had found the place a ragged blackened oblong on the veld, the house burned down entirely, one barn wall still drunkenly standing, the garden plot a scorched echo of its former self. A detachment of Rimington's Tigers, armed with a map with no compassionate omissions on it, had ridden through two days after Matthew and set fire to everything, even the native rondavels. The Kaffirs had gone, no doubt accompanied by the cattle, and the mealie fields lay ripening and unregarded under the high early-summer sky.

Matthew, under the pretence of needing information about the enemy, had inquired at both camps to the north of Johannesburg for the Van Heerdens and received no help. In each one, exhausted medical officers sat in huts in a sea of flies and questions and chaos and waved dispirited arms at the squalor outside. At Hekpoor, the camp commander was sure he sheltered no such family.

'I would remember, Captain Paget, even without my records. She must be the only woman of this whole infernal race who is not pregnant. I would remember that, I promise you.' He looked from his hut doorway at the lines of military tents in their encircling prison of wire. 'Five children born last night alone – '

At Vaalplaas, where the Boers were housed in lines of depressing tin structures like sentry boxes, hot as ovens at midday, the commander could not help either, but he had a suggestion. 'Try the fever hospital in the city. They are supposed to keep a register of all the inmates of all the camps in the district. And while you are there, would you be so good, Captain Paget, as to explain that unless I have more assistance at once, everyone here will be dead, including myself?'

Thus it was that Matthew found himself confronting Adelaide. She had a small office, no bigger than a generous cupboard, in which she offered him a camp chair. They talked of Will for a while, interrupted frequently by orderlies with requests for lists, and then Adelaide said, 'I can only suppose you have some request to make. Otherwise I do not flatter myself that you would come to seek me here.'

'I had no idea that you were here. Until a quarter of an hour ago.' He paused. 'I do have a request.'

She smiled at him. 'A friend?'

'A Boer girl.'

Adelaide looked startled. 'A Boer – '

'Please,' Matthew said, 'please say nothing to anyone.

I've made inquiries so far under the guise that she may have useful information for us.'

Adelaide regarded him for a little while. He looked back at her and then dropped his eyes and began to turn his slouch hat slowly in his hands.

'I think you should explain rather more to me – '

'I spared her farm. Her father's farm. She had a sick brother, an aunt, lots of children there. She had taught herself English, she had books she had collected – ' He looked up again. 'Believe it or not, she is Hendon Bashford's cousin. And as unlike him as black from white.'

'I should hope so.'

'I got laudanum for her brother. She gave us all coffee, I talked to her; she was remarkable, extraordinary, so self-sufficient, so enduring. I went back to see her some days later and the Tigers had burned the place to the ground. I want to find her, find out which camp she is in.'

'How can you ask me to help you?'

'I do, Adelaide. For personal reasons. There is nothing remotely unpatriotic in my desire to see her. But I must find her, make sure she is still alive. I want to talk to her.'

'You have such effrontery!'

Matthew stood up. 'Then I must find her without your help. She is not in the register at either Hekpoor or Vaal-plaas. I'll just go on until I find her, even if I have to look in every camp in the Transvaal.' He turned and put his hand on the door knob. 'I should not have asked you. Forgive me. When I saw it was you, I should have gone away.'

'You are doing a very dangerous thing. A very foolish one, a lone search for a Boer woman. If I helped you, from the hospital – '

'I don't want sacrifices,' Matthew said. 'You know I have never known what to do with them.'

'I shouldn't make one for you, I promise you. I have myself to think of. But we have British inquiries, military inquiries, about women in the camps most weeks, some for information reasons, some – many – for humanitarian ones.' She looked at him. 'Leave me some information as to where I can get hold of you. And the girl's name. I will do what I can.'

238

'Adelaide – '

'If you thank me,' she said, 'I will do nothing. You are a routine inquiry. Good day to you, Captain Paget.'

In ten days she was found. A message was brought to Matthew in camp containing the information that a Miss van Heerden and a Mrs Bashford and sundry children by the name of Dreyer had been admitted three weeks before to a small, newly formed camp out to the west beyond Roodepoort. At the bottom of the message Adelaide had written, 'Please report to the hospital afterwards. It is standard procedure.'

It was thirty miles and more on horseback, skirting Johannesburg to the north, riding along pale dirt roads lined with the extravagant houses whose owners were beginning to trickle back from the Cape now that the mines were in operation again. Beyond the suburbs the land rolled green and pleasantly, northwards to Pretoria, west to the gigantic farming plains that stretched all the way to Bechuanaland, to Mafeking, with its railway lines and its stones. The camp was well situated on a western-sloping hillside, but it was built like Vaalplaas, of corrugated iron, row upon row of harsh stable-like sheds, a number crudely stencilled above each door, a trodden space running down between each row, and around the whole place a wire fence some eight foot high, stretched between iron poles. Across the valley, one could see fields, ragged and neglected, and here and there, a dark blot of a burned building, but in the camp there was nothing to look at that was not utilitarian and ugly.

The camp commander, a small and energetic man, was proud of the standards of the place. 'No nonsense about cleanliness, Captain Paget. Anyone caught using anything other than the latrine trenches – even at night during curfew – is liable to confinement in their huts. I'm not having cholera here and I've told them so. They aren't on the veld now, they can't just squat where they choose. Who was it you wanted to question?'

Alecia was brought to him in a small bare cell known as the Inquiries Room. It had no window, only a door which opened onto the main thoroughfare of the camp outside the commander's office, and it smelled powerfully of disinfectant. Alecia and Matthew sat opposite each other on camp chairs, a small rough table between them on which was a dented tin ashtray. There was a guard outside and, the commander said, Matthew had only to raise his voice and assistance would be forthcoming directly.

Alecia's face was pinched with strain. She wore the same dark stuff gown that Matthew now regarded as inseparable from any Boer woman, and over it, instead of the white apron she had worn at the farm, an apron of coarse sacking. Her hair was drawn tightly back from her face and screwed into a hard bun on the nape of her neck.

'They burned my books,' she said.

Matthew nodded. He pulled a small volume out of his pocket and put it beside the ashtray.

'It's Mrs Gaskell's *Cranford*. It is all I could find in Johannesburg. But I will look for more. An absurd thing to read here – '

She snatched it up and hid it at once under her apron. 'No,' she said, 'No, no – '

'Gaspar?' he said gently.

'He was dead before they burned the house. He was dead the day after you came. Your soldiers – they rode all that way for nothing.'

'I went back. I went back to the farm to bring iodine in case the laudanum had done no good. I am so sorry, so very, very sorry – '

She bowed her head. 'Why are you here, Captain Paget?'

'To see how you are.'

'They told me that you were here for information, that I must tell you everything I know. I know nothing. I do not even know where my father is.'

Matthew said softly, 'I had to say that. I had to, in order to see you. Are you hungry? Are you fed sufficiently?'

She shrugged. 'We eat what we used to give to the Kaffirs. Almost there is enough. But not always for the children, so Tant Johanna and I must give them ours, especially little Martje who is hungry always, always. But water, there is not enough. And I am afraid that it is dirty. The women here, some are from so far, miles out on the veld, and they do not know that water can be dirty. And there are too many people. Oh, Captain Paget, it is people, people, people – ' She pressed her hands to her head. 'Always babies crying and children and women scolding and shouting, even in the night. When you have lived always in the silence in the veld, it is terrible to be with so many people.' She smiled suddenly. 'To think how I used to want to leave it sometimes and see something new!'

'How can I help you?'

'You cannot.'

'I must be able to, some way – '

'You are kind, but you cannot. You are a British officer, I am an enemy woman, there is a war.'

'It is so stupid,' Matthew said angrily. 'We don't even dislike each other very much any more, Boer and British. We have half forgotten why this war began; most of your original leaders have gone – '

'You are now fighting for your empire,' Alecia said. 'We are still fighting for our independence. That is the sharper spur.'

Matthew looked at her and then said in sudden triumph, 'But I can help you! I can find you books!'

She put out a rough hand and touched his lightly, smiling. 'That is the biggest gift. We may be here many months, the volk will not give in, time is nothing to us, we have so much of it, and space. Books will change things for me. But you. Is it wrong for you? Is it safe?'

'I shall make it safe,' he insisted.

'But you are a British soldier – '

'Miss van Heerden. What is your Christian name?'

'Alecia.'

'Alecia,' he said, 'Alecia. And mine is Matthew.'

She rose, holding the book hard beneath the sacking of her apron.

'Must you hide it?'

She nodded. 'It is in English. The feelings about the English here run high. But I can hide it. My aunt will understand. I must go back to them now – '

She glanced towards the doorway. It was empty. Quickly

she put out her free hand to Matthew and he clasped it in both his.

'You will see me again.' he said.

'I have come to report,' Matthew said, 'as instructed.'

Adelaide did not look up from her desk. 'It is not me that you must report to, Captain Paget. It is to the military intelligence. They keep an office in this building near to the main entrance. Perhaps you would call there on your way out.'

Matthew shut the door of her office behind him. 'I had rather report to you.'

She put her pen down and looked up at him. 'What did you find?'

He shrugged. 'They are not starving, they are not dying in inordinate numbers, but it is a degrading place, an inhuman place – '

'I know,' Adelaide said, 'I have worked at Vaalplaas, I've seen others. But it isn't any use raging, it isn't for us to decide policy, only to do what we can with the results of it. And your Miss van Heerden?'

'Very thin, strained. I think it might be living herded all together like that. And so many of the women are so coarse there, different – '

'Aha,' Adelaide said, 'I see. A pearl among swine – '

'I want to get her away,' Matthew burst out, spinning his hat into a corner. 'I want to put her back somewhere decent, give her the books she craves, the open spaces, the ideas. I can't stand seeing her in such a place with those great fences round and the stench from the latrines and children crying, I can't stand seeing her enduring it.' He stopped and then said vehemently, 'It's worth deserting for.'

Adelaide said nothing. She picked up a pencil and began to roll it slowly backwards and forwards across the green blotting paper on her desk.

Matthew shouted, 'Did you hear me?'

'Oh, yes,' she said, 'I heard you. And I have this to say in reply. If you desert, I shall at once inform upon you.'

'Adelaide!'

'Sit down. And listen. I have watched you, Matthew

242

Paget, do several destructive things to your life since we first met, and I have no intention of being spectator to yet another. As you seem incapable of looking before you leap, others must look for you. Usually you are in a position to ignore what they see but in this instance you are not. I should have no compunction whatsoever in informing upon you if you commit any breach of military discipline while we are in this area together, let alone anything so extreme as desertion. You are in such a habit of self-indulgence, it does not strike you to consider the consequences to others as you blunder from one escapade to another. You have caused untold pain to your family already, may I remind you. If you desert, I shall inform upon you and you will be shot by firing squad, as you know. And then conceive of what value you will be to Miss van Heerden.' She paused and said more calmly, 'Love is not doing what you please so much as doing what pleases the object of your love. I should know.'

'Oh, Adelaide – '

'I am glad to hear that tone of voice from you. I had begun to feel that you were indeed the unfeeling brute you seem determined the world should take you for. I will give you another reason why you might be guided by me. It is for my sake. Once, at Oxford, you were influenced by me, not for long, but profoundly for a little time. If everything goes as you wish it to, and as I in truth wish it for you, this will be only the second, but also the last time that my opinion counts with you. It would mean a great deal to me if you let it, Matthew, and I cannot pretend otherwise.'

He leaned across the desk and clasped the hand that was still rolling the pencil. 'I am listening, I do take heed – '

She drew her hand away and folded it with her other in her lap. 'You only need a little patience, after all. I gather Lord Roberts is encouraging the Government in London to release all colonial troops and volunteer regiments and yeomanry after a year's service, and you have served that long and more. A few more months and melodramatic talk of desertion may not even be relevant. What could you do if you deserted in any case? Carry her off on a white charger like a knight in a medieval poem? You would have to hide on the veld in fear of your life, you would have no access to Miss van

243

Heerden at all. So, let us face things as they are. As a British officer you can visit the camp. As a British civilian you can. Is that what you will do when you are once more a civilian? Or shall you go home?'

Matthew shook his head. 'No.'

'I thought not.'

'I should like to farm here. Cattle ranching – '

'There is certainly enough room for you. Will you assure me of your prudent behaviour?'

He nodded, smiling. He coughed and said awkwardly, in a phrase not at all his own, 'And you, Adelaide? Aren't there majors languishing for love of you from here to Cape Town?'

She regarded him. 'Why should you think that? In fact I have received a proposal of marriage this week, from the chief medical officer of this hospital, and I declined it, I think much to his relief. He followed it with a proposition I much prefer. There is a plan to start a college of nurses exclusively for the benefit of soldiers, once this war is over, and there will be a number of administrative as well as senior nursing posts available. I can think of few things I should like better.'

Matthew got up, holding out both hands to her as he had once done in the hall at Norham Gardens, calling to condole with her after her mother's death. She put hers into them.

'I shall remember what you have said to me. And when all this is over, I shall bring Alecia van Heerden to meet you.'

Adelaide drew her own hands gently from his. 'Thank you, but no. It is certainly the old Matthew who would suggest such a thing but then, of course, it was the old Matthew who – ' She stopped and then said, smiling, 'Off with you, Captain Paget, and find a blockhouse to man. The rest of the world has work to do.'

19

Under discreet military escort, Will was allowed to proceed from Wellington Barracks to Hans Place to see his family and his lawyer. He was in uniform at all times – it was one of the conditions of open arrest – and he was brought in a closed carriage since public places were forbidden him. The first visit was only a few days after his arrival in England and was to see his mother.

He had known that the interview would be impossibly difficult and it was. She was waiting for him in the drawing room at Hans Place, dressed exclusively in black, motionless beside the chimneypiece with one hand resting on its empty surface. As was her habit, she had only ordered the dust covers removed from two essential chairs, and the rest of the room was still shrouded so that Will felt he was surrounded by a mutely disapproving public crowd. There was a small and unenthusiastic fire burning behind the black sweep of Beatrice's skirts but it had no chance against the November chill of the room or his mother's mood. He stood in the doorway, cap and gloves clasped before him, and saw his breath plume palely in front of him.

'Mother – '

She did not stir. He felt a sudden rush of resentment. Surely she had had, just as he had had, the long – so long – weeks of the voyage home to consider thoroughly what they might say to each other. He had hoped she might speak first, give him some idea of whether anger or disappointment was uppermost in her mind, but as she had remained silent, he had had to speak.

'Will you not even look at me?'

Beatrice gazed straight before her, out of the window between the heavy festoons of the velvet curtains to the gloom of the London November afternoon.

'I shall not come to London after today,' she said. 'I could not bear it. You have made me quite ill.'

'I have made myself so,' Will said. He advanced into the room, laying his cap upon a sheeted chair. 'May I sit down?'

'You will not be staying long enough to make it necessary.'

He waited, a yard from the doorway.

'It was my duty to come to London to see you. I wish you could have seen your duty as plainly as I see mine. I should never have allowed you to have spent so much of your time with the Pagets, you are infected with their headstrong selfishness, but I was sorry for the solitariness of your childhood. Your conduct is unseemly, dishonourable, and cruel. It is my duty to tell you so. And whatever the rights and wrongs of the matter, the public notice you have exposed me to is wicked enough in itself. The house is presently besieged with disagreeable people from the newspapers. There were even three of them hanging about here this morning when I arrived.'

Will took a step forward, crying, 'Mother, will you not hear me speak?'

She looked at him for a fleeting second and then she said, 'There would be no point. Nothing you can say could undo what you have done.'

'I don't think,' Will said unsteadily to Frances a few days later, 'that I have ever been so angry in my life. I felt – quite blind with rage, helpless. It was really something of a relief, you know, to feel anything so positive, so violent, as anger after all these weeks and weeks of remorse and shame.' He put his head in his hands. 'I am exhausted by remorse,' he said.

'I can see that – '

'I even feel guilty that you should have had to get special permission to come up from Oxford to see me, though if I am honest, my thankfulness that you have outweighs my self-consciousness that you had to. Frances – '

'Yes.'

'There is really no one else that I want to see.'

She said, smiling, 'I hope you have seen a lawyer.'

'Oh, yes. Twice. We go over and over the ground together,

246

every detail. All he really wants to know is the extent to which I was provoked to react, which means going back long before Matthew was sent down from Oxford, and, to be honest, because Bashford hardly mattered to me then, I didn't really pay him much heed and of course can't supply the proper details now. All that I know, black and white, for absolute truth is that through him I am the poorer, one way and another, by £3000. And, Frances, I wish it wasn't about money. I hate the vulgarity of it. I shall hate having to speak of it.'

'Has he tried to see you?'

'Bashford? Oh, yes. He is tucked up snugly at Claridge's and he wished me to wait upon him there. I am forbidden to but I should have refused anyway. His lawyer tried to see me here but I refused that too. I should probably only hit Bashford again – '

'Will, to think he embezzled your money – '

'I know.'

'But the court-martial will be a formality. Everyone says so.'

Will got up and began to wander about the room, hands in his pockets. 'Frances, I really must talk about something else.'

'Oh!' she said, instantly contrite. 'And that is what I vowed to do all the way up from Oxford. I'm afraid anxiety makes one obsessive – '

Will leaned on the back of a sheeted chair. 'How awful it is having to talk in this room.'

'It's like a morgue, isn't it? Or at least as one envisages a morgue. I must tell you, but I had such a childish revenge upon this house. I came and changed here once before a concert and Aunt Beatrice was deeply reluctant to let me do so but knew that saying no would not stop me going, so she said yes. There was a bedroom and a bathroom unlocked for me and I went in and found them as absolutely ordered as everything is here, and I went out of them and left them a perfect disgrace. I took some trouble over it too. I pulled towels off the rail onto the floor and I threw a handful of hairpins into the air and I sat on every cushion and pillow I could find and bounced on the bed – '

247

'And then you went out with Mr Stansgate.'

'Yes.'

'Mother wrote and told me.'

'Will – '

'Oh!' he said vehemently, 'I know that you are at complete liberty to see whom you like, talk to whom you like, go to concerts with whom you like. It is just that when one gets that sort of news thousands of miles away it is not at all easy to be balanced.'

His pacing brought him in front of her. 'I don't change, Frances, I can't. I have tried because I think in many ways you would be so much more comfortable if I did, but I cannot. I've done a lot of stupid, impulsive, high-spirited things, but it's always you I think about when I am in any kind of need. You see, apart from all the other aspects of it, you are, quite simply, the best companion I have ever had.'

'But Matthew – '

'I can't even talk to Matthew as I can to you. Perhaps once, not now. In any case, we have to start doing without Matthew.'

She rose hurriedly. 'What do you mean?'

'He told me he would stay in South Africa when the war was over. He wants to farm. He has fallen in love with the country. It's really a very suitable country for Matthew, you know, large and red and energetic.'

She said faintly, 'Oh heavens, Will, what did we start, sending him out there?'

He took her hands. 'Perhaps we started him on just the life he wants.'

'I am tremendously apologetic, but I am going to cry – '

'Yes,' he said, dropping her hands and putting his arms round her, 'it would comfort me enormously if you did that. I would like you to cry.'

She said, clinging, 'It's not for him that I am crying. It's for you – '

He said nothing, simply held her hard against him, his eyes closed.

'Any injustice done to you and I am ready to commit murder. I can't bear it. I couldn't bear it when you were wounded and confused in Cape Town either. Why should these things happen to you when you are so good, so untroublesome, so honourable?' She took a sharp breath. 'Please forgive me. I only mean to comfort you and here I am needing comfort myself – '

'You do comfort me. More than you know.'

'Wouldn't Matthew despise us?'

'Should you care? In any case, he wouldn't. We are only slowly learning what he always knew, that you must do what you want.'

'Steady,' she said, laughing faintly. 'Remember where that led him! In any case, I'm not so certain that I know what I want. Do you?'

He gave her a small and rueful smile. 'I think I'm learning,' he said.

Twenty-four hours before the court-martial, a charge sheet was brought to Will in his quarters. The first section of it stated that he was being charged under section 16 of the Army Act with behaviour of a scandalous manner unbecoming to an officer and a gentleman. He was further charged under section 178 for conduct prejudicial to discipline and was reminded that the existing state of war made such an offence even the more grave.

The second part of the charge sheet was a meticulously detailed account of all that had taken place that night at the Mount Nelson Hotel. Will had recalled it, or had been asked to recall it, so often that the reality of it had escaped him long ago. He could remember the curiously black and white moonlit garden with Hendon's body white on the black grass, but he remembered that as an image, a picture clearly seen, not as an episode in which he had taken part. The half-hour over the billiard table at the Reform Club in which he had agreed to hand over £2000 for investment in Eckstein's was more vivid to him; he could remember that much more powerfully, even down to the mild exaltation he had felt returning home that night, warm with the rather worldly appreciation of himself as a soldier with his business head screwed on right.

He read it through several times most scrupulously. There was absolutely nothing to be done except what he was told to do, just as had been the case since that morning in Durban when he had been ordered to return to the Cape by the next ship. The bewildering sensation that he had somehow blundered into some other man's life had never left him from that moment. Nothing seemed to bear any relation to the familiar things of his own life any more and he was suddenly powerless to do anything but obey. All the people who had questioned him, his senior officers, the commanding officer, they had all been reasonable and unemotional to talk to, but however normal they seemed, nothing in their attitude could alter the bitter fact of arrest, the shame of being in uniform at all times but without his belts, without his sash, without his sword. It seemed to have been going on for ever, the confinement and the humiliation, and it was with something very close to relief that Will sat with his charge sheet before him on the table and realized that the end of it all was in sight.

Of the four of them in the dock, three were lieutenants. Because of Will's rank, all the members of the jury were either captains or senior in rank and the president of the court, a man Will knew nothing of at all, was a full colonel of the Guards. He sat in full uniform at one end of the panelled room on a low dais with crossed regimental colours rising in a draped triangle behind him. The members, stiff-backed along one side of the room, were equally formal. Through the high windows to the southeast came irregular gleams of pale sunshine, lighting irreverently upon the bald head of the judge advocate, a major of the lancers who was known to have a special knowledge of military law.

'Captain Marriott, Lieutenant Prior, Lieutenant Hermon Hodge, Lieutenant Judkin. Do you object to being tried by any one of the members of this court?'

Two faces were mildly familiar to Will. It was a relief to see them. The red army handbook on military law which Will had devoured since his arrest had stated that there was nothing to preclude a member from being a witness for a prisoner although it was generally to be desired that they should not be. All four shook their heads.

'Then you are required to take the oath.'

They stepped forward one by one to lay their hands upon

the Bible. The charge sheets were read, four times over, hardly differing. Rigid, his hands at his sides, Will stared before him, at the apex above Colonel Evelyn's head where the triangle of colours met. The sense of unreality was so intense that he felt quite light-headed. The president, the members, the judge advocate looked to him as highly coloured and stylized and insubstantial as playing cards. Hermon Hodge beside him was holding himself so rigidly that he was trembling. Will thought he would like to touch him, for reassurance, to calm him, and only with a gigantic effort could he restrain himself from doing so. Far away the president was speaking. Listen, Will said to himself, listen, listen, listen . . .

I am afraid [Oliver had written to Frances] that you may have misunderstood me in your eagerness to see your cousin set free without a blot upon his character. However much I might wish to champion him for your sake, however much I might deplore the behaviour of Mr Bashford, I am afraid that the *Speaker* can take neither of those personal opinions into account. The trial must be reported in accordance with our principles – our, may I remind you, socialistic principles. And I am afraid that those principles do not much care for upper-class horseplay in any context, let alone that of a serious and costly war in which the hospitality and susceptibilities of other nationals, in this case the Cape Dutch, are abused. If I misled you, I am sorry for it.

His letter had made her feel that her own complaints had been shrill and poorly thought out. Since the trial began, she had bought a copy of every daily newspaper she could find on her way to the first lecture of the morning and had read them there and then, standing battling with crackling sheets of newsprint in the November winds that sped down the Oxford streets. Court-martials, wrapped in seclusion, seemed a very slow business and repetitive to a degree, if the morsels of information that were parcelled out so sparingly to the waiting press were anything to go by. Again and again the newspaper reports went through the details of that July night in the Mount Nelson Hotel, the mock trial, the stripping, the ducking, and the final grotesque picture of Hendon Bashford slinking naked and half-moustached around the sleeping streets of Cape Town. Whatever evidence was being given in support of the officers' behaviour, the press, it seemed, was not to be told. Without the information they conjectured, some declaring staunchly that 'it is privately asserted that Mr Bashford is a Boer sympathizer and writer' and some that, whatever he was, 'this case is not one which rebounds to the credit of the Army'. *The Times* in its frustration even declared that 'the method of administering justice prevailing at courts martial does not appear to advantage'.

If *The Times* was frustrated, Frances was doubly so. For as long as the trial took, she was not permitted to communicate with Will, which was anxiety enough in itself, an anxiety sharpened by an acute apprehension that he would not, out of a mixture of shame and reticence, acquit himself at all eloquently when it came to giving evidence. She could quite see him, faced with all those senior officers in Wellington Barracks, shrugging off the loss of £3000 as if it were no more than one of life's regular little annoyances, it not being quite gentlemanly to emphasize the point as fundamental to the whole case. He had said he might shrink from saying so and she was so afraid that indeed he would. And she could not even write to him and stiffen his resolve, she could only hope that his revulsion from Hendon Bashford's behaviour and the collapse of all his gleaming ambitions for the war in South Africa would combine to give him some kind of energy to defend himself against the charges of disgraceful behaviour brought against him.

There was, however, another matter to preoccupy her apart from Will, apart from the unsatisfactory fragments of news about Matthew, apart from the chill silence that still reigned at Salisbury – and that was her own prospects. For the past eighteen months, she had believed that she had worked conscientiously. Her marks had been honourable, her reports, couched in the equivocal language of all academic reports, respectable. She read what she was instructed to read, delivered essays on time, wrestled commendably with the syntax and vocabulary of other languages – in short, dutifully followed the course of hundreds of other young women in the new teacher-training colleges of England.

'It is not, Miss Paget,' the principal said to her, 'sufficient.'

'Have there been complaints of my work?'

'A complaint would not be an accurate description. A complaint would imply a neglect of what you are here to do. I would prefer to describe the attitude of the teaching staff as one of disappointment.'

Frances gripped the arms of her chair.

'You see, Miss Paget, that I pay you a compliment in asking you to see me. If I felt that your talents were merely those of industrious application, I should not trouble myself about you. But I know better. I know that you are capable of more than industry, admirable though industry may be as a quality. I would not be so unfeeling as to belittle the effect of the war and its consequences upon you, but it is unworthy of your sex and its new opportunities to be unable to rise beyond these considerations. I like to see the young women of this college interest themselves in the issues of the day, but those issues must remain secondary to their studies. So too, without of course behaving with any degree of inhumanity, must the claims of those who are used to requiring your ready acquiescence to their demands. Do you understand me, Miss Paget?'

Frances said, chin high, 'Oh, perfectly.'

'Unless young women of your intelligence show themselves capable of professionalism in their lives, the way will never be open to their sisters. It is a privilege to be in the vanguard, Miss Paget, and one that I would not wish any pupil at St Hilda's to forget for one moment. You will leave this college for work in the new and foremost girls' educational establishments of this country and the influence you will exert will be incalculable. We are not, here at St Hilda's, a pleasing way of passing three years for you, Miss Paget. We are a preparation for the future and for more futures than your own.'

Frances had gone to fetch her hat and walked out into the Meadows after that. It was a sharp, clear November afternoon with yellow leaves thick on the grass and the air faintly flavoured with smoke from the bonfires lit behind the walls of the Botanical Gardens. It was not really in Frances' nature

253

to be melancholy but she certainly felt reflective to a point that was sobering indeed. It was difficult to know, however truthful she might attempt to be, if what the principal had said to her was to be resented or in truth a welcome articulation of what, in her heart of hearts, she had known to be the case. Had she let the single-minded enthusiasm with which she had sought her place at St Hilda's ebb away because it was easier, always easier and mostly no trouble to justify either, to succumb to the emotions and pressures of the other claims upon her life? Was Oliver right? Should she have refused to go home every time she was summoned, should she have clung tenaciously to the independence of which St Hilda's was the beginning? It was, after all, only a part of the same thing, this willingness to respond so swiftly to any cry for help, any demand. If you regard your work as secondary, the principal had implied, who can blame those around you who eagerly will do so too and who will have no compunction in demanding your attention. On the other hand, was not the prospect of a female life where work was always primary a barren thing to some degree? Was there not part of her – a large part of her – which responded willingly and lovingly to the people in her life? Was it greedy and unrealistic to want both, to expect the one to feed the other, enhance it, balance it?

'I must warn you,' Oliver had said to her, 'that you will get very tired and find yourself very divided in your loyalties.' He might say that but he would not himself be prepared to make concessions to women achieving both loyalties, one to themselves and one to others. Nor would Matthew. Might Will? Will would always have tried to understand it, but the old Will, the prewar Will, would have been saddened to see a woman even wanting such things. Now, schooled by his own harsh experience, would he understand her desires and her confusion?

She leaned against a tree and looked down into the clear brown edges of the river, the water hardly stirred by the current moving swiftly along in the centre of the stream. Far behind her, the clocks of Oxford in their spires and bell-towers began to chime four into the still, pale sky. In her room Celia would be waiting, and there was a barely started essay on Wordsworth on her table and a passage of Molière to be translated. She took her shoulder from the tree, wound her scarf more tightly round her neck, and set off slowly home.

Hendon had known all along that Will would be acquitted. He had said so to everyone, hoping to elicit from at least someone an avowal that the military had no business to shelter behind the privilege and privacy of a court-martial in a case like this. There had been a moment of hope when he had encountered a Member of Parliament in the Reform Club, who, because of some particular grievance against the army, had seemed likely even to ask a question in the House of Commons. But what a man seems ready to do late at night and full of port he does not always seem to see with the same urgency next morning over smoked haddock and coffee. He had promised Hendon that he would think about the matter and had hurried away.

Hendon himself had thought about little else for almost five months. The facts of the matter were entirely swallowed up for him by the enormity of his sense of injustice and injury. Nothing that had happened in England since his arrival in October had done anything but deepen these feelings, and when the trial was over and it was revealed that witnesses for the accused had described him as a man 'very much disliked' in both London and Cape Town, 'undesirable company for young officers', and even 'not a man that any decent person would be seen talking to', his desire for some kind of redress was almost too much to be borne. Any personal letter sent to Will was ignored and attempts to see him were met by a soldier servant with instructions to admit no one.

It was the senior partner of Holkam and Crabb of Mincing Lane, in whose hands Hendon had put his affairs, who had a scheme.

'I am to take it, am I not, Mr Bashford, that you wish to take civil proceedings against Captain Marriott for libel?'

'Certainly – '

'In that case, sir, may I make the following suggestion? I recommend that we place advertisements in all the well-known national papers suggesting that Captain Marriott has behaved in a manner inconsistent with his claim to be an officer and a gentleman and that he is content to take the coward's way and shelter behind a plea of privilege. You may challenge him in that manner to defend himself and to answer the vile charges made against you on his behalf in court. The moment he responds to your challenge, it becomes proper to take proceedings against him and bring him before a civil court of law. Do you follow me, sir?'

'Perfectly,' Hendon said.

'And may I make a further suggestion, sir?'

Hendon nodded.

'Copies of these advertisements and copies of all clippings and correspondence relating to the court-martial should be forwarded by ourselves – with your permission, sir – to the committee of Captain Marriott's club and any other body to which he belongs. We do not wish anyone with a connection with the captain to be unaware of these things.' He paused. 'I imagine, Mr Bashford, that there will be no trouble over the expenses incurred in this campaign.'

Hendon looked at him squarely. 'None, Mr Holkham,' he said, 'none whatever.'

20

The visitors' room at St Hilda's College had been arranged with nobody's comfort in mind. The long windows looked over a garden remarkable only for its orderliness and were bare of curtains. The floor of boards, polished to a high gloss, was adorned with a crudely coloured English-made copy of a Turkey carpet and the only furniture, besides a number of upright chairs pushed firmly back against the walls, was a large central table which bore a castor-oil plant in a brass pot and a copy of yesterday's *Daily Chronicle*. The walls, half panelled in wood stained the colour of gravy, were hung with a series of reproductions of drawings of religious processions in sixteenth-century Paris and were universally framed in black.

'Is it,' Frances said nervously, 'even worse a place to talk than your mother's London drawing room?'

She had pulled one of the upright chairs to the table and was uncomfortably seated on it. She had tried to persuade Will to sit near her, but he had declined and was standing by one of the windows looking out onto a rose bed where a few brown-blotched flowers still struggled bravely in the chill.

'It makes no difference,' Will said.

He was in civilian clothes and looked gaunt and ill. When the news that his sentence had been no more than a reprimand came through, she had written joyfully to London fully expecting his exultant reply at once. Instead he had sent a brief note from his club. Could he see her? Would she spare him half an hour? She had hoped that she could take him round Oxford, introduce him to Celia and Rose, amuse him, but he had seemed indifferent to any suggestion. The visitors' room would do very well, he said. It hardly signified where he was.

'When the president pronounced no more than a

reprimand,' Will said, swinging the blind cord with one hand, 'I did not feel anything. Nothing at all. The whole trial was like that. I felt nothing. The moment it began I stopped feeling, I could hardly even hear them.'

Frances said, 'You must be so tired. You need a holiday. You have lived with it all too long – '

'No,' he said sharply.

'But how can you not feel relief? How can you? I wanted to sing and shout when I heard, I felt as if a huge load had slipped from my back. Will, the world now knows what we have known all along!'

Will half turned and gestured towards the paper on the table. 'There are those.'

'Oh!' Frances said impatiently. 'Those! Do what your commanding officer advised you, what your lawyer advised you. Ignore them. He can't keep it up for ever. Ignore them – '

Will said with an edge of desperation, 'I can't.'

She rose from her chair and went over to him by the window.

'Will – '

'I can't. There is a new one every day, always on the front page. He has started naming the regiment now, he has written to my club – '

'And what did your club say?'

'Nothing. They said they would take no notice.'

'There you are!' Frances cried in triumph. 'And that is what you should do!'

'Frances – ' He let go of the blind cord and put his hands behind his back. 'Frances, I am going to resign my commission.'

'No!' She said, horrified, 'No, Will! No! Don't be absurd, you cannot, not because of this, not – '

'It is only partly because of this. But this has something to do with it. It's made everything so squalid, so sordid, dragging the regiment's name in the mud. I don't care so much about mine. Please don't cry – '

'I have to,' she said, helplessly, 'I can't stop it, I can't bear it. You mustn't resign, Will, you haven't thought about it properly, you can't have, you can't let him defeat you like

258

this, horrible little man, you can't let him make you suffer so!'

He put out a tentative hand and touched her shoulder. 'I will suffer more if I stay. Nothing is as I thought it would be. It was like that in South Africa too. You used to laugh at me for my feelings about the Empire, for England – ' He paused while he found a handkerchief which he handed to her and then he said sadly, 'I think I left rather a lot of those out there. Why is it that life always comes down just to eating and sleeping and walking about in the end?'

She said furiously, blowing her nose, 'Don't be so weak, Will! How can you give in on all those things that meant so much to you? How can you turn your back on the army like this? How dare you let a scoundrel like Hendon Bashford triumph over you? No one believes him, you know that. No one cares twopence for his silly advertisements.' She gave a last blow and said more calmly, 'I am perfectly sure that your commanding officer won't accept your resignation.'

'On the contrary. He has told me to go away and think about it, but he understands my feelings. I told him that I felt that, whether it was my fault or not, I had in effect disgraced the army and the regiment and that the publicity to both was damaging, particularly as we are at war. He agreed with me.'

'But the others! There were three others!'

'I was the ringleader. And Hendon had a – particular grievance against me. And the others were junior officers.'

Frances walked away from him around the table, her head bent. When she came back to the window where he stood watching her steadily, she said, 'You are being stubborn and melodramatic, Will Marriott. There is no need to resign. You exaggerate the whole affair.'

'I *want* to resign!'

'But the army! It was your whole life, you never wanted to do anything else, be any other thing but a soldier – '

'I've changed,' Will said.

'And will nothing change you back? Is this not just temporary, the effect of the relief of this long ordeal being over?'

'No.'

She peered into his face. 'What will you do?'

He shrugged. 'I'll go abroad for a while. Switzerland perhaps. I want to go somewhere that has never heard of war, I want to be far away from everything, the newspapers, everything. Maybe when I come back I could try my hand at farming – '

'Will,' she said, 'could you not just go to Switzerland, if you must, and decide about the army when you return? Must you decide now?'

'I have decided. It's all over. I have to do something else. I suppose – ' He paused and looked at her intently, 'I suppose I couldn't ask you – '

She stepped back. 'No,' she said hurriedly 'No, Will – '

'I'm sorry. I shouldn't even have thought it. I shouldn't have mentioned it.' He picked up the acorn at the end of the blind cord again and began to toss it from hand to hand. 'When something dies in you, it isn't to be expected that something else will come at once to take its place. I was so sure that I was going to have a part in something glorious and noble, that although lives would be lost, they would be lost while we struck a swift clean blow for what was good and just. And, as is all too obvious, I knew nothing of how these things turn out. I saw muddle and delay and confusion and frustration and, in the midst of it all, lost my own sense of decency to an extent that made me behave like the most God-forsaken idiot upon earth. I always believed it would be easy to keep one's head even if everyone else had lost theirs, I always believed in my own good sense, my own standards. It's because I don't – I *can't* – believe in them any more that I don't want to be in the army any longer, even in England for a while.'

Frances said unsteadily, 'Your faith in yourself will come back. Of course it will – ' She moved closer to him and put her arms around his neck. 'Dear Will, oh, my dear Will.'

He held her tightly, his face against her cheek. 'You can't always have what you want – '

'I wish you would not say such things. I really don't want to cry any more.'

'Then listen.'

'I am, I am.'

'It is my choice to leave the army. It is my choice to go

260

away. It will be my choice to return or to go to India or to Canada or to Australia or wherever I choose to go. You never objected to Matthew choosing. Why me?'

She freed herself gently but left her hands lightly on his shoulder, reluctant to let go of the feel of him. 'Because I was never used to worrying about you. Because you always did what met with approval and sanction. Because you didn't break rules.'

He gave her a ghost of a smile. 'I told you,' he said, 'I've changed.'

She was about to say, 'I think I have too,' but suddenly found herself awkward, afraid of the new resolve in him born of his defeat, uncertain of the unfamiliar but welcomed feelings he inspired in her. Instead she said, 'Please say. Please tell me where you will go.'

'Why should you care?'

She took her hands away. 'Because I want to know where to find you.'

He shrugged. 'To Lake Geneva. I've a friend in Montreux, a chap called Tom Blacker who has to live there because of his lungs. He had to leave the army because of them. He reads all day. He won't bother me. After that, I don't know.' He looked at her. 'If I thought there was anything to come home for, I'd come home. Maybe I'd farm.'

'You must write to me,' she said, suddenly desperate.

He leaned forward and gently kissed her cheek. 'No, my dearest Frances. Not any more. I shall never care about anyone the way I care for you, but I can't go on pouring love into the sands, not any longer, not after what has happened. I'm going now. Back to London and then to Europe. If you want to hear about me, it is you who will have to do the writing.' And then he turned away from her, picked up his hat and gloves and overcoat, and, without even a further glance at her, quietly left the room.

'I have so much to tell you,' Frances wrote to Oliver. 'More, indeed, than I can easily put on paper. I shall be in London at the end of the first week of December – Celia's elder sister has most kindly offered to put me up for a few days in her house in Bayswater and I should welcome a chance to see you. And – I mention this with some little apprehension – I have written your article for you. Is that inducement enough for you to call?'

Celia's sister was married to a stockbroker and lived comfortably in a solid house in Gloucester Terrace. She had been warmly welcoming to the idea of Frances as a guest for several days, had provided her with a bedroom and a front-door key, and begged that she use the house freely as a hotel. Under such friendly circumstances it had been easy to ask Oliver to visit, although less easy to be sure when he actually would, and Frances had spent several fruitless afternoons, while her hostess was out on a seemingly endless round of calls, hovering in the window of the first-floor drawing room and gazing vainly down towards the park for a glimpse of the familiar loden overcoat. It was almost her last day in London when her vigil was rewarded. A cab stopped at the house opposite and Frances was watching it with no more than the idlest curiosity when Oliver stepped from behind it and crossed the street towards her.

He came into the drawing room with the air of someone who had often been in the house before.

'I think,' she said, going to meet him and laughing, 'that you would look just as at home if I were to ask you to meet me in the Sahara desert.'

He looked about him. 'The house of the husband and the sister of Miss Miller. And very prosperous too. I particularly admire the Negro slave boy holding up a lamp.'

'Hush, please! It is very good of Mrs Compton to allow me to stay here and to allow you to call.'

'Quite so. Now then, where is my piece from you?'

She wished rather that the papers were not so neatly, readily at hand, clipped together and lying on a table. 'I am a little doubtful – '

He smiled and held out his hand. 'Of course you are. It's only maidenly. Would the slave boy be persuaded to put down his lamp and fetch some tea?'

She rang the bell. 'I have ordered prodigious quantities of food.'

'I am hugely relieved. I had to miss luncheon altogether.

Frances, I must go no further without saying how delighted I was at the outcome of the court-martial. Your family must be relieved beyond measure.'

Frances sat down in a low chair by the window. 'Will came to see me in Oxford. He has resigned his commission and left for Europe.'

'My dear girl – '

'I really cannot explain it,' she said hurriedly, afraid that tears were gathering again, 'I hardly understand it myself. I think all his great ideals suffered terribly in the fighting, I think he rather lost his way all those months that he convalesced in Cape Town. I don't know – I don't feel that I know the whole story. He seemed to want to be punished, it was as if he punished himself because the military authorities would do no more than reprimand him.'

'You cannot suggest he would have preferred to have been cashiered?'

The door opened and the two parlourmaids – who had discussed with scorn the state of Frances' wardrobe and the smallness of her hatbox upon her arrival – came and set on the table in the window an array of kettles and cups and spirit lamps and covered dishes. Oliver gazed at them. 'I am almost too much shocked to be interested in the contents of those. Did you say he had gone to Europe?'

'Three days ago. To stay in Montreux where he has a friend, a man he was at school with who has weak lungs and lives there.'

She poured tea into a cup and held it out to him. 'And Matthew – '

'Ah, yes,' he said, taking his cup and settling opposite to her, 'tell me of Matthew.'

'I had a letter from Adelaide. Matthew is to be released from his regiment at any time now, but he is not coming home, she says. She tells me – ' Frances paused and took a deep breath before saying rapidly, 'She tells me that he plans to stay in South Africa, that he cherishes ideas of farming there. It appears that he has lost his heart to the country, that he could not bear to think of leaving it. And that he has met a girl, a Boer girl – oh, Oliver, this sounds so improbable but this is what Adelaide tells me. Matthew rode to the farm which belonged to this girl's family and found her there alone with her dying brother, an aunt, and a handful of little cousins. He was supposed to burn the farm but he told Adelaide he could not bring himself to do so, particularly as the girl was so courageous, so calm. So he disobeyed orders, he spared the farm but when he went back some days later, other soldiers had done the work for him and the girl and her family had been taken to one of the camps. He tracked her down there, he visits her, it seems he is only waiting for the end of the war to release her and carry her off with him – Oliver, is it really proper to laugh?'

'Yes, indeed. It is the effect that high romance always has upon me.'

Frances said sadly, looking at him, 'Matthew's story fills me with nothing but desolation.'

'My dear – '

'How can it be otherwise?'

'If you are consistent with what you used to tell me you felt for Matthew, it must be everything otherwise. You sent him off, my dear Frances, to find his cause, his goal, his place upon the globe. That is precisely what he has done for you.' He lifted a muffin from the dish with each hand and rose and began to pace up and down the room, gesturing largely between mouthfuls. 'It seems to me – and I must always remind myself that I only know these young men through your eyes – that what disconcerts you now is that Matthew and Will have changed places. The one, the perfect sub-altern, the kind and honourable and romantically tender one, has had his ambitions put to a test in which slaughter and tedium played equally damaging parts, and the test has proved too much for him. It has taken away the shining sense of purpose which inspired him so much before. He is temporarily disarrayed. Whereas Matthew, profoundly at odds with himself before, believing in no force but the anarchy of his own wild inclinations, has found in that huge untamed country something that for the first time in his life makes him actually want to subdue his energies to an end. Partly a place, partly perhaps a woman. So what do you have? For the moment Will has lost his way and it is at the very moment when it seems that Matthew has found his. No wonder a desolation strikes you. The inconsistency of human behaviour is a most puzzling and disturbing business.'

Frances cried with enthusiasm, 'I could listen to you for the rest of my life! You see things so clearly, you perceive things that only serve to baffle me.'

'Of course I do. I have had twenty years more than you have had to work upon the conundrum of humanity.' He stooped and held his cup out to her. 'Should you like to listen to me for the rest of your life?'

Then he retrieved his cup from her and took it down the length of the room with him. She watched him, horrified and thrilled. When he came back, he put the cup on the tray beside the kettle and knelt by her chair.

'I am not a man for protestations, I am not much of a man for gallantry and I am most certainly no man at all for half-truths.' He paused, gazing earnestly at her, and then he said with great gentleness, 'I saw long ago how it was with you. I saw it and it warmed me and flattered me and I knew that I was the first. You delight me, you interest me, you arouse my admiration and my affection.'

She looked away from him out of the window into the early December darkness, lit with the flare of the gas lamp on the pavement below.

'I'm afraid that I cannot,' she said.

'Have I made myself seem a fool?'

She looked at him. 'You couldn't do that. You have too much self-confidence. That is one reason why I could not marry you. You don't need me, you see, although you might like to have me and you would not care patiently for my struggling to decide what I want for myself.'

'Is that what you want – to be necessary?'

'Yes. Yes, I find that I do. And to spend my life with someone whose self is not as settled as yours is, someone with whom I can grow. Even grow up.'

'I see.'

'Forgive me,' she said, 'I am being childish and ungracious. Perhaps I lack all the proper capacities.'

'Oh, no,' he said, 'you behave with all the consistency of the nature to which I am so much attached. It is not you who lack capacities. It is I who do. I envy you your need for love,

265

your distress over these young men, your dutiful preoccupation with your family. Through all these you participate more fully in the human race than I shall ever succeed in doing.' He rose to his feet and drew up his chair so that he could sit close to her.

She said in a voice that was almost steady, 'I cannot help having the sensation that things are falling away from me.'

'My dear, you mistake the sensations. What you feel are the birth pangs of new beginnings.'

'But, Oliver – '

He leaned forward and took her hands in his warm capable grasp. 'You cannot discard me, you know, just because I am not allowed to play the accepted lover. I am here as your friend, your devoted and admiring friend, for as long as you want me. I will take you about, introduce you to people, guide your writing, but I want to see a strength in you, and independence in you, even a little ruthlessness perhaps. Your studies at Oxford are not simply a means to fill the time between the demands of family, the issues raised by letters from South Africa. They are the key to your future life, either as a professional woman or as a woman of education able both to bring up children and to write papers, deliver lectures. I suspect that sometimes you have said to yourself that you can attend fully to nothing until the war is over, but that will not do, you know. The war is still a long way from its finish, it takes time, as I said to you long ago, to subdue a people fighting for their nation, their identity. But your active involvement in it is done. Those young men are grown men and must now do what they have chosen as a result of what they have known. And so must you. It is the issues that the war has raised that must occupy you now, not the lives of Matthew and Will. It is new beginnings. You are free, my dear Frances, free to make of your life what you will.' He stopped and gave her hands a little shake. 'Heavens, my dear girl, how you do submit to my lectures.'

'I like them.'

'And what shall you do now? Christmas at Salisbury?'

She nodded.

'And then?'

'I shall return early to Oxford and take a room before the term begins.'

'Ah,' he said. He dropped her hands and leaned forward to kiss her lightly. 'Then I shall see you there in the New Year. Goodbye, my dear.'

She heard him descending the staircase and then the sharp sounds of his steps on the tiles of the hall and the muffled conversation with the maid handing him his hat, his gloves, his green loden coat. And then the front door was opened and shut and his steps went down the pavement towards the park, fainter and fainter. She lay back in her chair, her arms upstretched, her hands folded behind her head, and surveyed what he had left, the dented chair cushion, the empty teacup, the plate strewn with muffin crumbs. Free, he had said, that is what you are, what you must make yourself. A new year coming, new beginnings.

Six o'clock struck from the hall below. In a moment Mrs Compton would be in from her bridge party and her arrival would set the house in motion for the evening, the lamps and fires, the children's bedtime, her husband's dinner. Six o'clock. There were fifteen hours then until nine o'clock the next morning, the hour at which she, Frances Paget, would be outside the offices of Thomas Cook, waiting for the doors to be unlocked so that she might enter and purchase for herself a second-class railway ticket from Victoria Station to Montreux. Christmas in Switzerland . . .

Softly, her eyes fixed no longer on the remains of Oliver's tea, but resting with amusement on the Negro boy by the fireplace holding aloft so tirelessly his lamp of clouded glass fashioned like a lily, Frances began to hum.